The Vampire Squid and Other Stories

LUCIA BARTLETT

Copyright © 2021 Lucia Bartlett.

All rights reserved. No part of this book may be used or reproduced by any means, graphic, electronic, or mechanical, including photocopying, recording, taping or by any information storage retrieval system without the written permission of the author except in the case of brief quotations embodied in critical articles and reviews.

This is a work of fiction. All of the characters, names, incidents, organizations, and dialogue in this novel are either the products of the author's imagination or are used fictitiously.

Archway Publishing books may be ordered through booksellers or by contacting:

Archway Publishing
1663 Liberty Drive
Bloomington, IN 47403
www.archwaypublishing.com
844-669-3957

Because of the dynamic nature of the Internet, any web addresses or links contained in this book may have changed since publication and may no longer be valid. The views expressed in this work are solely those of the author and do not necessarily reflect the views of the publisher, and the publisher hereby disclaims any responsibility for them.

Any people depicted in stock imagery provided by Getty Images are models, and such images are being used for illustrative purposes only. Certain stock imagery © Getty Images.

Image Credit: Lucia Bartlett

ISBN: 978-1-4808-9924-7 (sc)
ISBN: 978-1-4808-9925-4 (e)

Library of Congress Control Number: 2020922106

Print information available on the last page.

Archway Publishing rev. date: 03/31/2021

normal isn't near

This work is dedicated to my son's and their technical support, to my sister Amy and Granny Ruth

Introduction

The Vampire Squid begins in the Fall of 2019, blows past New years into frightening spring and summer of 2020's covid pandemic. It's a cautionary tale of heroines, (and heroes) battling emotions during the lock-down. A psychological thriller and battle of the sexes, this novel invents a future with far less freedom, if the Sergeant Major has his way.

Some people come to Maine and hide their true intensions. A Sergeant Major, Physics PHD and MD relocates to Piscatiquas County and is power unchecked at Fort Charon, a new underground military facility located in the shadow of Mt. Katahdin. He extends an invitation to The Lane School for a science based field trip where they see many unexpected advancements.

Young female characters my readers may find familiar, grown to teenagers, became aware of social justice. Anne, (Mrs. Stevens), Director of The Lane School and mother of three is alarmed when she learns children are in danger at the woman's prison not far from Fort Charon.

It was suggested by a reader that <u>The Vampire Squid</u> would make a great video game for women. Children in danger, women and girls to the rescue… The old Levesque Mansion, MacPhee's stately log home and Stan's home behind the old granary, beside the disused rail-bed, plus Fort Charon's sci-fi network of underground caverns are great backdrops for gamers.

While <u>The Vampire Squid</u> may be a female nightmare; 'Papercuts' is definitely a male one.

'Papercuts' is sci-fi/futuristic, year 2030…, our hero; Wesley an innately good young man in his early twenties yearns to become a CERT, part Central's inner group, but he's seduced by a beautiful co-worker. This short story bridges the ages, as Wesley's caught in a time warp; a healthy young guy in a inhuman world.

'The Community' takes us back to years 1975-1985', where a close-knit upper-class housing development unravels into epidemic suicide and explores the possibility that expectations of a perfect life may not be healthy.

Contents

Introduction ix

1. Nigel 1
2. Dan 17
3. Stan, Fall 2019 23
4. 2019 Christmas Party 40
5. Post Christmas Deconstruction 57
6. Lucy 68
7. The Base 80
8. Flu Season 121
9. Pandemic 137
10. Leah MacPhee 155
11. Havin' a Ball 182
12. A Major Issue 202
13. Undocumented Time 218
14. Couplings & Other Problems 229
15. Saving the World 260
16. Ada's New Job 270
17. The Vampire Squid 274

Epilogue 313
Papercuts 321
The Community 363
About the Author 373

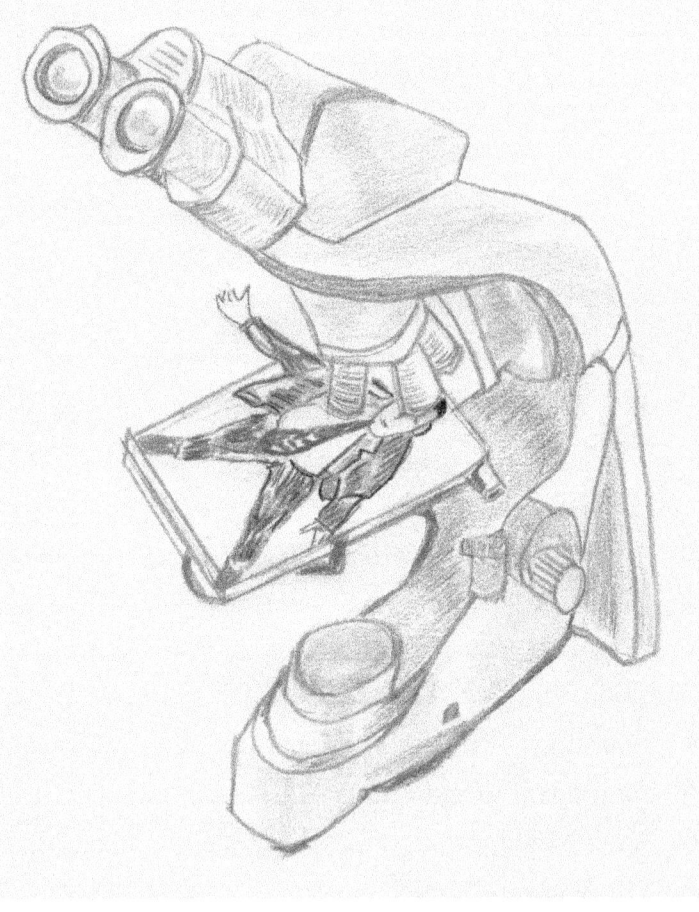

1
Nigel

The beaver came and went, spending days perfecting pond and dam until his inexplicable absence.

Beavers took care of everything, built a beautiful pond, removed poplars, padded mud, carrying construction material by mouth … swam in close, noticed Nigel's binoculars, slapped the water and dove. Like a prep-school teacher slapping the table with a notebook, it got his attention … Nigel loved the rodent, soul expanding with a desire to protect all living things and gratitude towards the furry friend who helped him avoid local and state requirements. It was a beaver pond … not manmade!

Sightings diminished, winter threatened and still no sign of the creature. "Damn him!"

"Could be he needed an emergency vacation," Ada pointed out over Thanksgiving.

"He wasn't anxious," *gnawing everything in sight.*

"He worked so hard and the wood had to come from somewhere…" she smiled, in a mind reading way and left for Carlisle Academy. Fall turned to winter, the vacant beavers lodge crumbled under the weight of snow … Nigel put his binoculars down.

2019. ONE HOT SEPTEMBER weekday before the beaver left and before Cov-19 lockdowns were ever imagined and social distancing forced on all of society, Nigel paddled alone …canoeing on Foster Lake. If only he could persuade his wife Leah or the boys or even thirteen year old Bett to join him. They were over occupied with The Lane School and Farm, he was too of course, however as teacher he had the privilege of playing hooky, push chores aside, take the rest of the day off and head up to camp for a moment of peace.

But time was spoiled by loneliness, made more acute since seventeen year old daughter, Ada was away. It's not like she was an avid naturalist, but she loved the little stories he told of wildlife and people sightings and was as happy hearing them as other girls with real gifts. He'd walk in the door and she'd approach him like a wrapped present … wanting to hear everything.

In leisurely paddle mode, no longer looking for God's intent in the sky, totally grounded in the service of others, he none-the-less cast critical eye on camp owners across the lake.

Ol' Frozen Pipes, defended his microscopic frontage behind Swans, flamingos and shrieking kids whizzing around in tubes blithely oblivious to his wealth and status. Nigel empathized and but for the grace of family, saw his own lonely end game while nearly capsizing, *damn pontoons!*

Out on patrol, Park Rangers ignored them and made Nigel hold up a life jacket. Still … it was nice to be recognized, even suspiciously. Sportily dressed, three hundred dollar sunglasses dangling, they knew him and the brief eye contact, while acknowledging his full compliance, bobbing in their wake, erased solitude and invisibility, the consequence of pressing the wrong button, *life is full of wrong buttons.* Nigel day traded and made two hundred thousand dollars disappear. He remotely viewed himself, rising on the crest of a perfect buy point … winning the two hundred thousand dollars back, while the Rangers revved engines and instantly became a black dot, white plume waving.

At least I'm just a lonely guy out in his canoe and not a mentally disturbed patient. He forgot time musing ups and downs, graphs, charts, irritating bankers, lawyers and the consequences of doing nothing, blind to the approaching dinner hour and the disappearance of all other water craft.

The wind dropped to nothing and smoke plumes stood in pillars along the shore, slowly ascending to heaven like Indian spirits. In simple remembrances Nigel acknowledged their contributions, (corn, squash & potato) while smelling grilled hamburger.

He didn't worry about getting his own family dinner. It was someone's birthday, unmarried volunteer, a girl/kid party; they were always having, piles of presents and piles of spent paper afterwards.

A slight breeze rippled the surface; he floated towards a spectacular sunset, so much beauty it made him ache when up popped three figures in a long aluminum canoe, same material as his big old Grumman square stern. Awe ... like minded men, taking in the beauty of the hour, Nigel saw his childhood ... if he could only reach them he might reenter, reclaim, find a father figure, with a mustache like his... their canoe identical to his Dad's! ... dearly cherished, in the family for years, although he scarcely remembered going out in it with his Dad.

There they were again! Tantalizingly close, moving in an important way ...with conviction ... if only he could catch up, his fellow canoeists, pull alongside, have a little chat. The lake attracted wealth, they were important men, military, fit, in full relaxation mode, taking a break from what men do ... putting lives on the line for a greater good! He was tired of the 'girls just wanna have fun' atmosphere of the barn, the silly lack of consequence ...He might that evening reclaim, revisit that way of being, that manliness, have it rub off... he paddled hard ... but as if his mind reached out and touched, they veered away from stimuli! He slowed ... they rested, paddles on gunnels looked back at him, gave a tantalizing wave. He had another go, bowed over, put in maximum effort, but they did the same ... speeding up ...dipping and pulling. He paused, they paused then the game resumed, blades flashing away in the sunset, nostalgic, serene he got lost in gold sparkles.

No rude wind to combat, he forgot the chase, distracted by loons ... looking up the men were gone. He waited ... the loons reclaimed surface, popped up, looking around like nobody's business but not the men. It seemed impossible, the banks distant... last seen in the middle of the lake!

He paddled towards the spot, beginning to doubt his own eyes ...awareness. Silhouettes left out details... was it really a Grumman? Or some later watercraft, up market or down, age, race impossible to tell...he was sure they were male but that was all ...and now gone...poof... He wished for a corroborating witness, a passenger ...he was falling apart ... deep in self doubt ...more than that, it was very possibly an hallucination...too much time alone! He had to get home and paddled speedily back to camp, put everything away, locked up and drove back to ordinary life.

On the way he had on the Rovers excellent system, tuned to news, so much out there and so narrow the focus, (impeach Trump) things he was interested in would've to wait, like the story of day traders discovering a glitch in the system that allowed positions borrowed on margin be collateral for endless trades and accumulations of debt or profit. *Fun while it lasted*, Nigel sighed. *Everyone's up to no good in these end times.*

Still he couldn't imagine investing three years of time and treasure to impeach the guy and coming up empty each time, the target hugely annoying and fatter than ever.

Planning a future and not caring about political parties or green energy or global warming,(in favor of it, actually) or their next hustle… but focusing daily on little boys and girls; teaching, reading, showing American History …

Is that the reason they're so angry? Up here in the second district he no longer followed politics. But Connecticut born, Massachusetts raised, graduate of the University of Virginia … Nigel was a life long Democrat. *The burden is to be called mean spirited for not contributing …* They knew he had money, small amounts wouldn't do, buried in the country, desperately wanting to leave past behind, solicitations went in the wastebasket, suffering as he was from generalized happiness disorder; distance a contributing factor.

However there was the dollar. *What if money didn't matter and we had to barter our way through life …* He wanted to grasp life while he had it, own bit coin before it vanished, buying the March 2009 bottom AND the chance to socialize with fellow canoeists, everyone in motorboats.

Canoes were synonymous with monetary serenity on quiet open water, having the means to glide along. He longed for the clubhouse atmosphere …all his old friends in similar circumstances never called… paddling buddies at his old job, youthful acquaintanceships … gone! Like his position at Winslow and Company; puff Gone! Massachusetts played, the past coming at him, rearview mirror more real than windshield. *Better watch where I'm going. Maybe loneliness is a deception, a turtle drawing into his shell, escaping a world of pain only to find it hurts more to be alone. Like 'Ol Frozen Pipes, snarling at neighborhood kids, I really should visit him…*

Sun winked between layers, shadows moving up and over the Rover and he tried to bring to mind new friends. Their interconnected groups, messaging, tweeting, face booking, camaraderie of like interests, while he was connected with private home-schooling teaching groups, he didn't belong to any sort of sporting club. He couldn't ask female teachers to bring their husbands over to his camp, when all he needed was someone to go canoeing, going solo made the mind lose focus, imagine things. Dan might pry himself out of his office, drive up for a swim, Nigel mentioned it before, a second request might be awkward.

The changing light and setting sun eased him into better mind-frame … where an odd dream from several nights previous replayed. He'd gone to the Mall, new memory for comp. on his purchasing mind. The Mall was packed, he couldn't get through …a 100% female mob! But he soldiered on and managed to squeeze in between elbows and hips … find a small opening, push towards it, gasping for breath. Then like being forced out of a pelvis and landing in hostel hands, hundreds of women formed a blockade facing him. Smoke gathered and wah-lah one by one they were in face masks, then gowns, full scrubs, flashing lights, techno-beat … 'We think you're better off alone… we think…your…' *Right. … Better off alone!*

He wasn't sure how to interpret it. It was too early, more than half a year before the lock-down. Premonition? The idea didn't enter his mind. It seemed a pure statement of fact. He knew other people were much closer than he and Leah. Dan and Anne and other couples mired in emotional clinging gobbledygook. Dan mans-plaining and spreading all over the place to Anne's high spirit and ample figure. Nigel preferred Leah's and his physical fidelity and emotional detachment … *too much glue can be a bad thing!* He liked his position of caretaker to other's, (primarily females) neuroticisms. He was kind and aloof, chin held high … clean perspective. *Perennially social distancing with near & dear ones.*

Home. Where he actually liked being alone because with Leah it was never peaceful! Leah had a problem with life in general and more specifically everybody; the Volunteers, Anne Stevens, Dan Stevens even the children autistic or otherwise. As always it was some imagined slight, small hurt, that she'd never own up to … instead the 'hurter' was disparaged to the nth degree, thereafter hated until the number hated outweighed the 'soon to be hated'. So Nigel retreated …. venturing out to the beaver pond hoping for fresh evidence, a downed tree or other gnaw marks… it appeared all animal life was in a state of retreat, just left, left tracks. *Why does every living thing have to hide?* He was sure they were watching him, waiting for him to leave.

The vanished men played with his thinking, perhaps they were farther away than thought, pulled canoe up on the far shore, safe inside with their own families. Was this the beginning of an adventure with water? Water, forever in flux, sight cresting surface … one can only imagine the floor. The 'silent service' on occasion never pop up.

Water, Nigel didn't like putting his head in it. Water suffocated, killed, disposed of, spent life trussed up for burial at sea, slid off a plank, everyone at attention, Fair winds and following seas! Only gulls getting that last glimpse of the dear departed, the disappearing shroud. He wondered about preauthorization, naval inductees, signing a waiver, *dispose of me at sea!* That way all the family had to-do was go to the beach, as vast final resting place, their sons or daughters incorporated, (swallowed), made into new life, *memories are like that, dropping out of the picture then suddenly appearing alive… the odd friend…or enemy.* At least burial at sea was permanent, one never heard of corpses washing up on beaches. *I wish that was the case with guilt!* Nigel was a guilty man, turning into his drive, waves of relief washed over, *Good no Cop with his pad out or worse the Sheriff with a summons.*

It happened two weeks ago at a plant nursery he frequented, liked their staff and stock. Familiarity had him parking with the workers near a cache of shrubs, he walked up and down the burlaped rows, checking tags, leaves … needles, pushing the envelope, discovering a row of beautiful juniper he dearly wanted to Fall plant, enticed by bright green, the tag read $85. It only got worse, *they want upwards of $100!* Nigel eyed their quaint little shop with disgust, leapt back in the Rover, ready for a quick exit.

Backing up while eyeing the display with negative vibe … he rammed a car, rode up on its bumper, half his driver side window filled with the sight. Heart thumping he backed to his original position, leapt out and onto the shop to find a worker, some unkempt strong back, weak mind type and throw himself at their mercy but no one was there! He walked up and down…it was ghost town, cash register left unattended. Exiting without looking into the eye of security cams, ducking head low he jumped back in the Rover then, slowed to examine the victim's car. But nothing was there!

Not that he could tell in the multitude of scrapes and dings. *They'd allege I did all that!*

Once home, in the safety of his garage with the door down he examined the car. The only mark was on the driver side mirror … must of collapsed inward then sprang back, the driver's side door 'self healing' in some inexplicable way. He went from nervous wreck to peaceful fellow to nervous wreak, they'll go over footage… probably old style two week loop.

Great I'm safe already. But what about social media, the cloud …. archived adinfinitum, … *I'll never out live it.* He imagined himself ten years from now caught in some other real or imagined semi-criminal behavior, the DA saying; "back in 2019 you hit & ran, you a wealthy man hit a poor workers car and fled!" *It will follow me to my grave.* But the imagined arrest didn't happen …yet. The heavy weight of the law was like a student's drawing, he retrieved from the floor. The assignment was President's names…

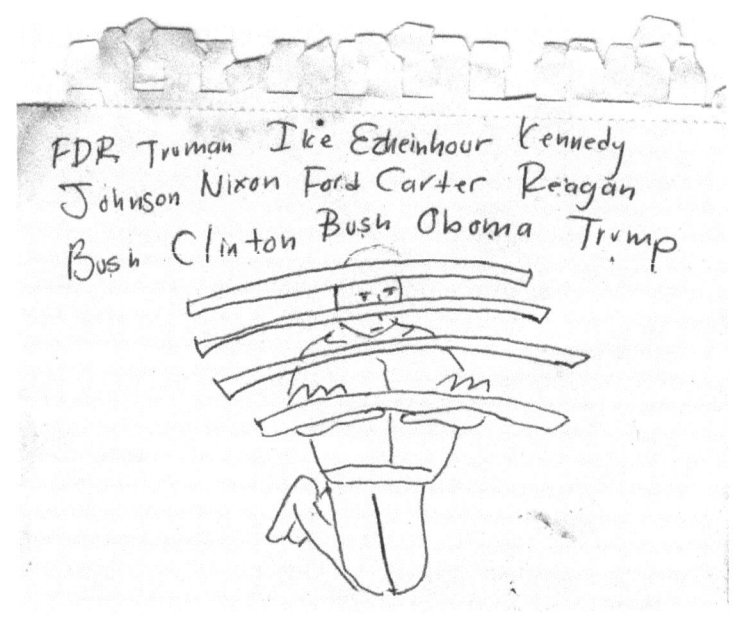

He wasn't that burdened with quilt ... only teaching history, he understood greatness and felt he'd somehow tarnished the American system of justice by running away... and drew comfort from Stan's restoration projects.

Freedom rang in fake chromium steel and over the years Stan became permanently ensconced. Nigel was planning on having a problem with it, reclaiming the space for his boys but the words never came and years brought more.

He liked the evidence of progress, engines torn down, parts refinished, repurchased and replaced, the launching days, interesting clutter, Stan's tears of Joy…it was all too real, too close to the heart, *Machines vary greatly from animals, animals* are complete, tinker at your own peril, and they are apt to-do what they want; kick, bare teeth, growl, bark, bite … *run away!* When a perfectly timed engine's a work of art. Better! God like, Machines give without needing anything in return… oh right God wants love and praise, and I give money. He admired his reflection in an old pair of hubcaps … A gutted automobile lay in wait, tools winking like half asleep spirits ready to rock & roll.

Little did he know Stan actually had nightmares about a parts pile growing bigger; the engine grown smaller, but Stan had to fix things … *Aad laest I can baing dem baack ta lafe.*

Fall 2019 turned his nest quiet, Nigel rummaged the frig., poured himself cold coffee, grabbed a cookie, headed for his computer corner, considered his wife and her slim chance of happiness.

They all love animals, their time at the barn …. Women and animals … while men are preoccupied with the mechanics of life; commerce, law, politics, medicine… women are present there too, always having to prove themselves. But at least now they have a chance. It's not preordained, (you can only be a preschool teacher, nurse or mother)… Calvinism. Why bother to live when your path is all laid out, weekly preaching, "stay in your place" Some went to their great reward early having found life on earth pointless *Had to Change that messaging!*

He fired up his comp and right off there was a message from Ada! He felt her presence, as if she was leaning over his shoulder holding onto her hair, ear inches from his ... she'd find the screen, funny, engaging...congratulate him on a discovery, be sad over a harsh news story, hand lightly on his shoulder then gone...

Ada was attending the prestigious Carlisle academy, found a tutor, trigonometry, calculus, cramming for the ACT. She informed him of how hard the math and how simple the languages. He told her about the men disappearing in the lake and she told him to get his eyes checked. How he loved her! But couldn't say a word. She had that complexity of depth, expressed in changeable mood, never went lightly about... and as always there was that devotion. Life was less stark, with her home. The boys; ten and eleven and all their desires, (mountain bikes and ATVs) His wife, Leah and her brittleness and thirteen year old Bett; Ms. Aloof, unwilling to engage in conversation at least not with him ...she had her friends.

There was an odd incidence at The Lane School with Bett and one of the four year old Steven's boys. She was reading to them in the Mansion's huge subterranean kitchen/classroom when he started to choke. Bett leapt from her chair, with the desire to save life, pent up future career energy, she grabbed and held him upside down striking him between the shoulder blades. Thump Thump Thump! Flat-handing the spine.

The room went silent, but nothing came out of his mouth, he didn't gasp for breath but wriggled to get free and once free stared at her backing up. "He's got a quarter in his mouth!"

But before anyone could catch him, he'd run to his bedroom and hid it under his pillow.

Witnesses weren't sure if Bett saved a life, or a fake, done on false pretences. Bett ignored the un-accepting vibe, in her heart she knew the action was justified, she was there at the right moment, had presence of mind, followed choking protocol for a child his size and saved him. Evidence held stubbornly in his mouth, she didn't care if they never knew the truth, she'd do it again, over and over … for any kid even if they lied like the twin did, denying the quarter, saying he'd never-ever put one in his mouth.…when he'd figured out the power of money and was afraid his parents would take it.

Odd looks continued 'till Dan started removing quarters from both boys mouths… The looks changed, cloud of suspicion lifted, nothing said… time mended.

Vindicated from that, Bett was cast in a different light. Quiet and physical, turning into a beauty in her own way, with curly light brown hair, golden skin and brown eyes, like her mother, (except Leah's hair was straight), she had an amazing practicality of world scope. *Comes from being on stage as a little girl, she understands things don't last forever.*

While Bett remained centered during suspicion and acceptance, Leah's life revolved around reacting to others, she wasn't centered or solitary…everything was always about somebody else! The result was instability and with Ada gone no one was there to temper her swings. But at least she no longer took it out on family. Friendship with Anne and time at the barn and mansion changed her from neurotic and defensive to self assured and proud.

LATER THAT WEEK Nigel lay down with a pain in his shoulder. He was out to the lake a second time looking for mysterious boatmen …. *Paddling too hard.* Like a mission of the absurd, chasing a mirage, he none-the less had real muscle stiffness but didn't take aspirin.

His eyelids closed, Leah sleeping peacefully next to him, *sleep is the only time she's happy* …he fell into a deep sleep. In his dream, he was in a big city and found a hospital, clean and glowing, yellow and white stone, steal framed windows, emergency room doors. He entered, *I'm here so make me better!* But Nigel wasn't reassured at all, Doctors were flesh and blood ….and….don't know a thing about healing.

He was whisked along to a treatment cubicle filled with light, out of the walls came robots, smiling like gas fireplaces, barbeque tong hands gently probing, examining, applying light with a musical element, they moved serenely on air, like God's understanding, a great mind cognizant of the pain he'd endured, how he worked so hard and remained unrecognized, the questions he still wanted answers to, the people he missed. It had accumulated into a toxic buildup that was removed, clattered like an exhaust pipe on the floor, his parts pulled together ….

Man fixes machine… it's only right to return the favor…

2
Dan

Thunderbolts crackled through social media then clouds parted and rays of hope fell on their little Town of Foster Lake. It all came to his attention when a little immigrant boy was denied admittance to The Lane School. Dan offered him a scholarship as a new American but the oversight committee for The New Citizen's Initiative refused his parents request. They said public school was his only option. Private Schooling misrepresented true American ideals and since the boy was a recent immigrant he needed to be given the best opportunity and advantage.

Dan was asked to join the group, (The New Citizen's Initiative) being a solid member of the community and along with his wife Anne, owner and founder of The Lane School with it's therapeutic riding, donkey rescue program **and** member of the town council **and** executive position at the plywood mill... but he quietly declined with caveat, "I'd be happy to help, if others don't work out." knowing more excuses would follow. He wasn't sure about the group. *They want to create true Americans while denying the little boy and his family the right to choose!*

With fresh political velocity in his bones he arrived at Town Council only to be mired in committee and decorum. Officials of Foster Lake had no interest interceding on his behalf with 'The New Citizen's Initiative'. Dan might've pressed the issue but he was distracted by a plague of building inspection. Aware of the shadow patriarchy, fraternal order's brain fog ...while choosing compliant women to run his own domain, Dan knew why, in their great wisdom and compassion, they were using a little boy to draw the line. So They could state as fact, PUBLIC SCHOOL WAS BETTER.

The 'new citizens' found a place in the environs around Foster Lake. Dan saw them in the fields and forests but always in the most menial tasks. They lived apart, how could that be fun, separated out in federally funded communities, learning regenerative farming and carbon trapping. "More like human trapping," Nigel replied in conversation.

"Easier to send them back," Dan half smiled, "If it doesn't work out."

Nigel never considered that but knew various think tanks did a lot of preplanning.

Dan thought back to the donkeys, when they first arrived. Some were in tough shape, separated from their pair-bond rolling eyes suspiciously while they health inspected. Donkeys didn't know friend from foe, trust was won with gentle words, brushing, hoof trimming and …time. It took awhile.

Likewise the immigrant. Unless they have kids, settle into jobs …*having family helps* Dan considered, no family and they're looking for roots … *no family to bring you up to date and you're left with what? The past.* Childless contemporaries went on endlessly about their French heritage, returning to it, made trips to the 'old country' north or south (New Orleans or Québec Canada where his family the Etiennes, (that he never saw) …lived. Now with thirteen year old Olivia and four year old twin boys he was totally grounded … *they're my life.*

The New Citizen's Initiative meant every third Tuesday and Foster graciously let them use council chambers.

"It's like they need to be rescued from bondage, Underground Railroad, Harriett Tubman, like that," Nigel said.

"Yeah, 100%," Dan looked down … The last thing he wanted was to go up against other 'do-gooders' … especially with the force of government on their side. They had the power to crush his sweet little set up and make him irrelevant. *At least locally we vote them out, to face the pinch of their own legislation. Not so Washington where they gyp the vote and we're confronted with many buildings and people who dress alike.*

Buzzers, flashing lights and other warnings about the future had him wanting to step up but he said nothing as it seemed a career ending move. He understood injustice and physics *They're bigger*, and out of habit he checked himself. Inside a swelt physique and carefully crafted manners, a fat angry man waited to be let out.

Housing blocks. They'd found a solution for homeless families and everyone was for them at first. Located in Bangor, The idea was communal living, shared facilities, kitchen, laundry and storage room areas. Intricate social oversight committees, integrated with FB. used public shaming instead of fees and fines as a means of control..

Nigel was briefly engaged, helped with the charter. He floated the idea of low interest loans in combination with donated lots, "help bring out their individuality,' … but the idea was immediately flattened. *Afraid of favelas popping up overnight.*

They tried to fit the philosophy of condo cooperation into new housing, only instead of contributing money for upkeep; ground work and maintenance, 'grateful' residents' were to provide services themselves … they were 'blue-collar' after all, in the trades; plumbing, heating … grounds-keeping but nothing got done! When asked why? The answer was; 'It's not my effen' floor, window, wall…grass.'

The NCOCPH (New Citizens Oversight Committee on Public Housing) with great patience explained; "yes it is yours, ours is yours … in America, we control government and your neighbors pay taxes. All that's asked that you … is to return the favor in general upkeep."

"Where's the deed? I got title to my car, and when I sell it the buyer gets title and I get paid." Capitalism the scourge of man-kind reared its ugly head.

"Yes but don't you want to 'give back' to the community? Keep the place nice for the next tenants that need it?"

"That's not my problem, my problem's working two jobs, saving money so I can get out of Dodge before winter."

Still they followed rules for the most part, knowing convicted felons weren't allowed, likewise gun ownership forbidden. Courtroom style metal detectors featured at every entrance and anyone under the age of eighteen had a 10:00 pm curfew, completely ignored during summer months, basketball in the wee hours, it was only used as an add on for eviction… Saved for the truly bad actors. The family had to go because their kids were future pharmacists, graffiti artists, musicians and community organizers who had the audacity, the unmitigated gall to ignore curfew.

All this went on before the pandemic turned normal life into crime, and government decided on freedom. Cops brought German Shepard's to Community parks, to bark at people recreating. Instead of a 10:00 pm curfew … the curfew lasted all day, everyday. No basketball, tennis, baseball …soccer or paddling on the river and especially no going to Foster Lake State Park. A shutdown was coming to flatten the curve and spread out death.

3
Stan, Fall 2019

Stan walked shotgun in hand. It had been a long time since he'd had that happy security needed to hunt alone… four years since his son died, two years since his wife had another, a wiggly little charmer with a head of golden curls, blowing raspberries, pulling his beard, little arms around him, he was in heaven and his wife cooking another! His fourteen year old daughter a mother hen! Life behind the old granary, beside the disused rail bed was better than he deserved, imagined in those dark days. *Govena' save me … led me stay a' 'is plase 'ere lak 'ome. I'd bay dead ba fa' 'em.*

He started off that morning, hiked the disused rail bed, beside his home. No 'rails to trails' in the area, it was considered too remote, his quad stayed parked.

Decked out in camo, wanting to get away from other sportsmen… walking slow, thinking of life. He liked being alone, brought snacks and water enough for a day, his house while perfect for a pregnant wife and small child was claustrophobic to him.

He was after grouse and turkey. Shot at a few Toms causing major alarm but nothing for the pot. *Godda show up 'ome wiff a burd,* It felt good to be out on logging roads, wandering in mud, looking at tracks or even false claims, he yawned not used to long walking, the sun over that little rise ahead, land all streaky with shadow.

He came to a huge maple feeding off a little run and sat at its base, leaning back, removing cap, empting pockets of gear, making himself comfortable, put his head back … surrendered to exhaustion.

He sat on a stool at his favorite woods bar, men like card board cutouts drank while bright three dimensional women circulated. Moosehead pale, frothy hoily grail, bottles dancing in trays by his head, women's sympathy brought more and more, a table full he couldn't open, all men drinking and he didn't have a key… then a giant appeared, like Rt. 1 Freeport only instead of an ax he had a chain saw. Grinning piano keys, revving the saw, knocked cap

after cap… Foamy essence of life lifted him to the ceiling, he floated up and up.

Spirits of heaven he was there, licked his lips, woke in pitch blackness, no stars, no moon, no nothing and no flashlight, he had a cell, lost on the ground …. felt around like a blind man, crawled to the stream.

Like youth in a bar, he lost sense of time, rubbing his face, the water tasted like trees, he was at home, the social atmosphere of men and drink, Paul Bunion helping him out, no panic over moose, deer… bear. He had two weapons; long barreled shot and G- 4 semi-auto.

He thought of climbing to the ridge, they'd planted wind towers, ugly as sin … high up, in the faint displacement of air he'd figure a way out. …then imagined himself on their thermal imaging cams, remotely viewed by security men in vans ….and just didn't want to deal with it, … *alwaays some un watchin*. Instead he crawled back to the tree, found his cell… nothing.

He'd follow the stream that was the plan, it flowed to a pond, he'd been there before, but more recently on a map, *lass I waas 'ere 'tees waas smalla'*. The cell's face just bright enough to collect the rest of his gear.

Instead of leaving he sat down again in the same spot, gun across his lap, *dis es rid'iac'lass I caan't see nothin'*… A little bird, hopped on a branch, white chest too big for his suit coat, complaining in his ear.

"Ya gat wing, I done."

But the little bird kept up the racket, reaching back to his dinosaur roots, *ged id on U-aube*. … pressed record but it flew away.

Thinking of nothing, drunk on life, hat pulled over his eyes he again surrendered to sleep.

I'm still 'ere, he sighed dismayed at the pitch-black. …Staring at the star-lit sky, glittering between boughs when, out of the stream the water stood up, a woman surrounded by a pillar of silver came towards him, apparitional and talking but he couldn't make out what it was, "Spaak up," … he felt love and recognized her. She was the old psyche nurse at the hospital when he went to identify his son's body. Words she said then were unintelligible too, his grief so great, now the transmission was pure spirit. "Yaur daad," he pointed out, he'd read her obituary, her pic. young like now…moved towards him and disappeared.

He shook his head, said out loud, "Daa'll neva baleif dis," then noticed his eyes had turned into flashlights, faintly shining on the ground like almost dead batteries. And his body wasn't sore, "I cun do dis," …he started down the edge of the stream.

It was immensely quiet; he checked stars, keeping a north-easterly direction. gun in a shoulder sling, arms free to push aside branches, there were plenty, kept an elbow raised, fending them off. Light footed, enjoying the air, quiet, sense of peace the image of the woman like a candle in his mind.

He came to the pond, circled, slogged the outlet, picked the trail up again, down a gentle incline and continued tramping across swamps ... abandoned fields, up a logging road, looked back and saw the towering forms of wind mills, turning on their gas fired 'cheat system' rotors grinding that his ear paused to diagnose, music of failure, he understood the noise, could fix it, but there they were ... towering overhead, ... *day used ta bay crosses poking aat heaavan*, shook his head, *prayeah warks; day done.*

Following instincts, prancing onward, expecting the mythical elk to appear, wave antlers in right direction ... but instead got a dose of reality, walked right into a chain link fence, ten foot, with a red electrification tag, topped in razor wire, ... *I'm 'ere? Can' be, dads tewenny-'ive maile fam 'ome.*

He tried for a signal but his phone was dead, killed. *Caan' aksess' gaagle maap, awr GPS.* He remained hidden, nothing made sense. . . what reality, distance traveled? The ground covered in storm litter, last storm washed the woods clean, took all trash evidence, ... *Ef dis isn't da Naavel baase ... whaere am I?*

I'll ged ta da anntrance dey'll bay a gaard. I'll aan'once ma pra'sence. He'd have them contact his wife get a ride home or have them drive him...*na daay'd neva giff may a 'ide.*

Gradually he moved down hill but the fence didn't stop, turn a corner as expected, *maan daay naad a lodda spaase.* Then he started to see buildings, *hausin'* The structures formed an inner and outer semi-circle around a court-yard, flagpole in the center, arching security lights cast blocky shadows, he stood awhile, *dane loak lake wad I 'memba'*. When his family first moved across from Quebec, he was a child, on a fieldtrip with his third grade class. Later it became less accessible, then disappeared off maps.

He didn't wear a watch, cell dead, estimated the time at around 4:00 am, mostly he always woke then. A habit left over from when he lived at MacPhees, sleeping on their living-room couch, he'd have time to doze, prepare for the drive to Bangor; his job at Public Works.

Reaching the front, cameras angling, double drop gate, striped reflective flagging … he found the small entry door … opened in …. guard post but no guard … decided to wait until morning, moved back in the woods, *day wone warry*, picturing his wife, he'd gotten lost before, never LOST, lost … but late home.

NIGEL SAT before his gray screen, imagining Poseidon, in gigantic form, Hercules with a whale tail, sleeping in the bottom of Foster Lake, waking up from a long summer slumber, grabbing the men, dropping them in his mouth, terrified faces squashed like grapes. *There's a monster at the bottom.* But no one was missing, let alone three large military looking men or hapless off season vacationers, no one unaccounted for or at least unreported.

Only one missing was Stan, his wife called that night, her easy going question as to his whereabouts was answered by,

"Don't worry about him, blindfolded in the middle of Baxter and home before dinner." Nigel knew Stan was born in the woods, hardy as a bear.

At 9:00 am, next morning his cell vibrated. "Morn'nan Govena' daa, you?"

"Stan, where are you, your wife called."

"Caal 'er back, I'm a' ah gas sta' shan, jus Narth a' MoreKaul Mao'nan." Shay cun pic may auh 'ere."

Nigel phoned Stan's wife Rosalie and although immensely relieved he was found she wasn't that keen on the drive up to get him. Her sweet contralto, over weight women often possess and know how to use … swayed, besides she was pregnant.

"I'll get him, no problem," Nigel was actually looking forward to the adventure, pushing the Rover's trip comp. into territories unknown.

"Should be back before dark," he optimistically texted Leah and set out in high spirits, enjoying the change of seasons. Branches stripped bare up there, hurricane rim blew through, rain and fog digesting all litter, the bare hills rolled at him as he went by abandoned farm after farm … everything turned to hay, he loved the look, it wasn't depressing, rolled hay left to rot … but… *hard to live up here … hard living in Foster … impossible here.*

He tried to reach Stan but to no avail. *Wonder how he got through.* After a few blind turns and roller coaster hills he found out. A Circle K Convince store out here? Behind the gas pumps was a 'remote' Ranger's Station and behind that a medium sized communications tower, good for bouncing calls, hunters trucks parked, owners hunched over cells, 'did ya get a deer?'

It was drizzly, gray, pepperoni aroma clung around the entrance, everyone tanking up on coffee, he quickly used the washroom. Crowded tables, male voices amplified excitement had Nigel wanting to join in but like any battle everything's great until the slaughter.

He bought coffee, returned to his car, decided on gas, paid with dusk falling, waiting to see Stan's face, knowing he was close, their long acquaintance's ESP in full gear.

Like an upright bear Stan padded towards him just as he replaced the pump. "Ma bad'draay died a'wale baak, day lad me barra d'eir's." Stan, holding his cell only briefly glanced at Nigel.

"At least you're found, thank God for that," Nigel happily rubbed his hands together then looked down. The man appeared different. The sadness that clung to him for so long was back.

"Tank-ya Goven'a."

After packing the back with Stan's gun and gear, he sat quietly next to Nigel, looking out the window and sighing.

"You hungry?"

"Nah, aad sam'din a' da stare."

"What happened," Nigel tried to keep the tone even, *the man was 27 miles from home, in the middle of nowhere, with no explanation.*

"I waas waalkin' an fell asleep."

"You fell asleep?!"

"Yeah, pad ma haaed agnse' a taer an wake ap an id waas patch daark a'out. Caoudn' saee ma han'. Ba' I gat movin' fallow' da sream, foun' ma waay ou'"

"Then what?"

"Nathin' ya knaw da' raess." Stan was still processing ... he wasn't ready to tell anyone, *I'd aalmose eanded ma laafe. Neva' saae ma waif an' baabies again.* He thought of the close calls in the past as a long haul trucker. *Haa' ta gaav' ad up too dangar'is.*

They bumped along for awhile down terrible roads, "I swear they're depopulating Northern Maine one pothole at a time."

"Wea'll maake id ta Fosta' aany ways."

Nigel, accessed location on his onboard, but it didn't show settlements or the Navy Base he'd assumed was in the area, jets periodically boomed in daytime hours.

Nigel thought back to the previous Fall, 2018, Dan reported infantry in night vision goggles, behind a stone wall, (ghillie suits !)… Gripped by reality, they eyed each other and said nothing, Dan making the first move…retreat! Plus rumors were ripe about white survival gear and cold weather training. More recently reports circulated of convoys slogging up I-95 ... personnel carriers, with black-out windows, taking different routes, splitting up at the Newport exit, Irving's parking lot.

"Scarry stuff," Nigel said, the next spring, 2019, making conversation with Dan.

"Cold weather training for when we invade Russia or North Korea," Dan told the future by penetrating the present.

Nigel believed in the fantastic, *first imagined then made*. But a war with Russia? Insanity. They were our allies. Like erasing history. AI, (CIA's) probably working on the book right now or at least generating a lot of comments.

Rescuing his friend, bringing him safely home, the old fellowship of cause feeling had him wondering how men could want otherwise. What about the old promise from his school days that technology would unite people, races and culture. The nineties, World Wide Web ... the late eighties, 'Hands across America ...Hands across the World' An image of his sons grown to men came towards him. The theater of war. *Those old Bastards! ... leave my kids alone!*

He glanced at his passenger. How Stan got from point A to B. where he picked him up was a mystery, the man had pulled into himself. "Did you light a fire?" Nigel knew he hadn't, no smoky odor emanated from his clothing.

"Nah warn't col'"

"You were hunting deer?"

"Nah, Ta'kay. Ta'kay 'n sea'sin"

"You walked twenty-seven miles after a turkey?"

"Da' Faar?" Followed by silence.

"How did you get to the Ranger's station?" Nigel clutched the steering wheel.

"Ranga' baough' me."

"How did he know where you were?"

"I caal'ed em." Most everything he said was true. Circumstances surrounding the call emotionally tumbled. He had no desire for revenge and didn't want another confrontation with the women, just wanted to get home to his wife, buy her a gun, maybe tell someone, *daay pra'bably knaw alreaady*. Their freak-out was unexpected, they didn't hurt him, but did place him inside a cell with nothing in it except a chair, 'time out room' they said. It was the narration of his son's death, four years ago that saved him. Hearing it, they were unsure of themselves, *caaugh' em off guaad'*, ... and eventually gave him his guns back, drove him out to a road, called the Ranger Station.

It happened when he followed the chain-link down, rounded the corner to the entrance and found an unlocked door cut in the gate. At first he decided to wait for dawn, but tired, hungry and anxious to get out of the woods, see his family, *day maay waory*, he chanced it, opened the door and made entry.

The guard house was empty. People were present, evidence of use, activity marking the ground, his spirit enhanced night vision interpreted it to be a low security part of the old base or training facility for young recruits, he waved at the security cameras. Nothing. He paced the entrance gate like guard duty. Deciding against firing three shots and running out of options he moved in…

Approaching one of the buildings, he peeped inside and saw cots with children sleeping. He wandered to other buildings, waving his arms to be seen, peeped in more windows and he saw older kids and lots of very young women, teenagers, but no men. Moving to other dorms, up on tip-toes to get a better look, found little lumps under blankets, he was close enough to watch them move and breathe, suck their thumbs when suddenly he was grabbed from behind, thrown to the ground, put in handcuffs …

Women, smelled and felt … unmistakably female. They took his guns. Large beautiful women. One was very nervous, "Lets get rid of him! No one would blame us, we've orders. He's seen them!"

"I can see nothin' wiff-ou ma glaases." He put his head down and cried, humbly explained how he was hunting turkey, got lost, followed a stream, found the fence, the open door ... he knew how they'd respond and they did. They were gentle lifting him to his feet, marching him through a deserted building, with no electricity.

Handcuffs removed, locked in a cell, he was unafraid ... almost amused. *Women.* They returned with a tray of hot tea, cookies and a banana ... didn't respond positively when he laughed at the sight of the banana so he looked down and asked in his quiet humble way to be let go, told them again about his kid and ..."Ma wiff as as'peac'kin' are dard chil'."

They left in a state of mental confusion. He waited in the dark and thought of his life with women. They always trusted him and he loved them back, if they needed his protection he'd give it, car fixed? He'd do that too. Richer men courted his wife, but Rosalie chose him and she returned after the break-up when their son died. He always felt comfortable around women and settled into a kind of lively stupor wondering what would come next.

"You'll have to wear this." He was blindfolded, handcuffed and led out, placed in a vehicle that was inside the building, a garage door opened. Dawn was just breaking when they left him on a road, guns returned without ammunition ... told a ranger would be by, explained that he was in a restricted area and if needed he'd be brought up on charges.

"Wha' I do?"

Four pairs of very serious eyes bore into him," You want to find out?" A well made woman with a sweet face, looked steadily at him, "make up some stupid story… and you'll find yourself in Federal prison."

At home, dangling his cherub on the knee, reading from picture books, *laife waas badda' baack den.* Snow covered castles, horses and blacksmith shops. He'd always wanted a forge, hammer ringing things into shape, *maak ma oawn tool* or like a hobby; turning out iron gates and fences. He was building a new shop at his place. Big metal building to repair trucks, *daecant manay, if da tawon waant shaut mae dawn.*

He hadn't told anyone about that night and his head was at floodtide, revisiting the scene of sleeping children .... girls and threatening women; *"make up a story... and you'll find yourself in Federal prison."* He was ready to spill the whole thing. *Da bass pear'sin ta caal as Dan.* But he didn't bother, knowing Dan would call him and like clock-work he did.

Dan wasn't a lazy man, only disliked working on certain things if he could avoid it, and ready to help Stan with heavy stuff, mending fences, righting doors, bracing beams ... Gentle donkeys and mules were also destructive, knocking over fences and escaping to pond and woods for bathing and hiding.

There were better/easier ways of doing it but Therapeutic Riding's autistic kids, might not be able to understand; "electrical fencing is to keep animals safe," .... (welcome to our farm, noted place of healing ZAP!) as a result nothing was electrified.

Dan and Stan were replacing posts on that gray November morning when Stan described what he saw, not mentioning the encounter with the spirit. "Day caalled da war' dan. ..I mean Raan'gar an Nay'gal gad me."

"You called the Ranger station?"

"Day daid, yeas. Da un dawn' dare."

"He picked you up."

"Yaeah, eaven doe I waern't of'f"aacially maissin' an didn' kaanow where I waas neva' heard a id ba'far, no saaign, na nathing saom kain a wamans fa'ci'lady'" Stan fibbed, because he had seen it before, as a school child.

"Oh, you mean Lanzee, women's minimum security prison," Dan smiled imagining the scene, "It's all women now, no men working …there period"

"Bu' Waa' a'bou da kids?"

"Kids?"

"Ya Kids … do daorm fall a kid, an anotha fall a yaung garl."

Dan put his head down remembering from two years ago when he and Anne were invited to a photography exhibit at Lanzee.

Anne received written invitation and he was her 'arm candy'. It was a women's empowerment series and the photos were done by inmates. Anne was a judge but they arrived late and someone else took her place. All of Maine's women of note were in attendance, the Governor, councilors, civic coordinators, ranking members and their husbands, directory heads, it was a big audience, mixed murmurings of female voices and plenty of cupcakes. Photos exhibited on rolling board, were enjoyed by all and a small speech was done by the Governor; … "We need them…they are coming across the border to help us." She went on about the importance of inclusion in today's fractured society, "Art is a universal language and blooms here at Lanzee."

At the end awards were handed out. First place went to a puppy with overly photo-shopped eyes, staring pleadingly at the camera, titled: 'Looking for my Forever Home.' Second was for two three little girls, arms around each other, titled: 'Winners.' Third place was a hundred or so children in a dusty yard wearing different colored bandannas titled: 'We Are Americans Too.'

4
2019 Christmas Party

D an and Anne Steven's Therapeutic Riding Center held their annual pre-Christmas party/fundraiser. Many notable Maine personalities were in attendance, plus Volunteers and their families, Stan, Nigel and their families.

Dressed in holiday-wear, everyone showed up with gifts of food and non-alcoholic beverage. It was a typical chaotic scene, huge dining room table and sideboard groaning with plates of food. Volunteers in the kitchen periodically replenishing, shared joy for the past years accomplishments and optimism for 2020.

Leah arrived with husband Nigel and children Bett, Henry and Jeff (minus Ada away at boarding school). She mingled like a pro, having brought a plate of gingerbread men and donkeys, decorated with raison eyes and expressions drawn in white icing all looking surprised to be there. Nigel slipped Dan an envelope, "A small token of our esteem," he patted Dan's shoulder. Like burning his fingers, Dan made for his office and shut the door.

Suddenly shy after Dan's abrupt departure, Nigel tasted a spritz cookie, searching for friends over his glasses. The abundance of females, like plates of goodies, painted and highly edible, he choose instead to find a paper plate and loaded up, noticing no others did the same he was suddenly embarrassed but couldn't return what he'd already taken and quickly ate two to prevent avalanche.

"That's Ok, Nigel, take it all … Go Crazy!"

"Government money."

"No, silly,… Christmas!" An attractive woman squoze his elbow so tight he almost lost balance, puffed out crumbs, only great presence of mind kept him from answering to feelings he was having inside.

"Humm," he chewed.

She didn't drop her hand but massaged his arm, leaning affectionately, "Can you believe this?! Some clean eating… Look at all this junk …and she's a health foodie, … do as I say not as I do!"

He looked coolly down, "antithetical …say, can you hold this for me?" He handed her his cider and disappeared with the plate. *One has to-do what one has to-do.*

The Wiznowski family appeared soon after. Stan's wife found camaraderie in Anne, once their baby declared independence. Although there's a big difference between two and four year olds, especially when it came to boys, her rugged little son didn't know that, his fat baby arms reaching for the floor, body wriggling away. Luckily their fourteen year old daughter, Marie bent forward, gave chase and ran herd, her red Christmas sweater disappearing in the crowd.

Family occupied, Stan was free range. In parties like this he was a somewhat invisible man. Proportions on the full side of mid-weight, dressed in a dark blue pullover sweater, 'dress' blue jeans, long black wavy hair and beard glinting in the shadows, Stan 'eves-dropped'.

Because he was handyman to the, (with the exception of Nigel and Dan) all female farm, he knew them all, addressed them by name and they responded, "oh, I didn't know you were there! (blending in with a shadow) Stan, I'd like you to meet my husband."

The men merely nodded or waved, leading their wives to safer types of the same class, no alcohol to dull distinctions, they were stand-offish, well educated, had money, he wasn't and didn't. Stan barely passed his GED after dropping out of school at seventeen, even baseball couldn't keep him, most of the boys in his group did the same, couldn't wait to be out working, earning a paycheck. He and Rosalie were married at eighteen, had a son and daughter. Four years ago their son died from fentanyl poisoning, they were reconciling their loss with babies, *as many as God gives us.* Rosalie saw cherubim in clouds reaching for her.

"One must really put everything on the fast track," forty-seven year old Nigel was expounding while the young married's listened politely, she a pretty young volunteer, he like 90% of the others worked in the woods industry, "before the old noggin gives out," he tapped his high forehead knowingly.

"And for you, it's art, your art?" politely asked but not waiting for an answer when another man horned in, captured his attention and the discussion turned to hunting. Nigel sighed. He'd seen the spilled guts of a deer in the woods and felt at a loss for words. *It's like committing murder and bragging about it afterwards.*

Stan came forward from the corner, radiating warmth, "'Low Govena'… soam paddy"

"Stan, how's it going,"

"Gud," Stan responded with a nod over warm cider, eyes lighting around the room.

"Did you ever bag a bird?" Nigel was relieved, he had a friend to talk to and turkey hunting was something he was in favor of, they'd become a nuisance.

"Nah, neava' daid ga baack aoud dare."

"No I don't imagine you would want to repeat the experience, twenty-seven miles is quite something. How did you do it. I imagine you paid for it in pain."

"Nah, jauss a laddle taire." Stan thought for a moment, 'e mia' bay innearst 'ed 'en da saaupar-naduarl ... "I waas wiacked tiard bu' 'en an wam'man 'oh waas daead awl'reaady ba' na daead, en rael laff, rael tame, shae waas staandi' lake a appahar'atin' taalkin' bu I caouldn' unner' har. An aafta' shae laef I waas raedy ta gad oud'da dare ..."

"You couldn't understand each other ... you and the ghost"

Naat a Ghaaos, naw Ghaaos, bu a 'eal sparit foam da sparit warl.

"Scared you and you took off running?" Nigel crooked a finger over his mouth hiding smiles. Separating his own strange tale of the disappearing boatmen, Stan's was the preverbal guiding light in the woods ... while his was an unsolved mystery.

"Nah," Stan collected his thoughts, although it happened more than a month ago, her spirit helped him find his way, forgetting the women's prison and the rest, it was like the dead woman's soul dissolved in his own consciousness, she became part of him, he was supported, helped... but in this instance it was only to make conversation with Nigel who liked him and Stan wanted to keep the friendship alive, being in good terms ment garage space, Marie's tuition and unreported income. He felt a slight guilt as he hadn't broken the news that he was planning on moving out of his garage as Nigel in his generosity had just added heat and insulation.

"Nah I waasn' scaar a har, sha wa same'un I knaw." Wanting to change Nigel's quizzical look, he tried a different topic. "Daares a prason aup dare; wam'man's"

"Really, I wasn't aware of that."

Through the crowd Stan spotted his daughter talking to Bett MacPhee and Olivia Stevens, his baby son nowhere in sight, he was about to go look when suddenly something locked onto his pant leg, cherubic face looking up. Nigel quickly bent down and placed him in Stan's arms. The Baby looked from man to man and buried his face in Stan's beard, thumb in mouth, the other hand played with Stan's hair. Stan rocked him side to side, thought of the babies he saw in prison, too numerous to be born from inmates. "Thay'es baabies in da priasin, an yaung chail an taenaag guil.'"

'Really? are you sure about that."

"Saaw id wiff ma aown dow ayes."

"An overnight respite daycare is now run out of that prison... more than that" a tall man neither of them recognized was speaking to a woman holding a cup and saucer of warm tea. Stan and Nigel looked at each other, the man had answered their question! The man turned his back briefly but they caught the continuance… "but by far the most prolific human trafficking was done using forged passports. You know how middle easterners all look alike? Add the same beard and mustache or in the case of kids, dress them in the same outfit and bingo, they're in the country." The man pulled a flask out of an inside coat pocket, offered her some, she declined, placing a hand demurely over her tea while he poured carefully into his.

Nigel turned sideways, moving behind Stan, who edged back as well, rocking his baby. Both men had excellent hearing, Nigel found it annoying while Stan cultivated his from years of tracking game.

"They'd simply bring passports over; get counterfeit stamps and return with person unknown, identity hidden under similar facial growth. Kids were even easier … five offspring the norm."

"That is so wild and you helped to put a stop it?"

"I ran surveillance, if that's what you mean,… underscored the mission, he wagged his body like an important guy, dressed in form-fitting slacks, tan shirt, gold tie and brown sport coat he bore the look of status. "Theirs was a large well run organization, and hard to trace it back to the source and you realize some were allies so its tricky, a lot of high level negotiations taking place on both sides."

"And you were part of them?"

"On the lead team, made preparations, held briefings, ground floor, advanced decision planning, made them look good. Appearances … you know … top translators. But you know, as long as they weren't hurting American citizens it was left to continue, human trafficking" …he sighed "…kids…"

"But is it still happening? It can't still be happening, that's so wrong."

"It's hard to say … but," he looked briefly at the ceiling, then down at his cider, "I can say it was watched very closely," he sighed at his 'cider'… "sometimes I put too much faith in others,"

In the shadows Stan and Nigel held their breaths, the man pulled at his jacket. "Would you like to go for a walk, it's hot in here."

They waited for them to leave, finally able to exhale, "Whaa da 'aell!"

"Yeah," Nigel looked down suddenly wanting a drink, when he hadn't for almost twenty-two years, a choice he made during post graduate years and renewed as his wife Leah couldn't handle alcohol. His mind cleared, "Stan what did you see?"

"Dwo baaeek an maore faull a laddle kid, slaepin en an'naotha', big'gar an only awl gual an … id waas dat naigh' I waas missin'." They were silent, on solitary mental voyages, but didn't find safe port, some moral sanity to call home.

"There's strange things done in the midnight sun by the men who moil for gold"

"Haugh?"

"Robert Service. Look!" Nigel whispered, the couple had reappeared through the dining room door, acting like they were trying to hide an acute excitement in each other. Stan and Nigel were of like mind, he was drunk and might spill the beans. "Introduce yourself!" Nigel hissed. Stan paused for a sec. eyeing his friend, then smiled in his most disarmingly simple way, golden haired tot sleeping on his shoulder added to the aura of total harmlessness. "Perfect," Nigel said in his ear.

"Sdaan Wiz-now-ski," Stan let them come to him and nodded, cocked his head to the side hoping to get a name.

"Bob Mason."

"Naise ta maet ya Mas'ta Maa'sin. An' das as ma fraen' Naegil,"

"Nigel MacPhee," he corrected, "and are you Mrs. Mason? I didn't catch the first name." he smiled charmingly at the young woman.

"Oh no," she said with some alarm as if caught, "I'm here with my sister, she's a volunteer …I'm just…oh my tea's cold … catch you later," she smiled at her companion and light footed away.

Waman, thought Stan, *daay laoke ya an den day don'*. He turned towards the man drinking 'cider', "Ya waor'k raoun' haer Maes'ta Maasin?"

"Over at the base, Fort Charon," he paused rocking, "I was ROTC, earned a medical degree, taught College briefly in Bangor before deployment, that was back in 2001 after the attack, was part of that first enlistment wave."

"An naaw ya 'ome,"

"The world is my home …The military is interested in ventures like this so we reached out and Steven's mentioned the party as a way to learn more …they've a large well run facility here."

"An whaa' da yah dao ova' dare."

Stan's thick Maine accent along with a slight lisp, had him pausing to decipher. "Oh you mean rank?"

Stan and Nigel nodded.

"Sergeant Major, if you'll excuse me," he headed to the dining room.

DING DING Dan called everyone's attention by ringing the glass. "Please join us in the Library for another round of Video Madness!"

With contagious excitement they funneled in, awed by the high ceilings, ancestral portraits, crackling fire, it was a Victorian masterpiece and the Stevens knew it; sharing it was key to their livelihood. A trash can placed at the entrance suggested spent items be deposited before entering.

All evidence of 'home schooling stored away in the basement, chairs from all over the mansion, a few from the MacPhees stately log home and several hastily made pine benches with store bought cushions, set in a semi circle were eventually taken after time spent noisily admiring portraits, dark landscapes, framed maps and fire. All eyes coated Dan with admiration, he was their handsome host, children sitting cross legged in front, faces upturned.

Dan pressed a button and a projector screen slowly lowered, manually was quicker but even at the end of 2019, technology awed. "Thank-you for joining us on this festive occasion, we look forward to having everyone here with us. All of you have played significant parts, with your energy, dedication and support, The Lane School and Rescue Farm keeps reaching and surpassing goals, Anne and I dedicate the evening to you … you made it happen." he paused while his heart filled with joy from a room of friends, in the back row he saw a man hastily dump something from a flask into his cup, a much younger plump woman sitting next to him pretending not to see, *someone new…*

"Ok lets get started, there's a lot to be worked on, ongoing projects … that's why it's important to have a look back. And for that we need the heart, soul and brains of the operation, my wife Anne…" Dan paused pacing, he wasn't reading, had eaten too much and wasn't prepared to turn over the microphone. "It all began with her love of the retired woods horse, she tended to their care from childhood, at the rescue farm south of here in Dover-Foxcroft … but had to give it up to look after her elderly parents… Then responding to need she convinced me to adopt not one but twenty burrows from the southwest … well adapted to our winters they did great up here… so a year later we added the two mules, Jack & Jill, they grew thick winter coats too. …and then as you know we increased our capacity with the new indoor riding ring, five new stalls …fifteen new arrivals." Anne quietly appeared to his left, she'd changed to a Victorian gown, glowing like a spirit from the past, "I now turn the stage over to my wife," he gazed fondly down, taking in her beauty enhanced costume.

"Oh, thank-you so much for coming here sharing our joy and evening with us and thank-you Dan for being our strength, our inner core. We look forward to having everyone together to celebrate Lane Farm. I'm wearing this gown to pay tribute to my many greats-grandparents, the original Lévesque's who came to this area from New Orleans, shortly after the Louisiana Purchase …they were on their way back to Quebec when sidetracked by the sight of this forested land and large flowing rivers and settled in Foster Lake. After many successful generations in the timber industry … in order to honor their past the Victorian era Lévesque's built this mansion from stone, like mansions in New Orleans, one can see the many stories of their lives reflected in these walls, in their portraits, the wealth they brought to the area, their gentility, I can feel them smiling down on us for what we have done and why we're here tonight."

Her crisply curling black hair, the sweet gentleness of her voice had everyone convinced not only of the purity of their mission, but the purity of her gene pool, *she carries authenticity well*, Nigel thought sitting next to Leah who was likewise was spellbound, (even though she saw her friend everyday). Bett and the Boys occupied cushions in front and Stan, sleeping baby and pregnant wife were one row up from the back, having strategically placed himself with in ear-shot of the Sergeant Major.

"Better drink up, don't want that cider evaporatin'" the young woman giggled. Stan smiled, sitting to close to look back. Personally he hadn't touched a drop since Nigel put him on a alcohol free diet, four years ago to prevent drowning in sorrow. *Laife Daon't Madda' 'dan.* He thought of how much it mattered now.

"And now to begin our recap of the last five years, I pass the baton to one of our most capable volunteers… the mic. was handed to a tallish much rougher individual, totally devoid of feminine graces, to the point that all eyes followed Anne off the stage watched the rearranging of her ruffled skirt, bare shoulders glistening, kiddy-corner to Dan, they could see each other and everyone witnessed their mental exchange.

"2015.. was when it got started, first we had the donkeys arrive from Utah," she waited as the scene played out of forlorn looking creatures, tails to winter wind, stranded in the high plains, captured, corralled, the long journey across country, stopping along the way to water and feed, somber looking creatures not knowing what was coming next. Then with music trilling, a joy filled noisy arrival, herself in a barn coat, pretty little Olivia running around, Dan calmly waving the trailer back, adjusted the ramp, opening gates. Everyone exclaimed, it was unbelievable so many fit in one trailer.

"And we can never forget Jenny!" Jenny's heavily edited story played, the narration told so many times, the clips of her growing from sick three week old to a large gray emblem, her image an early selling point.

"About our plans for tonight, we could drive down to Irvings in Newport." the Sergeant Major whispered.

"Irvings."

"Or … I've access to a friends camp… he keeps it open for snowmobiling."

"And lets not forget The Donkey Club." A new scene played, a tall, thin girl with delicate features smiled sweetly into the camera. It was twelve year old Ada, (away at boarding school,) leading donkeys in a circle, rows of brushing at cross ties, carrots being fed, and Bett playing with Jenny. The rescue when Bett and Jenny fell in the 'well' hole was deleted but not the blue cast, her robust form featured in a sequence about cleaning the barn, dumping manure, sweeping out … "Everyone finds fun at the farm …"

"I'm working tomorrow… look let's see each other again …I"

"So tonight's off! But you!"

"We just meant!"

"You agreed."

"No I didn't … It would be like killing myself."

"And let the fun begin!" (The rough woman worked, too distracting if Anne kept the mic.) … Children with obvious deficits holding tight to saddle bars, led by volunteers, wide open eyes looking directly into the camera, they appeared transformed by the experience and the volunteers all business, expressions marked with mission, they taught the kids as much at they were capable of learning, difficulties deleted, it was beautiful.

Then came the creation of the new indoor riding arena, shown at warp-speed, Stan riding a gigantic dozer gave finishing touches to a flattened one forth acre next to the barn. The sun rose and set over days of Dan mounted on his big yellow tractor, back-hoe elbow articulating in repetitious trench digging, water pipe and wire laid, covered, foundation posts poured, steel beams lifted by cranes, a pause in the middle for a terrific rain storm, fast action resumed, it suddenly had roof, fiberglass skylights, doors, windows, interior wiring, ceiling fans, suspended lights, five huge stalls. A long silver horse trailer arrived backing in and eight little, three mammoth donkeys and two pair of mules, dutifully off loaded, ears pricking up at the sounds of other animals. They spent two weeks quarantined in their new stalls ….the 'Release Day' in the general population a cause for celebration …. Crowds of people enjoying a tour, three piece Country Western ensemble, picnic tables of food.

A slow gentle scene of a riding lesson followed. Six kids on mammoth donkeys and one on Jenny riding at a walk without saddle bars, serene attentive expressions, reins held tight, sunlight streaking through the skylights, it was cinematic.

"Is this place for real, the kids looked like they're on something … some medication … drugged." The irritated voice of the Sergeant Major spoke unaware Stan had pressed record.

"No they're not, 'on some medication' some take pills to control outbursts, but none are drugged/drugged … my sister has stories of kids getting off meds … improving that much. The Lane School kids ride too you know and they have classes, riding …"

"Why spend time over them, their just a bunch of imbeciles, they'll never get better."

"If that's how you feel, why did you come?"

"I'm on assignment … they're being studied"

"Really … well that's interesting … but … what is there to learn … their lives are pretty much out in the open, everyone knows about the place, Anne is the most assessable friend I have, she's always there helping and she's got four year old twin boys."

"We look at things like net-worth, civic involvement, Dan Stevens might run for Governor someday he needs to be investigated ahead of time otherwise he'll be totally out of control, on his own, not in a party … we need to learn his weaknesses … help where help …is …

"Since when has Dan had an interest in politics?"

"They start with Town Council, get noticed…"

The video over, Anne was back, sweet voice ringing out, "we have thought of incorporating, instead of being a simple non-profit, but include The Lane school in our mission, allowing more participation by special-needs kids, perhaps a second building … wouldn't that be wonderful! But to-do so … we need your input and help. There's so many things to be thought of and we need better minds. Dan and I are so fortunate to be part of this and we both feel our journey with you has just begun."

"How the hell did he find her." The Sergeant Major, now clearly drunk, red in the face.

"So please if you have any suggestions don't be shy, just email, twitter, instagram, go to the Farms website, Face book …and" she put her hands together and leaned forward smiling seductively…like a rendering of timeless femininity.… "let us know …oh and there's one last treat waiting in the dining room so please come and join us there." Anne lead the way, poised and self confident she emptied the room.

His seating companion quickly departed, leaving her cup and saucer. The Sergeant Major, void of deferential hardware, 'body armor', or even scrambled eggs, got nary a second glance as the crowd funneled around him.

5

Post Christmas Deconstruction

Later, during a pause of days and weather, as night descended more slowly, Nigel requested an audience with Dan, said Stan had something interesting to show him.

8:30pm, the twins settled for bed, thirteen year old Olivia in her own room, the men meant in Dan's office.

Warmed by a bright fire, surrounded in redwood paneling, Stan pushed play on his cell, placed it on Dan's desk. The men eyed it like a life-form with background noise, Christmas party, brought the scene back, they heard the SGM's voice collaborating what Stan already told to Dan in earlier conversation.

After the cell stopped talking Stan and Nigel reiterated the SGM's claim of being an inside man working against human trafficking. They also retold Stan's misadventure in the woods, (minus apparition) that Dan had also already heard.

"So he didn't recognize Stan …"

"Nah."

"No, curious you'd mention … that … but he was very chatty."

"Woat do ya thank's goin' on … do ya thank wae shaad en'tar'vaew da garl."

"The one in … augh conversation with the Sergeant Major?"

"Da ary un."

"I don't know, maybe he left his army shorts in the dryer too long." Dan's attempt at humor was meant with dismay.

"Dis es se'ious."

"Yeah… he talked so freely," Dan considered, "like a man on a mission…like he don't have worries about guilt."

"But it's more than typical prison life. There's something undercover, only I can't quite put my finger on it," Nigel pressed his lips.

"Yeah, something bigger. He's an army guy, they're organized, but at the same time he seems kind of 'out there.'"

"Oh you mean outside the 'chain of command."

"Yeah, like he's a one man show … or sent here for some special purpose."

"Unruffled."

"Yeah, …Let's get my wife in here … pour water on it and see what happens… err shed some light.… " Dan leaned back in his chair looking from man to man, their mansplaining pact, security for the female majority, echo-locating threats. He liked them, felt zero threat *they can study my achievements; possessions ...chock full office...*

Cha-ching, numbers lined up, there he is again scooping up coin... Dan had returned with his bride who even in simplest attire, void of makeup, was beautiful, seductive.

With heightened awareness, the men were able to absorb more, the recording played several times, the pleading Sergeant Major, the uncooperative girl.

Anne listened, head sideways, each time it came to the part of Dan running for governor she giggled, when the SGM vented on the kids she laughed out loud. The men failed to see the humor.

"Can't you see it's just all made up to impress the girl ... and then ... when she wouldn't just jump in his bed ... he was angry."

"The whole thing? ... about that?"

"It's a universal feeling," Anne smoothed her clothes.

"Trending." said Dan, supportively.

"But why would he say it like that ... it's like propositioning her with reasons to say no." *unless he's used to having his way.* Nigel considered, crooked finger on his lips.

"Waad abaoud da waman prasan? an da kad?"

"I don't know about that, seems like they were playing a game ... and not totally serious. A man, someone like you Stan, you're a hunter and dressed like one ...a hairy bearded stranger' appears in their safe space …. they might of overreacted… but there was more of them and only one of you…and it may be respite care, I know the state provides it for Foster Homes …I didn't know if that's happening there or what you saw in the middle of the night … you walked miles …must of felt very tired." Anne's soft voice had a quieting effect on the men, they felt like calling it a day.

"Reasonable," Dan tapped his pen in agreement.

"The women caught you peeking in windows, disarmed you, locked you in a room, fed you and let you go…"

"Daay dreadened mae."

"Yes they threatened you, but you also threatened them … you must see Stan, from their perspective they were the humane ones." She leaned forward looked in his face, "They could've called the police, had you arrested for trespassing and being a Peeping Tom…could've made up stories," she noted Stan's blush, straightened her back addressing her Husband and Nigel … "They could've connected Stan to us, made it hard on the farm's reputation, instead of simply reacting, going by the book, like … other people might … you were treated with compassion. A woman's prison run by women would necessarily be defensive … but when it comes to core beliefs … behavior … you'll find understanding and forgiveness." She looked away, didn't turn to Dan for support in her theories, *toxic masculinity*, "Well if you'll excuse me I've test papers waiting." She independently left, shut the door.

The men looked at the door and then the fire …the ceiling.

She's 90% right, it's that 10%. "Women want the whole thing to be about them,… that will never change," Dan broke the silence. He felt his wife had evolved, since the birth of his twins, the additional attention, support … Lane school in its fourth year. No more the shy diffident trusting creature but a model of self possessed strength. He'd delighted in the transformation, now he wasn't so sure… "And… they don't improve with age."

They meditated on that age old problem until Nigel brought the topic around again. "He was a bit braggadocios … must of seemed like a good idea at the time. Unless you take in the fact that he blew it, didn't get the girl, got drunk and had his conversation recorded." He smiled, finger to his mouth…"the rest of her analysis was rather spot on." *'hairy bearded stranger!'*

Ya dan'no… ya waren' dare. Stan knew better that to correct Nigel. "I wanded ta caall da pal'lase bu' caoud'dan 'caase daays da uns ad caugh' mae. " Stan couldn't believe they would take her version over his.

Dan brooded, became less annoyed with his wife, "What do you expect to get out of this… disclosure project?" He smiled, "a meeting with secret relatives, Sasquash …"

"Big foot."

"Or Maine's brand of area 51 … connect something they obviously want unnoticed. Spend weeks, months, gather a million terabytes of information, that ain't going nowhere. And we don't know what we're up against or if we should be."

"Daares aotha' ave'va'dance."

"Yeah, personal carriers", Dan held up a thumb, "evidence of training in the woods..." a finger, then his hand went down. "You know as long as they stay in their own territory I'm Ok with it, but coming here to investigate me for whatever reason" He felt a jolt of pain, from four years ago, when he was a person-of-interest in Bett's disappearance.

"Saems paa'quialla' 'em caomin' ta a kaid paardy."

"Obviously be wanted to attend, asked for an invitation." Nigel knew Dan just didn't hand them out, half the town would come. They'd plan on sixty and get eighty.

"He's a Sergeant Major of course he's getting an invite." Dan thought for awhile, "So he didn't get the girl ... was drunk,... or on a mission? How serious was it... We got to let it go ...we're not effen investigators."...*show me a man and I'll show you the crime.* "What if they retaliate ... conjure something up about us... arrest Stan..."

"Not fix power outages."

"make our computers die."

"Na plaow us aout."

World's changed. Dan brooded and observed popularity was a threat to government, but out here? Government was synonymous with law and while law breakers were controlled, given prison sentences, liberty taken away... goodness was allowed to flourish unchecked, out in the open? *We're a free society*, our lives our own, unless in a political party, or other protective force, follow their lead. Was the idea to find fault, a chink in the armor, publicly humiliate even crucify the individual do-gooder? Dan wasn't sure. *Let them shadowbox.* His desire was to remain unattached, autonomous, not endorse anyone. *So I'm politically incorrect.*

The Lane School by its mere existence was an irritant …but for Therapeutic Riding serving the needs of Foster Lake Regional's special ed kids… *Good thing Therapeutic Riding came first. But who was their target?* Dan brooded, the Sergeant Major getting drunk at a children's Christmas party, in a household notoriously tea totaling. Hitting on one of his women, the college aged sister of a volunteer. He knew the Sergeant Major's behavior was normal in his world, the fact he allowed himself to 'get comfortable' gave credence to their low level of concern over Lane Farm/School activities … but not necessarily.

"Perhaps he was monitoring conversations … recording, trying to see if the girl knew anything," Nigel offered, "you know how the girls gossip, but one of us walks in their safe-space and it's quiets -ville. *Man shines light and cockroaches disappear.*

"That's it, he might of targeted her to see how far it traveled." …Dan thought for awhile then leapt to his feet. "My wife!"

But when he reached her, sitting before her huge roll-top desk, computer off, she was going over work books, ordered on line to help with the basics. The kitchen was her domain, as much as his office was his. While he cataloged piles of print-outs under quartz paper weights; hers was a scene of scrubbed fastidiousness, not a stray paper in sight. She glanced sideways then back at her task.

"You haven't told anyone about our meeting."

"You mean Stan and Nigel."

Dan nodded.

"I'm far too busy."

"No? …Good no gossip spread around."

The kindness usually emanating from her was touched with irritation. "We don't gossip."

"What you heard in my office stays in my office."

"All of it? You asked me in … wanted my opinion." She stood, brushing her sweater, annoyance dissolving in quiet, her home, after so many people, gave sanctuary and Dan was part of that.

"You sent messages … they already know," his voice on edge.

"No," she sat down, picked up a kid's schoolbook, looked up at him, "Oh honey nothing bad happened and really …. Stan … and Nigel? Stan's a … good man but you can't really believe his account and Nigel? It's not that they're untrustworthy… I like them both … the same as you … it's just you must know … you're on a different level, a whole different league, there's really no comparison ... and I won't say anything, my lips are sealed," she locked them with a pretend key, the key into a pretend pocket. "I've forgotten the whole thing already."

Her voice and manner had the desired effect, susceptible to flattery, he bent and kissed her neck, rubbed her shoulders, eyeing the school book. "How're they doing?"

"Good except that one girl, I've emailed her Mother… she so disruptive."

He put his head next to hers, breathing her in, seeing but not reading.

Nigel and Stan were at the door. "Guaess wae'all bay headin' hoame, naaght Caapin', naaght Anne. Stan opened the door.

Dan stood blocking their view of his wife, moving towards Nigel, incase he thought of staying.

STRUCTURAL ISSUES weren't noticed in winter, things totally covered in ice and snow. But the mind wasn't, Nigel was on fire with many new events. The Lane School. Winter; 2019 - 2020 had Lecturers they never dreamed of … they needed little encouragement, only travel money and lodging, staying in the Macphees guest room or the south wing of the old Levesque Mansion. It was holiday time around the world and their area turned into a resort for cross-country skiing, snowmobiling and sledding, the lecturers brought family, it warmed Nigels heart and removed the stone that threatened to form when Ada returned to boarding school. She'd showered them with presents, the UPS truck making daily stops until she appeared in person, quiet at first, letting people come to her and they did.

Christmas doesn't last forever, Ada was gone and New-years had an ominous feel. Just the other day Anne, who never shared anything personal asked if he might help interrupt a dream. In it she woke up blind and had to grope around. Feeling the floor she discovered the reason for her blindness was her own head moving around but when she tried to grab it, it rolled under the bed…

Guest lecturing continued, Five Star reviews, unpaid mini vacation. In the Steven's Library, The Lane School learned about diesel engines, from an executive at Caterpillar, (Stan's idea), large scale farming, timber harvesting from one of Dan's associates, followed by a presentation about the mill, with a promise of a tour. An exceptionally well dressed woman, Maine's Senator's Aid from Washington gave a talk about the inner workings of Washington,; how bills were passed etc., it was a little different from textbooks.

During the Aids visit an incident happened on the road to the women's prison. No one would've known but for a post and images on Foster Lakes PD FB, (police departments face book). During a January snowstorm trees brought down power lines and CMP, (Central Maine Power) repair trucks hightailed over for emergency clearance. Trapped by arching wires, a busload of kids upgraded to critical … they ran out of gas and temps well below zero! No images of them, only the bus, same variety seen crossing the New Hampshire border heading north to Maine … dark blue or black with black tinted windows. Foster Lake's PD's FB page's pic. had the license etched, but Dan and Nigel could just make out white lettering and blue background, US Government. The image subsequently deleted, 'children' changed to 'passengers' and a day later the story disappeared.

Maine's senatorial aid from Washington was asked about it, "It's a state matter," she explained, smiling, "handled internally by Maine, Washington gives advice and grants but everything else is done by your state." pausing to gather thoughts she picked up the original thread, "They did a very good job getting emergency services out there …and so quickly."

6

Lucy

No school would be complete without a problem child, enrolled out of love and respect for her mother, volunteer and confidant, she'd known Anne from the beginning, since Lucy was three years old.

Now seven, Lucy had no deficits, so didn't qualify for therapeutic riding. They'd added regular riding as part of the curriculum, the indoor ring made it possible, thrice-weekly classes held as long as temps stayed at twenty above. Modine blowers in ceiling corners, raised temps to 40 degrees Fahrenheit. The kids were 100% super excited, especially Lucy. Riding a mammoth donkey or mule was the only time she behaved herself, so ironically it was the only thing available to remove as punishment.

Lucy was a beginner reader sat at the beginner reader's table. She wasn't hyperactive, mean or hurtful to other children; only frustrated with herself for not learning as quickly as they did. No other differently-abled kids attended so no one was available to make a separate table with, share a safe-space of similar aptitude and ability, instead Lucy sat with the other beginner readers, … she was at least a year older, albeit smaller in size.

If she misspelled a word, she'd snap her pencil in two, even when Anne said, "misspelled words don't matter at this stage, I can still read them."

"But they're wrong!" Tears of frustration wetted her papers, she balled into angry wads and dropped them on the floor. The first time it happened Anne took her on her lap. but instead of cuddling up like the other small crying children, Lucy wriggled free …looked straight at Anne and said; "I don't like you."

It got so bad Anne would hand her tests back without correction. Still she'd break a pencil, crumple papers into a ball and kick them around the room. When Anne told her it had to stop she hid under the table, moving with it when they tried to get her out.

It was decided at a meeting with her Mom and the other teacher/volenteers to try withholding riding privileges. Lucy was to be held in the kitchen/classroom, Olivia would keep an eye on her.

At almost fourteen Olivia Stevens was two inches taller than her mom, with the same beautiful coloring, black hair, white skin but that's where similarities ended. Olivia had a temper. When Lucy came home with badly blistered feet, the explanation was, "Olivia made me walk around the kitchen."

Upon further investigation, a call to Anne who questioned Olivia, it turned out, Lucy and Olivia were at the kitchen table studying together, Olivia had promised a game of jump rope, something Lucy wanted to-do, had suggested, they'd done before, tied a rope to a cabinet handle, Olivia swung; Lucy jumped … but Lucy wanted to jump-rope without completing her work book. She broke her pencil, tore a page out, crumpled it in a ball.

Olivia was going to make her do a time out but felt Lucy couldn't handle it … too much energy. Instead Olivia led her by hand to the kitchen wall and told her to walk around the kitchen until she was ready to say she was sorry, sit and do her work. Little did she know that Lucy wasn't giving up anything, but stayed walking, sometimes skipping, the whole time, all one and one half hours until the other kids came in. The 'walking' was done as noisily as possible, skipping, jumping, running and sliding, creatively tap-dancing, trying to annoy Olivia and she did until Olivia found a pair of headphones in her mom's desk drawer.

Sitting in head phones, concentrating on an e-book, deliberately ignoring Lucy she failed to see, (or hear) the last fifteen minutes of her walk was done in tears. When everyone came in Lucy hobbled to her seat, looking studiously down, like she'd been there all along. Soon after, her Mom came to collect her.

It was then decided that Lucy return to her riding class and take on the responsibility of extra chores. Olivia was again pared up, with corresponding sympathy or social experiment …If two high tempered girls, seven years apart in age, can work together anyone can.

Once she learns how to read, everything will be ok. Olivia observed Lucy hated being told what to do. But with a non-reader, handing her a clip-board or tablet, with a simple to-do list wasn't an option. Olivia soon discovered Lucy could keep orders in her head and so it worked, even if it wasn't really a punishment.

The arena had to be cleaned of manure and Olivia was humming to herself, she loved music, played the piano and was thinking of her best friend Bett, playing and dancing. Lucy was happy, making funny observations about the donkeys, "They all wait till they get in here then poop all over the place." and "The girls pee more than the boys." and "How come your Moms so fat?"

"She's not fat."

"Yeah she's wicked fat …I'm calling her fatty …here it comes …Fatty, Fatty Fatty! Your Mom's a fatty!"

"Finish up with the arena and we'll oil some tack," Olivia left the room, anger spiking and calming.

The tack-room was just off the arena and Olivia stood there thinking, she wasn't sure what to make of Lucy. When her Mother was in a room, Lucy spent the whole time staring at her … Olivia felt that Lucy loved her Mom, had a crush on her. Lucy was almost eight, not reading while the rest of the class basked in real praise for their achievements, Lucy got none … only stiff comments like, "I see some progress there," or "that's better." when actually there was no progress and she wasn't better.

A table under a window was set up near the sink for soaping and oiling tack. Olivia found a few bridles, girths and leather leads to-do. She was looking for more items when Lucy appeared in the doorway then ran over.

"All done!" Olivia was startled by Lucy's high screechy voice, one of the boys made fun of it. That was another thing about Lucy, although she seemed to want attention and approval from her Mom, she shunned the other kids. She wasn't unattractive, only a little thin, the smallest kid in class, with a wayward tentative hold on life, she was delicately formed with long brown hair and large brown eyes … Olivia felt she shunned the others because they were smart and she wasn't, so they had to pay. Olivia was suddenly sorry for her, she was like a tiny sick kitten ready to scratch and claw anyone who came near.

"Lucy! That was fast," Olivia gave her a hug and was pushed away. Olivia sighed, she remembered the feeling when everyone's bigger than you. "Why don't you get started with the soap and I'll go check the arena … incase you missed a few."

Olivia left for the arena and found the wheel barrow with the same amount of droppings as when she left. The ground appeared to be manure free, except for bumps in the once smooth surface. Olivia's Wellingtons kicked the bumps and yielded manure. Lucy had carefully covered the droppings with 'floor' material; a mixture of sand and shavings. Olivia sighed, but instead of confronting Lucy she went around with manure fork, carefully lifting and sifting, dumping the wheelbarrel twice until it was completed.

When she came back Lucy was standing on a pail in front of the mirror with scissors used for trimming animals, only Lucy was trimming her own hair. It used to be down around her shoulders now up to her ears!

"Do you like it!" She jumped from the pail and ran to the windows trying to get a different reflection, jumping and turning her head. "My Mom won't let me have short hair, says it'll make me look like a boy."

"Lucy you should've asked … her first."

"Why? She said no already." Lucy gleefully ran around the tack-room, hands in her hair then bent upside down and scrambled it unto a big ball, like the bride of Frankenstein; climbed back on the pail… making faces in the mirror.

"Did you bring a hat?

"It's on my hook."

Olivia ran back to the mansion's schoolroom and Lucy's hook. "Her head's cold," Olivia waved the hat at her smiling Mom. Anne was listening to the children read out loud, leaning forward, blossoming as was her class, glad the disruptive child found occupation elsewhere.

When she returned with the hat, Lucy was rummaging around in someone's tack box, hair on end. "Lucy what are you doing?"

"Get me a pair of those blue gloves, … please Olivia." Olivia found two pairs and they set to cleaning tack, Lucy working as hard as she could, trying to get everything perfect.

It was not long after that Lucy's fate was sealed and she was permanently kicked out of The Lane school and when her Mother didn't leave in a huff as was hoped she was asked to leave as well. "Your priority needs to-be Lucy …" It was the first time anyone was asked to leave and Dan was chosen to do the dirty work. He was far from despondent, more like in a state of controlled fury, besides Lucy's Mom was from the next town over and 'in-between dental appointments.' Anne was less upset with the situation but more at her own inability to reach inside the child, find the problem and pluck it out.

It happened the day after Lucy's self hair cut., In the arena during therapeutic riding it was discovered four of the specially made saddles had their cotton webbing girths cut. The other saddles had leather girths and so were spared. The cotton webbing wasn't cut the whole way through, just a majority of the strands, hidden under the saddles skirt it wasn't discovered until kids started sliding off.

Since Therapeutic Riding never went faster than a walk, it was a slow motion emergency, kids white knuckling the safety bar. Taught to never-ever let go they believed in the magic of compliance ...it had always worked before ...'do what you're told, nothing bad will happen, you'll ride donkeys and have an organic treat afterwards. With panicked realization that life was coming undone anyway, no matter about following directions ... shrieks of betrayal reverberated.

Prioritizing mammoth donkeys the instructor, nicked time and caught two kids while two others hung twisting just above ground. Feet tangled in stirrups one with a bruised ankle, that might've been worse but Olivia, Bett and three older girls, dropped their donkey's leads and ran to help.

Lucky thing to have Donkey comprehension working in their favor. Horses were known to shy ... runaway but the donkeys with dangling crying children paused and assessed the situation, the ones with dropped leads naturally ground tied, like they were taught. But calmly standing donkeys didn't prevent pandemonium, crying over stimulated children or the possibility of notice by authorities.

Internal investigation yielded the discovery of the cut girths, carefully done as to go undetected while saddling up and buckling billets. Saddling up was something older school girls could do without looking and never paid strict attention, as they, like their Mothers found the barn an excellent place for gossip.

ALL FINGERS POINTED at Lucy ... except Olivia. Olivia wasn't having anything of it, "But Daddy, Lucy doesn't know how to-do that! She's only seven and not strong."

"Eight in a month. She was a problem from day one ... we have to draw the line somewhere ... this is a liability issue ..."

"But what if she didn't do it?" Olivia was uncomfortable in his office. Only occasionally was she called to watch videos, about the farm. Standing behind him, he gave instructions, pen on the screen, about how to run things. (She'd listen nicely, agree he was right and then do it her or her Moms way.)

She'd never watched TV while Dan took in games with friends from work, had a yearly Super bowl party, her brothers with inborn understanding, waved along plays like miniature versions of Dad, she could hear them yelling from her room.

Dan was quiet, playing with a pen. His daughter at first impression was like his wife, only taller with long wavy black hair around her shoulders. He loved her but while Anne looked to him for judgment and reason his daughter had an irritating way of conflicting with his ideas, she didn't trust his mind, didn't really know him ... he was the Dad who'd take a bullet for her, no question, push her out of the way, ... she didn't know how proud he was of her, she was perfection, his most precious possession. Dan was a man who struggled, constantly checking anger, the obese child, bloated and unhappy became a socially aggressive man craving the public's love. Along with a beautiful wife and perfect family, he was always thinking ahead, positioning himself. Olivia didn't see everything around her was made possible by him and her future would play out the same way ... he'd make it so, find her the perfect husband, build her a home on the property. Instead she questioned his authority ... *and it's getting worse... fourteen in two months, adolescence...*

The meeting with teachers and volunteers had already taken place, the decision was final but Dan had yet to enforce it. "She did it alright," he said, anger blanking uncertainty.

"But she's so little and it will hurt her so much, Daddy. I want to work with her ... discover why she won't read ... We need to find the right piece to her puzzle and that will take time. Oh please Daddy. Can't you see? It's so basic! I don't believe she really did it! She's never hurt anybody."

"The evidence is too strong," Dan wanted her to leave... he was angry, trapped, because she was right. Before the actual occurrence, odd stuff happened that only came to light afterwards, when they looked for corroborating evidence and found the hall security cams obstructed; the tack-room's cam with a bridle hung over it and the hallway ones smeared with mud. The barn cams were the old fashioned variety, not Yfied into their new system, and ran on two week loops so whoever was responsible for disabling them was off the loop by the time the girth-cutting occurred. *Took some know-how...* And twice when he did a random night check the manure trapdoor was unlatched, giving access to the barn. Dan chalked it up to Ada's leaving, she noticed everything, they were playing a game of catch up and someone or thing was playing them.

Lucy was a convenient scapegoat. Anne felt she'd be better served by public school, they had special classrooms, aids and psychologists. Even though Foster Lake Consolidated wasn't due to open until next year, she was certain the State of Maine would step in and help. The Lane School couldn't be the alternative for difficult children, it was meant for high achievers, therapeutic riding took care of the special needs piece, if anyone challenged them for not doing enough.

Dan spent many hours thinking and talking it over with Anne, they'd run out of options and here was his own daughter doubting him, "We'll talk about it later," he placed his hand on her back steering her towards the door.

"But Daddy I'm really shook over this! I know I could get through to her, remember 'never give up on a child?' You're going in the wrong direction … we're supposed to be a safe place for different kids … but you're not … you're a total boomer!"

Dan scarcely looked at her, "I need some tea," he left the door open …

She stood for awhile, before going to her room. *Dad's changed.*

Because it was handled internally without outside help or plausible deniability, the school was able to move on. Anne with sincere promises to both Lucy and her Mom … "Let me know if you need support at Foster Lake's PET, (pupil evaluation team) meeting." ….and in later conversations, "the door will never be closed to you or your daughter."

While Anne hid her tears, Dan was confident his wife had disarmed the threat, (kill two birds with one stone). Still the afternoon of Lucy's departure was traumatic. One minute she was there, with her Mom gathering their stuff and the next minute… gone. They searched everywhere … the secret library staircase, the stage's trap door and spiral steps to the loft, cupolas, under beds…in window box seats … boys ran across fields shouting "LUCY!"

Dan and Anne looked at each other and descended dusty stairs to the basement, opened the coal bin. "I thought you'd like me better like this."

7
The Base

Dan consulted Stan about the obstructed security cams. Stan lived only a quarter mile from the farm and promised to check first thing in the morning and again at 8:30 pm, or before he went to bed. Stan made ready for evening rounds; wore his glock four holstered in a belly band, carried a flashlight.

This continued as days increased light, night fall later … earth anticipating spring. He rode a bike over, enjoying the element of surprise, ready to catch whoever it was, prove his indispensability … but of course there was no one and no alarm raised. That changed one night but it wasn't a bad guy … it was Anne and Dan on a 'date' in the hay loft. Stan quickly left the barn but turned back to watch them meet up in front of the mansion, she in a century's old evening gown, bits of hay glinting in the moonlight, they had one little kiss before entering by separate doors, Dan by the front, closest to his office and Anne by the side door that led to the kitchen. *Nobo'day naed ta naow nothin'*

It was early February 2020 when Nigel proposed the field trip, "lets see if the Sergeant Major is amiable to a tour of the base."

"Class tour," Dan bowed head in thought.

"Get our foot in the door, discover what's 'hiding in plain sight.'" Nigel continued while Dan said nothing. "You'd be the one to ask them of course." (Dan finessed a tour at the mill … as a rule they never gave them.) "Just turn on the charm, they know you of course … it will be like returning a favor, you gave him an invitation to the party and now you want one back … his turn to show off. Say something provocative like; the barn Chicks are excited."

Dan smiled toyed with a pen, "You like the Canadians, Blackhawks?"

"I'm not really into hockey."

The green curtain pulled back from the big screen, Sunday afternoon hockey was on, 2020 wasn't cancelled yet.

Nigel leaned against the office center table, covered in stacks of paper and quartz weights… and stared into the fire, openly burning without modern improvements. He'd grown used to Dan's silences, the better he knew him the quieter he got. "Well, what do you think?"

Dan settled in, a practice game had just started, hadn't missed a minute, "They let it happen 'cause of Canada. This whole shutdown deal is BS. Canada has like what? five cases. They're mad at normal…"

Nigel still wearing his parka and scarf waited." Well?"

"Yeah, I'll look into it."

He called the number on the Sergeant Majors card and it was tentatively arranged for March ninth. Late February a package arrived with instructions. They wanted children ten and older, five foot height minimum. Safety railing wasn't in place to accommodate younger/shorter kids. The permission slips were lengthy along with instructions about footwear and clothing. Only 100% - 60% cotton and soft soled shoes. Girls may wear leggings. Jackets with hoods and scarves but no hats. An army transport vehicle had pick-up @ 8:00am; drop back @ 3:00pm. Backpacks are to be left in vehicles. Any and all recording devices, smart phones, tabs, body-cams, selfee sticks, go-pro must be left on the bus. Everyone entering and leaving will be wanded and afore mentioned items confiscated. Facemasks weren't mandatory but would be on hand. The time spent inside the compound will be from 10:00am to 1:00pm. snacks served @ 11:30am. Medical history forms must be sent in by Feb 15. Any and all children may be excluded from the trip, a Doctor's letter may be requested.

The ride over was done in a black-out bus. It looked 90s vintage on the outside but beefed up inside, with agronomic seating, shoulder harnesses, cup holders. "the eagle has landed," said one of the boys.

Nigel got a different vibe, *Space Shuttle Columbia. Totally unaware we're Doomed.*

Dan's natural propriety silently screaming, he had to make allowances, Anne was staying home.

All three girls had their Dads, Stan took the day off to accompany fourteen year Marie, the six boys had two Dads between them, five adults and ten kids total. After the bus two military hardened black Cadillac SUVs with tinted windows pulled in the barn's parking lot. One was going with the bus, leading the way, the other to Dan's astonishment stayed behind at the farm.

"You wouldn't want us leaving the farm unguarded," the Sergeant Major text messaged when Dan reached him on his cell, wondering was the deal was. Everyone was ready, he had to go.

"Its ok," Anne smiled excitedly, "We'll manage."

Women are all whores. Dan bitterly watched his 'girls', the Moms, smilingly waved bye-bye while the bus backed and turned, his wife talking to a guy fifteen years younger, gazing coyly at him, *she looks ridiculous a thirty-six year old woman acting like that...*

Anne still carried baby weight from four years ago pregnant with the twins... and while she seemed not to notice Dan absolutely did notice his once perfect head of hair thinning to a noticeable circle on top.

He stood briefly for a better look out the back, moving up the isle to a side window. The soldiers split up; two to the barn; four to the house.

"They'll do just fine," Nigel gave him an all knowing grin, aware Dan never took her anywhere. *He's that insecure.*

The scene of human failings grew smaller as the bus bounced along and Dan sunk unsmiling into a seat across the isle.

Good medicine, Nigel sniffed, there was a sort of noise canceling device in play, he couldn't hear his daughter or Olivia chatting away seated right in front of him. The bus turned onto paved road, heading north … he turned to Dan; "Aren't you kind of overrating them, they're kids in uniform."

"Yeah, and those kids might be in your house by now, checking your computer, this is a disaster," Dan whispered over the isle and stopped, fake smiled. "Don't you just love the scenery," he batted his eyelashes like a woman, rolling them up.

Nigel discerned a tiny ceiling camera lens disguised in a light, "You really must let me plant some of my winter hardy roses at your place, and you know flowers from heaven, the rose"

"The mill needs landscaping design, consider it a job offer, roses would go great over there." They talked about nothing then stopped, while the bus drove with escort leading deeper into uncut timber, moving roughly on terrible roads, past acres of mossy swamp where tiny ancient spruce grew. They rode a little fast for roller coaster roads, the boys with their hands up like Six flags.

Everyone gazed sleepily, the early spring landscape changing in dreamy lots of timber, broken by sun filled cuts in various stages of re-growth. After a never ending straightaway they made a easterly turn, into brilliant March sun blinking a morse code of promise at the traveling bus … summer in Maine! Right around the corner…. or after the next long straightaway.

Touristy crossroads, held in place by a river-bridge made ready with raft and canoe rentals, even though it was frozen solid, ice-out not happening till late April. Vernal energy had convenience stores prop a few sale items outside on rickety steps, depression era signage advertising Coke and Salem cigarettes. The unorganized territory was alive; laid out in grids, unincorporated tax free towns; population a hundred or less sent kids down to Foster Lake consolidated.

The bus climbed, made a corner around the bottom of a huge mountain. An arrow pointing over winged military logo made heart's race, a real eye-opening adventure.

Low hills surrounded the base, the next bend revealed a single runway with no visible hanger or planes. The bus circled and stopped in front of a gate. "Daddy where are we?" Olivia was standing, alarmed, afraid she'd be taken away from her life at the farm, she'd longed to leave but not like this, deep into the heart of Maine in the shadow of Katahdin. She held the seat in front of her, bowing to see out the windows, remoteness frightening. Her childhood fantasies were of dry places where donkeys lived free.

"Please stay seated until the bus stops moving."

She looked behind at her Dad, the force of her gaze turned him into superman, emotions coating his surface like an exoskeleton, inside a hard shell, impenetrable armor, he'd save her, save them all if need be … except he was forced to leave his Glock nineteen at home and was sure all six servicemen were armed, the lead vehicle bristling with firearm, *a kidnapping.*

"They always over due it, the military," Nigel sniffed.

"Totally," Dan sighed

"About that clemency request," Nigel tried to make light but Dan wasn't amused.

Nigel steeled himself but he unlike Dan (immersed in worst case scenario), he didn't have mortal fear …. his love securely held, golden cord stretching to heaven, Nigel was distracted by his gut. Without mandatory rounds of replenishing, incapable of consuming enough quantity at one sitting to sustain life for more than two hours, he was a snack-c-holic. Following their rules, role model for the kids, he had nothing with him and was starving.

A dark uniformed soldier opened the main gate and waved through their convoy of two. Rolling slowly they passed a patch of woods featuring Maine tree species, a hard surfaced exercise field and on the next bend low buildings, sidewalks and small shrubs.

The bus jolted around turns, a service man stood in the isle, cleared his throat and began a prepared speech. "Thank-you for accepting our invitation to Fort Charon. Unlike most modern facilities Fort Charon is all male ... but that doesn't mean we're amenity free ... You can see we aren't exactly Sparta." The windows framed a moving picture of sun burnt snow, paved basket ball and tennis courts... a soccer field / baseball combo dotted with blue puddles sublimely awaited players. "Fort Charon competes against teams at other bases, our men are new but some of the best."

Around the next corner loomed a communications tower, disguised as tree, a boulder pile hid other features; relay dishes and metal geodesic domes. Several men appeared from behind barracks, lab coats worn loose over khaki, they were hatless, had a civilian air about them. "We have many of the finest minds in the US stationed here, collected from all over; M.I.T., Cal tech, Michigan, Syracuse, Notre Dame ...we're very proud of the quality of our researchers.

Led by the SUV the bus made several more turns around one story structures. *Sterile but nice* thought Nigel.

Built low to the ground. Dan observed. The airfield lacked a hanger, until they noticed a low hill the length and width of football field, fronted by huge steel doors.

Stan stood to get a better look at a wide roof, open at the sides covering what looked like a hundred ATVs. "Look! Your dream job, Dad," Marie stood next to him, her curly blond head rested briefly on his shoulder, "Oh Dad, "she giggled, took his arm and squoze while the bus lurched, "look, … a repair shop too."

"Daay 'in a daffaren' bas'nass." The ATVs had large clips for mounting weapons and related features.

The bus continued, a second low hill came towards them and a black tunnel lead in.

The serviceman had more to say; "We're taking you to our science area, where you will see some of the latest cutting edge technology ever developed. Much is done in a lab environment, similar to what's easily accessed on line …but we've taken it to new realms, with whim and wisdom we travel different directions in the pursuit of excellence, opening up new frontiers all in the name of science."

Dan managed a smile of watchfulness, *playing dumb to disarm*. He'd seen it before.

Nigel sneezed, "must be allergic to clichés."

"In a galaxy far far away… a long long ago," a boy added dramatically.

"Clout cave." a second kid added.

"Flexing" said another. while shadows came forward until they were in total darkness. Huge LED lights glared from walls covered in an odd material, that wasn't present at the tunnel opening.

The SUV stopped, U-turned, the six soldiers disembarked, came to attention, then shook hands with their superior officer.

Inside the bus they stood preparing to exit. "Leave everything behind besides the clothes you're wearing." The two lead solders stepped off.

"I I Captian," said a boy. Six boys and two Dads exited, followed by the girls and theirs, last the four remaining soldiers who like-wise saluted their superior.

"Well, well if it isn't a Daddy/Daughter dance," The head man turned out to be their old friend, Sergeant Major Robert Mason, eyes hidden behind aviator shades.

"Qeaite ta please ya gat haer, Saaer'gan Maa'jar." Stan broke the ice.

"We try. The reason for the extra duty detail is to keep everyone in line, we found it works out better…" with twelve unsmiling soldiers flanking him, six on each side, everyone agreed it was a great idea. "As you may have became made aware of on the bus this is our service cave serving the cause of science. It offers the best protection and environment for discovery and we'll begin with our G-force walk way. Follow Me!" He turned started off at a fast walk. With six soldiers in front and six behind, there was no question but to follow. They formed a line, same as their seating arrangement, boys leading, with Dads then the girls and their Dads and lastly six soldiers.

Everyone was quiet. *Like being lead away to Federal prison,* thought Dan, *for the crime of being different...*

The cave walls naturally narrowed into a long unlit passageway. The tall elegant Sergeant Major pressed a button on his remote and a long isle with handrails, like an endless tread mill glowed dreamily under LEDs, the end disappearing in blackness ... *Carnival fun house The Gates of Hell. No going back now,* Dan blew out his cheeks.

"The G-force walkway was put in place to double footfall impact, it helps ... keep up bone strength, elevates pain and makes up for the lack of normal sunlight. Please grasp the hand rails for stability." The Sergeant Major pressed a button on his remote and still in single file they stepped on to the long elevated platform that sent a pulsing vibration through the bone structure, like a walking massage. What started out as a pleasant experience if not erotic was towards the end, 60 yards, not fun at all. The LED lighted hand rail rounded a corner into absolute disorientating blackness, eyesight vibrating along with lighting so they couldn't jump over the railing, and expect to find solid ground, they were forced between jiggling lights. Vibrating, glad the soldiers kept up the pace until spilling out in a circle of light.

"I think they're crazy Dad," Bett was on tip-toes, pulling her Dad's shoulder, whispering.

"To alleviate the slight vertigo we're all experiencing, we will now do twenty jumping jacks, form lines" The spot lit Sergeant Major blew a whistle and the regulars, took everyone by the shoulders pushing them into lines, soldiers flanking, the whistle sounded again. "Ok everyone I want to hear loud voices counting out, "ONE ... TWO" In the eeriness of sound absorbing rock, midpoint in blackness, everyone did what they were told.

I don't have a problem with that ... Dan jumped, added his voice to the chorus of called numbers, his defensiveness cracked, he relaxed, decided to enjoy himself, knew it was all BS, physiology 101 but he couldn't dampen an inborn interest in things science related, even in the dim light he noticed the floor material was the black shiny rock common at certain depths, crushed basalt from an ancient pyroclastic flow ... the odd wall covering prevented the sight of strata ... even so he was convinced they were in the geological depths of an old volcano.

The forced exercise was a great release of tension for all except Nigel. Energy flagging, his famished body demanding either rest or food, he eyed what he could make out of the space, imagining white tableclothes, ordering something caloric ...

"Everyone shake out tension then be at ease," they followed the soldiers example; shaking. The Sergeant Major pressed a button on his remote and a small brilliantly lit room appeared cut into the rock. "It's time to hydrate; my advice is to drink the whole container." In the room a table was covered in military issue pint sized energy drinks. The regulars handing them out. They experienced effervescent orange raspberry and again felt it was exactly what they needed.

When Nigel took a second, it was removed from his grasp by a much stronger/younger soldier "We're being had."

Dan ignored Nigel's irritated whisper. Suddenly he wanted to do just what they said; follow directions, be part of their team. Impulses to protect vanished, the kids were fine, there was no threat, in the cave, in darkness totally dependent on people he didn't know and formally distrusted.

"Wow this place is so cool!" said a boy.

"Like Christmas," whispered Marie, the LED's formed a dazzling ring, they looked up smiling.

Nigel considered his empty drink container, everyone was lining up to dutifully throw them away, *we've just been drugged,* he felt it, knew it but didn't want to fight, the only strength he had was riding a wave of pleasure and a desire to see more.

"We'll now take you down to our science rooms," smiling, sunglasses removed, eyes and teeth glinting, the SGM (Sergeant Major) led the way … two large double doors opened with a press of his remote, "since they're so many we'll take the freight elevator down."

"Oh Daddy this is so exciting," Olivia happily took Dan's arm and they all stepped in. There were no elevator buttons, the SGM's remote lowered them in an extremely slow moving elevator that paused, dropped and paused.

"Everybody I want to see big yawns, that's right, keep doing it." He was absolutely correct to remind them, everyone, except Olivia had ridden an elevator before and understood the inner ear and air pressure. But the men knew it was a ruse, *Disneyland*, they weren't dropping far at all, but yawned anyway.

Finally the elevator came to a stop, the SGM pressed his remote … doors opened into a large domed room, the class disembarked, awed by its size. "This is our 'Air Chamber', so named as it replicates a pressurized sports arena. The entire place would not be possible without Kevzar & Oxygen. It was discovered in years of lab testing that Kevzar seals itself against oxygen, grows and re-grows from substances normally found in Maine soils; silica, iron, aluminum, kaolin … we add the catalyst and it does the rest, like a beaver repair to dam it detects weaknesses and naturally, organically grows a patch, weaving into the already formed superstructure, it's in continual change." A tiny bit of dust fell at his feet. "It took some getting used to at first. We had to overcome man's desire for 'the look of perfection' … just like beaver's work, visual imperfections have nothing to-do with structure."

"How do you handle water," Dan knew he was inside an engineering marvel but underground meant hydrology, earth and it's core had everything falling inward and water must be dealt with. …. He was ignored. *power move.*

"Ya neva' sand axava'ta's dawn?" Stan hadn't finished his entire hydration ….drink.

"Totally unnecessary. First we had to find super thick deposits of both iron rich chesuncook and glacial till soils, Maine is the only state with an abundance of both in perfectly layered sedimentation, loose rocks forced to the surface by deep frosts. Then we send down a series of shock waves to loosen … going as deep in the crust as can be done, and drilled holes for the Kevzar. Kevzar needs water to grow, gravity fed it flows through tubes naturally bringing nutrients to the construction areas.

Once Kevzar grows a substantial layer under ground, flattened by the natural weight of the subsurface … We give it time, checking once a month with earth penetrating radar. When we find 30 centimeters, roughly a foot in thickness we pump in Oxygen. Kevzar is repelled by pure Oxygen but feeds off co2…co2 is the most abundant soil gas.

"Yes but…." one of the boys began.

"How long does this growth process take?" Dan stood politely.

"What does it cost?"

The SGM held up a finger, indicating wait… "To extract the Oxygen we use a splitter run on methane. Very Efficient, as Kevzar uses both waste elements carbon and co2 plus iron. We found that after a 'bubble' is formed the 90% Oxygen can be lowered to normal earth atmosphere, what we're breathing now is pumped in from the outside. Kevzar still grows and repairs itself on the roof side of the ceiling.

"Quick process?" Nigel's glasses reflected LEDs, he wouldn't have missed this 'field day' for the world.

"Not exactly," the SGM paused, "all together it used only 10% man power and in material it's hard to judge as we're dealing with the unknown quantities of soil abstracted substance. Construction costs even with lab time are breaking all records, when you consider the size, the 'self-repair' feature, the ability to form small chambers off the center without workmen onsite. And of course the lack of material expense. But as you can see, all piping, wiring, duct-work remains visible, but we find it esthetically pleasing. don't you love the red color," he addressed the girls.

"Red Orange," Bett corrected.

"My favorite color, it's gorgeous!" Olivia said without one hint of shyness.

Dan moved in front of his daughter, "You were saying about 'new chambers?'"

"Over here you'll see some of our scientist's storage areas, gene sequencing machines, uncovering origins and worthiness" he led them to a wall and pushed a button, a one-way window appeared, "this is our 'Genetic Transfer' room. The room was all tall black computers and no people. "You may've heard of the 'big bang theory?"

"Total bunk," Nigel's whisper was a tad loud.

"I did say theory … but …. and it's easy to project man's purpose …err design on outer space."

Giggles and smirks…

"Here we use the same proposal to deconstruct life forms, realizing we all come from one point, life's origin began with water H2O, 2 parts hydrogen; Water…star dust and … some energetic feature, lets say the sun, solar radiation caused a mutation into an explosion of life. Going on that theory by taking very small single cell organisms, back to the origins of creation; bacterium, amoeba, paramecium … viruses … analyzing genetic code for common ancestors … add a dose of radiation and a new hybrid is created, imagine ridding the oceans of toxic waste, dissolving plastic … oil spills, Pacific trash islands a thing of the past … and on the human front; genetic engendering ending world hunger, gobbling up cancer cells, giving people greater longevity, saving babies, Fort Charon is the perfect place for this kind of study; remote, underground, in a sterile air tight low oxygen clean room. Our scientists wear respirators. In a second room behind this one we have an oxygen rich environment, duplicating that of most ancient of life forms.

'Scientists?" Nigel was beginning to long for sunshine, the outside…food.

"Oh yes, a lot of computer power but it's still all about people, serving the needs of humanity, there are so many wants and so little time … computers speed up the process. Our scientists are constantly inputing to artifact … create xenobots … imagine programming organisms that turn waste plastic into clean burning fuel or fertilizer. Or a shot of xenobots to clean out clogged arteries… the applications are endless."

"Why is everything so quiet?" The only sound water dripping and Bett like her Dad was ready to leave.

"The entire station is under a 'kone of silence', free from electronic surveillance, satellite interference …. walls absorb what the kone doesn't."

Kone of Silence Humm, Nigel suddenly felt a pit open to inky blackness … *that kone once descended on me!* Post graduate, 'what's next' year, his life was squirrels in the park, until by a fluke of mistaken identity, he landed a editorship in a prestigious publishing house. Charm, manners and dress lasted twelve years. He was fired over having four secretaries, never-mind that two were interns. That's when the kone descended again, only he was better prepared, with Leah, four children and a nice cash reserve. A felt a hand from the past reached out and sent him off kilter. *My intentions were good!* Like a devote Christian diagnosed with stage four cancer, he did a mini life review looking for a reason, explanation for the sudden anxiety attack, *my commitment is real* … here on a mission to be the perfect Dad, teacher … *where the hell am I,* mind not channeling the present … *Earth to Nigel,* stomach grounded with a huge growl he was sure everyone heard. *It's the lack of external stimuli that brings out phantoms.* Nigle smiled to himself, *self diognosis rather spot on.*

The SGM hugging the wall motioned to follow. Pressing his remote, a section rolled open like a pocket door, introducing them to the 'Ant Farm' room. "This is one of our most important model. That's Kevzar weaving it's magic." Through the double window, they witnessed wall to ceiling ant farms only it was Kevzar forming natural appearing tunneling systems, bisecting large chambers. "Who knows maybe in your lifetime Kevzar buildings will be the norm, say goodbye to maintenance ... but ... we aren't ready for primetime...yet."

"Oh Daddy this really slaps!," Olivia by Dan's side, no longer frightened, but excited. *She's a lot like her mother, but... innocent.*

"Dan't dao ad unnar ma haouse." Stan made everyone laugh.

"How do they get inside?" a boy asked.

"Yeah where's the lab entrance."

"Yeah, how do yah?"

"Maybe it's a CGI, you know fake," a boy was walking back and forth in front of the window cupping his hands, eyeing the edges. Nigel copied, cupping to eliminate glare ... moving to the sides.

Everyone watched the SGM's face turn colors but only for a second before composing. "Lets visit the 3d imaging room, that is a real fake," and he led the way across the big empty center chamber. "The 3d imaging room is open to the public." He pressed his remote, a door slid open ...lights flicked on. The soldiers that had stayed in shadow suddenly appeared and everyone went into the room. Except for a long table with four PCs, office chairs and what looked like an oversized coke machine, the room was empty. Sliding doors connected to other chambers and hid closets and shelves set in Kevzar cubby holes. "This is one of our most exciting advances," his face lost it's stiffness, he was less formal rummaging around in a closet shelf. He found what looked like a light meter, held it briefly against his own palm. "We do total body replica imaging, here." He eyed the soldiers, "PFC Raymond over here." He pointed to a square in front of him.

"Sir!" Raymond stood briefly at attention.

"At ease soldier." With his hand held the SGM circled, at times the device touched him, for accurate hair and skin tones, images of his face hands; all sides, front, back and hair. He plugged it into a computer on the table. The next step is the virtualization booth. He opened, the 'coke machine' and PFC Raymond stepped inside, the door closed, a switch thrown and after a whirring noise stopped, in less than 10 seconds the PFC stepped out.

"Wow he's still alive," a boy said.

My thoughts exactly, Nigel was torn between fascination of what was to come next and repulsion at the possibility of science gone too far … but he stood with the rest watching the monitor as PFC Raymond twirled in 3d.

"Who wants to try it?" The SGM looked brightly at the group. I need a boy and girl to volunteer. No one answered or even moved.

"And what exactly are you going to-do with the information gathered here." Dan asked the right question.

"Nothing, it's only as example for the kids to see how it's done. Deleted and otherwise not stored."

"I'll do it," a boy spoke up and he was put through the painless process. "Do I get to keep the end product?"

Smart ass, the SGM almost said, but touching the boy's shoulder he reassured… "There isn't an end product. We are simply gathering information about the mechanics of replicating. This machine," he patted the 'coke machine' is still under development. It simply takes pictures, no radiology, ultra sound, magnetic imaging or CAT scan, safe and superficial … everything seen by the naked eye.

"But we already have that," a boy said, "3d imaging's old."

"This goes 'one step beyond' plastic models… we need a girl who wants to try it"

Bett stepped forward, smiling and waving. "I …do"

"Great!" The SGM looked past Bett, to Olivia, "Would you like to see how it works?"

"Oh Daddy can I?" Olivia's glance went excitedly from her Dad to the SGM

"I…" Dan was torn, was he going to allow this? Why not Bett? She wanted to, Why not the other girls WHY OLIVIA of course he knew why …but it was double jeopardy, yes or no held clear consequences. "I guess it will be ok."

"Great!"

With the room in dire anticipation was the boy, on the large flat screen, his image twirled featuring exact measurements, hair, eye and skin color ... perfect duplication.

"And now the girl." Olivia stepped blushingly forward. "Don't worry," he purred, "It will help with the advancement of science." He touched the wand to her skin and she trembled, with half closed eyes looked into the SGM's. face. He continued on and she swooned, grabbed the table for support.

Anne acts like that when she's... he glanced at Nigel and Stan to see if they caught it and to his horror they had! But he couldn't go back on it! A fifty year old man touching his thirteen year old daughter and her reacting like that! In all other circumstances he'd of bundled her up, taken her home ... have Anne give her the 'talk,' but trapped, underground, acknowledging the sexual charge would only make it worse, and she might not understand, the boys did; smirking. *It must be the uniform, he wears it well... the chiseled features!*

"Perfect." The SGM and everyone kept their cool, seeing Olivia displayed on the computer made Dan realize she was growing up, almost fourteen, 5 foot 7 125 lbs, all her proportions, her lovely bright eyes.. *like her mother except Anne was shorter, heavier ... homogeneous ... here I am underground, going through something all Dad's go through.*

"Gaetin' biga'" Stan smiled.

"They grow up fast," Nigel smiled while his stomach growled like a captive animal.

"Is everyone ready for refreshments?" The SGM looked brightly around at the room and led the way, allowing half the soldiers out first, followed by the girls, then Dads, boys, the other soldiers then he turned out the lights, pressed and slid close the door.

A little ways down a second door appeared open and the light went on in a room decorated with posters of fresh markets piled with fruit and vegetables, tables covered in little boxes, chairs placed around. "Here's where we put together something for you to enjoy… the perfect nutritional meals, from all over the world, all the right amounts, packed with nutrients and we believe you'll find …them …tasty," his remote made bins drop open, videos played above … on half screen…growing and/or gathering ingredients, factory processes for the creation of each variety, sound muted, subtitled, the 'food' in colorfully wrapped squares. "Please try them, if you don't like the consistency, flavor, don't worry, just place uneaten portions in boxes baring your name. Don't be shy, a variety of drinks are on the end, same deal with the drinks, if you don't like the taste just leave the opened container in your box … this is how you help us discover what kids your age have a preference for taste wise, …it's greatly supports our mission." Of course the Dad's need to eat too….so dive in."

A boy snatched a bar with the Eiffel tower pictured on the wrapper …the video had simply dressed people collecting truffles. Everyone watched as he bit, chewed and swallowed, "Wow salty…I don't know …you try it," he tried to pass the uneaten portion to his friend.

"Augh, augh … remember uneaten portions go in your box, how else are we going to know who ate what…" The boy stopped and everyone stood around, appetites gone.

Nigel was depressed, felt like weeping … *food, food everywhere but not a thing to eat!* Then something happened to the room, a faint scent of lavender then cooking smells, almost below audio sounds of people enjoying meals. Nigel's mouth watered.

The S.M. picked up a bar tore open the wrapper and devoured, the soldiers followed, along with noises of appreciation.

"So you don't care if we don't like it," Olivia looked into his face, blushing.

"It appears not," Nigel and boys ravaged the bins, taking a bite out of everything.

"Oh my dear no … please enjoy yourself," the S.M's voice purred, he noticed Dan, turned on his heels, got himself a drink.

Dan decided on a chocolate bar, after a few bites a faint taste of fish pervaded and the uneaten portion went in his box. He started to forget himself wanted to **eat the world**; the scrolling marquee's message.

"Great enhancements in the chocolate," Nigel winked at him. They'd been drugged again, something in the chocolate was making them ravenous, "The drinks delete it."

"Please don't forget the beverages," the SGM maintained control. There was something slightly narcotic in the drink too, the room was full of peaceful teens, preteens, Dad's & soldiers. "Everyone done?" Don't want to rush …you."

"Oh this is so fun," Olivia took Bett's arm in happy giggles.

"Weird flavors tho, salty and …."

"Ok, everyone please…." The SGM stood before them, please take as many as you want of the uneaten, wrapped bars home with you, see if your younger brothers and sisters like them. Be our Junior Scientists, fill out a form for each child, answering all questions, have Mom and Dad sign the permission forms first. Make note of what you find out, on the forms … if your brother's and sisters like or don't like …keep careful records, to the best of your ability like scientists for the experiment." The SGM found more boxes of bars in a cupboard and placed them on the table, "You're looking at the end result of years of study, experimentation… $5 million dollar candy bars. He produced woven plastic carry bags with a US military double eagle logo and when they chose boxes, two or three, he held the bags open so they could place them in, patted each child, saying "thank-you, you're real scientists, a real help."

"Thanks so much," said Nigel, with four boxes in his bag, thought he'd found the most perfect antidote to his gut issues, (he didn't get a pat.)

All was done and they waited outside in the large dome room… happily holding their loot, loving the free stuff, the military logo … the state of anticipation. "If you need to use the wash room, please do … we'll reassemble out here."

Twenty men and boys crowded into one, while the three girls had a room to themselves.

"OMG look at this place!" Olivia didn't expect a real girl's bathroom painted in purple and gold, her favorite colors with gilded mirrors and louver doors on the stalls.

"To be honest this place isn't real … it's like really fake … fake food, fake labs," Bett brushed her curly brown hair away from her face, she rubbed on lip gloss, everything stored in cargo pants. Topped off by a pink flowered sweater, she was,'girl-force', 5'5" muscular, fit…. loved mountain biking as much as riding… kept ahead of her eleven year old brothers.

"Fake but lit," Olivia's first experiences outside Foster Lake wasn't going down.

"And that Creeper following you."

"Following me?" They were washing hands under brass faucets in the shape of dolphins.

"Yeah," Marie was going on fifteen, her first year at Lane school, the balance in public, "eyeballs on you the whole time," she redid her face, red lips smiled, the mirror smiled back, "and saw everything, like that booth he sent you in …

that wasn't a dressing room, it was an undressing room … and now … he's got you in his comp, you'll be duped, passed around … a plastic blow up…thingee."

Olivia applied a faint line of eye shadow and gloss so her Dad couldn't tell…felt her cheeks blush but played it cool… "Like I don't know he's a dirty old man…"

"You were thirsty for it!" Bett teased.

"Was not!"

"You don't care if we don't like it," Bett copied Olivia's simpering look.

"Stop!"

"Oh my dear no … please enjoy yourself," she purred like the Sergeant Major.

"STOP!"

"Choosing you; check, eyes following you; check, you looking up at him; check."

"He's taller than me!"

"Bett, stop! Can't you see she's in total emo."

"She's always been a total emo."

"I thought you're my BFF but your not! You're the Faker!" She hid her face in her hands, moved into a corner sobbing.

Bett rolled her eyes at Marie. Marie had never witnessed an Olivia melt-down. Bett could handle physical injury, but not mental and wished Ada was there. "Olivia! You stop it! Right now! They might cancel everything."

"I don't care, you hate me!"

"Olivia I care," Marie, pried her arms down, Marie was only five foot one but had huge emotional strength like her Dad. "Come on you emo," she gently teased and quickly got out her brush and on tip-toes did Olivia's hair. The feeling of Marie's hands calmed. She cast sad glances at Bett.

"Quit throwing shade, It's the facts."

"Stop it Bett." Marie offered lipstick, mascara, blusher, pencil, expertly applying while Olivia stood like a big doll, loving the attention.

"I know I'm baby…" Olivia calmed enough to assess the situation, her normal mind forcing its way through emotion. "How did you get all that stuff in here?"

"Fanny pack." Marie lifted her sweatshirt to show it off, "my total beat garage." They all giggled, Marie bounced, stood back admiring her work. Olivia in red lipstick, eye makeup, pink sparkly blusher was a true French beauty.

"Olivia Kardashian!" Bett laughed.

"You really think I look that good?"

"Sic yeah! Totally snatched."

Marie did her own her hair again, stepped back from the mirror, "Come on lets get back out there, they're waiting for us."

The men were talking loudly, without females present, goofiness ceased when the girls stepped out. The all male audience instantly noticed Olivia's makeup enhanced face;

the soldiers in particular nudging each other, slanting glances in her direction.

"Good you're back," the SGM smiled and she looked at the ground.

He's older than my Dad!

Ignoring the rebuff he continued, "Lets take the ramp up it's really quite pleasant, not a long walk…come this way," and he slid open a set of beefed up steel doors, exposing a wide ramp, at a gentle grade, turning a corner into darkness, LEDs truning on and dimming as they passed. The thick rubber floor clung to their feet, like sports facilities running track, giving bounce. "Refrain from touching the walls, the Kevzar behaves like a life form, always growing, looking for anaerobic nutrition."

"Kevzar the killer," one of the boys fake strangled his friend and his friend fake died, fell to the floor.

"Cut it out," the SGM said in a serious tone and stopped, pressed a button on his remote, "this is the miracle of Kevzar," a lighted passage appeared. "It'll be completely ready in about a year." He bowed under the low passageway and entered a large room, LED's did their thing. He paused in front of a solid wall and pressed his remote … with a noise like plates in a restaurant, the wall telescoped into an area that appeared in flux, looking through a thick translucent material, it was hard to tell. Exclamations of amazement came from everyone.

"Can anyone guess what/where this is."

"I don't know but man this is lit!"

"Totally."

"A mudflow?" One of the boys ventured.

"Chocolate factory?"

"No … anyone else chance a guess?"

"Gaown wada'?"

"We are under the most northern edge of Foster Lake, 150 feet down. Foster Lake is of interest to us as its world-wide the warmest deepwater lake at this longitude and we think we have the answer as to why, but I can't say for certain."

Everyone stared, "No fish?" Nigel wasn't optimistic for an answer.

"Sometimes we see life," He turned on a high intensity spot light, but nothing showed … only falling sediment in dark clouds and on the bottom round lake stones. They watched while the light was directed upwards. "We're also experimenting with mirage. Focused images and vids projected through water. Why spend millions on the real thing. We're years away from implementation, but the applications are endless."

"Dads in'narastin'."

MY GOD Nigel bowed his head, remained mute then smiled to himself … *the better 'trick' is them not knowing it was me, while I know it was them. Some mirage.*

The show over they funneled out of that space and onto the ramp-way. The Sergeant Major turned addressing the group; "This concludes our tour, we're hoping you enjoyed it and return home with greater knowledge of what ignites the minds of the military. We are all about progress, the future and our concerns mirror yours… so everyone has the greatest chance for health and prosperity and happiness of course," he gazed at Olivia.

He was angled above them on the walkway that felt like a water tunnel. The boys rocked back and forth, in physical anxiety, everyone wanted to go. "I'm ready to go home," Bett blurted.

"Yeah!" The boys voiced their agreement.

"Thanks for the tour," Dan kept his tone even.

The Sergeant paused sadistically, eyed them for moments more … "Oh we're done here," pausing to enjoy their angst … "this way," he turned leading. The lights remained on for brief moments of their upward journey, so it appeared they were leaving total blackness and walking into the same, totally dependent on the man leading.

"Think I'm gonna KMS," (kill myself), said a boy.

"Totally," said another.

"Have a little torture with your field trip," said a Dad.

"The joker leading us to Hell," said another.

"Yeah, wad da Hall," Stan was actually angry.

"Where is this taking us?" Dan said in his Mill Job, hear me above machinery voice and was ignored.

"We all had a great time, didn't we kids," a Dad said, noises of approval followed, like 'nice' helped.

The Sergeant paused, turned his head sideways, "my pleasure," and back to walking up in gentle turns and switchbacks …the rubber flooring gave way to gravel and stopped ascending. A huge metal door appeared. Everyone gathered round sweating, oxygen needs just barely meant. He pressed his remote and nothing happened. "Hope it's the right one." He put the remote to his ear and shook it … held it at arms length squinting. "A pity you'd have you wait here in darkness while I fetch the other." He gave the group a sick grin. Then with a booming noise the door opened and they were at the opening of the cave, bus and driver waiting.

They made it back home without the escort SUV. The SGM speeding ahead in his personal escalade, drawing comfort from the black-out windows, he spent the entire time on his lap-top, ear bud in place … fingers rivaling the fastest transcriber's speed. He checked the hour … asked the driver to step on it. He was hoping to secure time alone with Madam Plush-bottom, (his pet name for Anne).

Everyone was outside the mansion, littler kids in the process of being picked up by Moms. Anne with her usual high energy blush giving each parent a brief synopsis of their day. The soldiers milled about, finding interest in the Moms, their cars … genetic profiles, button hole cameras getting it all. They saluted the SGM and lounged on the SUV ready to follow him back to base.

"Great you did this for us … it's was fun," Dan elbow butted cooly'

"Educational," Nigel, elbow butted.

"A 'ael 'earnin' ag'spaer'an.'"

The two other Dads elbow butted the SGM with cool words of appreciation. "Fun for the kids, … Thank-you greatly sir." The soldiers meandered over to get a better look at the Dads and the boys gathered round the group, elbow butting the SGM talking excitedly.

Anne watched it all from the kitchen windows, but didn't go outside, not wanting to upset their man-ball or incur Dan's reprisal … if she walked out there, *he'd call me an attention whore*, nine men in uniform, five Dads … six boys …so she went to her comp. briefly answered some mail, stood, cleared work off the table busied herself with various chores humming, *they say these guys… these guy's in love with … me….*,

She thought of going up to see Olivia, talk about their days…with adolescence Olivia had become more sensitive, a real help with the younger children… but seldom confided in her, kept most things to herself. Per normal the girls walked by without saying a word, bypassing the kitchen they took the front stairs up to Olivia's room … *I'll wait till Bett & Marie go home.*

She was in a state of bliss, but why? Was it the six young men and their questions, the way they entertained the kids with stories about military life and followed her around. It wasn't just attraction, it was something else … the feeling she was valued and appreciated for what she was. Six strange young men, she'd never seen before, had eyes only for her. The other women; teachers and volunteers, some younger … were barely given a glance. Anne spent time on her appearance; voice, manner…most natural, some contrived, but feelings of excitement for others was genuine … and much more intense with young men, the day was acutely exciting … her thoughts went to Dan.

But, in his office all Dan wanted to talk about was Olivia, her reaction to the Sergeant, emerging from the ladies room in make-up, how she needed counseling about how men think, "She's innocent of her own feelings." Dan ensconced in his chair looked up physiological changes from prepubescent to preadolescence and puberty in girls, from an all boy family the thing was mysterious.

"Oh honey, I know she's grown up in appearance but still a child inside and doesn't know," she kissed the top of his head, above the thinning spot. "She's a lot like her father, wants to-do good for the world, even with the tides against her. I have the most wonderful man in my life and he gave me our most perfect daughter." The syrupy words did little for his mood.

'So how was your day? Must've been enjoyable with the company"

"Oh yes…it was good" … she backed up, "I'll see to Olivia."

"Good," Dan deep in brooding, went to the security cams and separate monitor held in his office closet.

Per Dan's instruction to alert Olivia about the perils of men they had 'the talk'. Marie and Bett left with their Dads and Olivia was alone looking up different army uniforms so she could identify rank, when Anne appeared at her door.

Olivia had already giggled about who was cutest, who was darkest and who they liked best with Marie and Bett and felt awks about her Mom. But then Anne promised to sneak her into Dan's office and check out the security cams, update Olivia's particular dream soldier, now that she was absolutely certain of status.

"We can zoom the name tags" Anne offered.

"For real." Olivia excitedly clasped her hands together, soldiers in uniform were super exciting, the ones visiting the farm slightly better looking than the cave ones. Olivia told her about the Sergeant Major, Anne wanted details and they giggled. "At first I was like trapped but after the Ladies Room it got better. I mean Marie's so chill and knows…"

"He's fifty you know."

"Yeah but" … she paused, "Bett calls him The Creeper."

"The Creeper," Anne smiled.

"But Marie thinks he's super lit! Not like guys who protest, you know, not all Woke, on the street, like all they care about is some cause, when they don't really know what it is."

"If you were to ask them…"

"Like some are, SJW, total emo's like look at me I'm GOAT, I got it … when they really don't … I mean …"

"Hyperbolae."

"Yeah, they don't like business, like they think business is taking something from them." Olivia paused, a glance to her Mom brought a kind of joy others experience in Anne presence, a person thoroughly interested and supportive so she forgot about her resentment towards Valerie, that left her silent at the dinner table and going straight to her room afterwards …"Marie says the guys in High School were like that, like they'd burn and loot. You know Mom it's so dumb."

"Counterproductive."

"Yeah and some are totally gay, or confused. Like it used to be okay being a boy but to be sure they take a class and come out thinking they're gay."

"Activated" Anne sighed .

"Marie, she's almost fifteen, you know and was Sophomore at Foster Lake when she came here. She likes Lane School boys better, 'cause their not what you said, 'activated' or like hyperbolic and she said some girls are unicorns… you know what I mean…

"To each his err … her own."

"Marie likes the Sergeant Major 'cause he didn't go to struggle sessions like High school boys. I mean … I don't know.

"Different generation…. understands woke …go woke and go broke" … Anne smiled, felt sudden tenderness for Dan; always 'on' with their financial picture.

"I mean even if he's a Creeper, … he's not a looter."

"Has some saving graces."

"Yeah, besides he's lit."

"I wouldn't tell your Dad that."

Instead she told her Mom about G-force walkway, the slow freight elevator, the labs, 3D imaging room and packaged food. Ann asked her dozens of questions, imagining what it was like. "Can you believe a place like that all underground? The boys were so lit, I mean our boys aren't tools." She paused to collect her thoughts; "we're SJW like everybody is, but it's not like we'd burn down our forests, cause somebody went off the rails in Bangor. Dad said they're so far gone they don't care about a safe place to fall asleep at night. I mean … I'm glad we live in Maine. Remember when I was little and I thought Maine was the country's head, you know on the map … where the brains are. Dad said 'waking up in Maine is heaven enough'. I never want to leave."

"Me neither," *except when its hell.* Anne crossed her fingers while her daughter pulled up fiery news scenes, teens running out of buildings with their arms full.

Returning from Olivia's room she paused on the stair remembering a disquieting episode at Shop & Save parking lot. After placing her bags in the Rabbit's back seat, she removed her face mask, returned the carriage and walking back when a truck pulled up around her so she had to pass the owner. 'Black Flies matter' read the bumper sticker, he quickly exited and stood in front of her, said something about glue removal and time he tapped his watch and pointed to his shoes, made walking motions. He was at least six foot five, gaunt, luciferian, with a green hew. The parking lot was empty, under a gray sky on that particular day the grim reaper visited. But she got away, drove home wondering why she had no sympathy, he was so obviously sick … evil is sick. Then suddenly she knew why … he was like the Sergeant Major, stripped of all grace. *Maybe I'm being unfair.*

"OH YOU KNOW we're almost out of grain, we need the spring mixture, you know more alfalfa pellets, less oats." Anne had returned.

Dan had an old catalogue of horse tack propped up on his keyboard and was leafing through. He looked up at her for a sec. then down, not answering, got up and replaced it finding another, gave her one of his deep looks and resumed leafing.

"Find what you're looking for?"

"Thought I had one already."

"What?" Anne moved to him, lacing her fingers feeling how far down he was in his mood.

"A faithful wife."

"What made you say that."

"Ok, … explain this," and he led her to the closet and separate security monitor, accessing the sequence, zooming in on the detail of her smiling up at a tall handsome young solider, excitement crackling over the screen, she motioned him off camera, … They reappeared around a corner and Anne calmly watched her self lead the soldier to their recently built machine shed, so new it lacked interior cams… about fifteen minuets later the three more soldiers entered, then fast forward fifteen min and the last two entered, a second fifteen minutes was skipped until they all left, one of them tucking in his shirt straightening his tie. Five minutes later Anne emerged blushing.

"When I mentioned we had a thirty-nine HP, 1956 Case he wanted to see it, he saw that old Agritrac dozer outback and it was all over, they were smitten," she clasped her hands and brought them up to her mouth. "Then the other boys came in, you know they were in communication with each other the whole time, some ear-piece device… you'd think they were talking to themselves but I knew better… and in that new shed with all the old farm equipment… they're eyes lit up, just like you when you first came out here, saw what I got, imagined our life" she blissfully enjoyed the memory, while her beautiful mouth went on… "They were talking crawlers, cats, I gave them the ignition key … they tried to start it, found a can of starter fluid… They were like little boys climbing, sitting on the seats, pulling leavers. You see, darling when the choice was fat old me and a dozer… the dozer won!" Silly didn't work so she became circumspect, "Really honey they wanted to see the whole operation, like they're inventorying our stuff. But I kept them out of here … your office, let them peep in … then locked it. You know, your guns… I turned the younger kids over to Valerie so I could keep an eye on them…We spent a lot of time outdoors… they even brought their own food, in funny little packages." He remained silent, back to her, "really honey all I could think of was you…out there somewhere, worried about seeing you and Olivia again…" she touched his back, leaned against him.

Suddenly he turned facing her, took her by the shoulders, and squooze her arms until he saw pain in her eyes, the same pain he was feeling then, pushed her out of the security closet walking backwards … pointing at the door… "Get out!"

"Dan what has gotten into you! I will not go! You must explain this."

He said nothing while the grandfather clock told time. "It's Olivia she…she's acting like … you!"

"Olivia! No!"

"What kind of man am I if I can't control my wife and daughter." He let go… watched her pause, gain balance and regroup. She toyed with a top blouse button. She wore an old-fashioned form fitting wool vest, jeans, healed shoes, jangling earrings showed off her lovely white neck. One of the volunteers ran a beauty parlor and Anne's perfectly quaffed hair, nails and makeup gave her great glam and more confidence, the extra weight bounced, she sparkled …was alive, excited… completely transformed from the solemn beauty he married fourteen years ago. He was suddenly angry at the contrivance, angry that she dressed for other men.

"But everything I do is for you! You're the one who leads us … Oh Dan and…I … I want to stay home so you can go places …do things … and … and," water came to her eyes, she placed both hands on his chest and he held them in his, stroking with his thumb, feeling her warmth. She looked into his face, eyes magnified by tears, she was touching him, had control of his temper, "But for you I'd have gone home …alone…when my parents died …gone here to this crumbling place to live my life in obscurity. You rescued me …" she sobbed, forehead pressed into him, "you saved me, you … oh Dan … I'd be nothing and I can't stand anything without you, Dan, I do everything for you but please don't accuse me … Dan how can you accuse me of terrible things….I love you so much." they held each other until the sobbing stopped.

Later he took a flash light out, inspected the machine shed for evidence and found nothing, he smiled, … *had their hands all over the dozer and not my wife.* The very next day he had the machine shed wired and Stan installed security cams. "We've got to keep the whole place covered, the kids aren't getting younger."

"Dust bu Var'ra'fay" Stan nodded knowingly.

8
Flu Season

One measthma free day Nigel was stuck in traffic, downtown Bangor, enjoying shafts of sunlight between turn of the century brick when suddenly his passengers side door opened and a woman was there. ... She'd bypassed the Rover's self locking feature by reaching through the open window, unlocking and suddenly this attractive young woman slid in the seat, tight pink leather suit, wavy chestnut hair.

The light changed, "Where to?" Nigel smiled.

But she failed to see the humor, sneezed, and under her handkerchief and facemask said; "Why didn't you tell me?!" leapt out and slammed the door.

Why didn't I tell her? It was spring and the world had gone mad. Blooming trouble. An attractive stranger that smelled like baby wipes, odor lingering long past the affronted exit, brightened Nigel's belief that good things happen to good people. Why did he need this affirmation? Because Insurance for The Lane school had tripled. He sighed and still driving pulled a check from his breast pocket and parked on the street.

Nigel leapt out to feed the meter and saw everyone in masks, various styles, it had been so sudden, he couldn't tell a really cool mask from a complete dud and with some irritation retrieved an old fashioned one, tied around his bald head, the lower string missing so the bottom puffed rebelliously with each breath.

He arrived at his bank's door, yanked before reading the sign, arrow drawn indicated he was to use the drive-in window and the Rover three blocks away! He cupped his hands and peered, 'facemasks must be worn for admittance' was taped over the old message, 'no masks allowed in the building', *seems to be getting worse.*

Given the mixed messaging, Nigel didn't bother knocking but he did what he had to do; stood waiting in the drive through lane, inhaling exhaust, enduring stares, navigating potholes, he finally made it and waved up at the window. *Here I am, upper-class tweedy mahogany, 100% on your side, socializing losses; privatizing profits…watching my white privilege.*

The bank tellers staffed like an operating room, eyes above surgical masks, looked down. A brave girl snapped on fresh gloves and took the check, "may I see your driver's license."

"It's a deposit," he pointed out.

"All transactions require ID."

Nigel fed it in the shoot.

"This is you?"

"You want me to remove the mask?"

"No!"

After minutes conferring with other masks he was granted a stay of execution, transaction completed and huge check deposited, swallowed whole into the Bank's stomach in a reversal of fortune feeling … Like the inmates running the asylum … poverty; good, wealth; suspect … but at least sickness is still bad… *isn't that what we're trying to prevent here? The spread of contagion?* But why all the hoopla, Piscatiquis county's virtually virus free. Maine's statistics like a puny inchworm crawling around the bottom, while New York's a bed of nails. He rubbed his corona virus beard, fiery-red mixed with blond, the face mask made it itch … beard, glasses, baseball cap and face mask… he was in solidarity with a state of pissed off Mainers.

On the way home he took the Interstate south to the Newport exit. The Marquee read; STAY SAFE; STAY ALERT, *(drop dead)*. The next sign read; STAY SAFE; STAY HOME, (commit suicide). Nigel saw hidden messages. They were turning his heavenly place, bursting with springtime energy, into a coal bin.

Back at the Lane's School's near normal, Jeff & Henry walked around business as usual, mentally immune to Government's flip side when Anne came running into the library, (his classroom) with a word document his 10 year old son Henry wrote.

NO ROLLS

There once was a man who worked in a office. He was there all day everyday. He worked all the time because he lived all by himself in an apartment with no family and also he was a workaholic.

One day a pandemic hit and he had to stay home. He watched what was happening online. He didn't believe it until he ran out. No toilet paper. Luckily he was allowed back at work half days. At work on the toilet tank was an extra roll.

Now the man had one roll at home. But what if I run out? He wondered but didn't panic. Back at work he saw another roll on top of the toilet tank. Now he had enough to last him a week. But what if the pandemic shut-down lasted more than that?

Now the man had two and a half rolls at home but still he worried. Work didn't put out extra rolls anymore so he went to gas stations and unrolled theirs. Now he had plastic bags full. Enough to last him a month but he was out of eggs.

BY HENRY DAVID MACPHEE

THE LANE SCHOOL was hoping the Pandemic, (we comply mask-wise and practice social distancing) would quell the town's interest in them but the opposite happened. A shift in attitude arrived with the sudden increase of enrollment. Twenty-five new kids next year.

Because the Therapeutic riding/Donkey rescue program served autistic children The Lane School was granted dispensation from Maine's new 100% immunization compliance. The trickle of new enrollees became an avalanche and Dan, a Baptist Christian refused to turn anyone away. In the East Wing. four bedrooms with fireplaces were being formed into classrooms

Long closed off, the East Wing was reopened, time capsule photographed, documented and reclaimed for the present. Everything but the basement coal storage, dark and gloomy in windowless repose was doomed to remain the same. Coal made Victorian glitz happen, the mansion rested on that.

Coal was life itself, turning industry, fueling progress … now it's the devil, satanic polluter, scorned, made illegal.

But above the bedrooms a large airy sun-lit second story ballroom running the length was slated as art room/exercise area, its tower balcony with a commanding view over fields to the Piscataqua, beyond a ribbon of Foster Lake shimmered and Flagstone mountain rose out of the mist.

Nigel and Dan were aware of the contrast. Renovations were dizzying in scope including the expense of bleeding radiators, repointing and reinstalling draft systems for the many fireplaces, painting tin-tile, removing old bedsteads, (mattresses long gone), plumbing repair to adjoining bathrooms, re-glazing windows…it started small, then falling plaster made for a total rehab.

Several people from the State arrived in face shields and hazard suits, insisting on fire escapes and fire doors. Dan was tearing his hair out, over that and balances. Insurance increases meant the once reasonable tuition went up by a third …and all that money flew out the door. He had big plans of adding sports, didn't want to wait for accounts to settle … and sports added to ….guess what? Insurance. Riding wasn't a sport but considered therapeutic, helping kids focus and behave… a transformational experience for the not so normal … and so it had a separate clause and rider. Real sport; base ball, soccer and cross country would be played on the MacPhee property. Dan signed a rental agreement for… the amount of insurance and Nigel donated it back, a patiently obvious two way street deal but he'd never been examined that closely. No audit worry yet.

Building inspection wasn't fun but Dan didn't sit with bowed head for long, the noise of construction, his position of authority, used with restraint and humor, otherwise; delegating and retreating, the closed door to his office received many knocks. Except for his daughters and wife's he never knew who it was on the other side,. "Come in," he was problem solving from home, (sheltering in place, they'd closed the mill for a week to establish social distancing markers).

While ordering on line, he recognized Olivia's knock and looked up from an old book on Victorian Plumbing....

"Oh Daddy something's bad's happening in town…"

"Something you need to tell me about?" He wasn't about to be caught off guard.

"It's like they've canceled life. They're afraid of people dieing only its… totally sus."

"Yeah, I know, the Pandemic."

"But Daddy what they think isn't real. No one's sick or ending up in EMMC, It's so extra."

Dan didn't feel he had any responsibility for things under 'local control.' He knew they'd made a choice to close Foster Lake Consolidated School even though no one was sick. Teachers and staff sent home, as if no longer safe to operate. It wasn't a reality he belonged to. He smiled at his daughter, "Only the phantom knows…"

"But Daddy what if its facts? ... someone said, 'you're going to catch Corona Virus and die ... when they saw me not wearing a facemask."

"He said that to you?"

"Yeah, Mom and I were out shopping, you know Dad and no one was out. If it isn't real why are they doing it this way? I wish they'd all hop off ... leave us alone!"

"What did he look like?"

"I don't know he was just a man in front of the Shop & Save holding a clicker. But he let us in, we had to buy facemasks at the pharmacy. They were watching us and there's tape on the floor like arrows and 'social distancing' signs, like we're viruses."

"I don't know maybe it's a test ... they're testing us ... see how we handle it. See if we comply. It's like being inside an insane asylum ... only the inmates have unlimited power and we don't want to piss them off so we comply and wait ... they can't keep it up forever."

"But we didn't wear masks all the time! Are they going to go off on us ... swat us. I know it can't be true. No one's... dyeing ... I mean not here ... They're dieing in New York City. Maybe we have a different strain .... but maybe if we don't wear mask and or don't do 'social distancing' we'll get it!" Olivia was literally wringing her hands.

"Oh dear," he wanted to take her in his arms like when she was little but instead held her gaze in his... "Lane school was granted an exception. We can stay open and don't have to follow protocol. You don't have to worry … we'll get through this. The Sergeant Major had something to-do with it. He said, 'Out of a Coronavirus Pandemic, Lane School was his ray of hope,'" Dan shook his head; smiled. "He's using The Lane School as control in their test."

"Like a science experiment. How can that be safe?"

"If you want to wear a mask in town … that's good."

"Mom tried to get a whole box but they're all sold out."

"I'll try and find some on line … but here we don't have to."

She looked at him with dismay. "What if it comes here?"

"It won't … we need your steady intelligence … they need you Olivia, to set a good example."

"But they're all in one mood … and bigger than us."

He steered her towards the door, "God's bigger. Remember Thomas Aquinas from Sunday school; reason, natural law… wins…. eventually."

She looked at him like he'd lost his mind, "We didn't get to that part, they locked us out of Church because of 'social distancing.' And you aren't teaching the highest class anymore…remember, you said someone else needed the chance."

Dan paused …"They can't lock up our hearts." A year ago he'd dropped Church. His mill job, The Lane School, therapeutic riding program's new buildings (indoor riding ring and machine shed) and east-wing renovations all occupied his mind. But he wasn't totally spiritually absent *work is love made visible*, even as he lapsed in prayer, bought guns for protection, knowing the two weren't mutually exclusive...

Anne took the children. She needed the space to prove herself, he'd eyes inside the parish, reporting back, she wasn't provocative with men, joined an all woman's prayer. group, behaved herself at coffee hour. And he claimed precious hours of quiet at the mansion.

"But Daddy, why don't you go to Church? I mean way before the shutdown you canceled. It shook Mom, really shook her because you weren't there with us, sitting next to her ....and now you won't tell me." she turned to him ... chin raised defiantly.

He held her by the shoulders, looked into her eyes, refusing to acknowledge the challenge, his mind instead rested on her lovely face and quizzical upset expression. She belonged to him, didn't she know that? She was his ... and him. Her coloring, black hair, white skin was her Mother's, but the face, the set of her eyes ... stature came from him... if only she'd stop questioning she'd be the perfect daughter, smart, beautiful, kind. She's led a sheltered life and he was responsible for that. The contrast between home and town was upsetting her. It was important she listen to him and do what she was told ... how else could he protect her.

Olivia believed that if everyone went to Church and prayed, God would hold up his white gloved hand and send Covid 19 to Alpha Centauri. She remembered the rescue, (Bett fell in a hole one frigid February night 2016, and wasn't found for twenty-three hours. Everyone else searched except the residents of Maries Lane, they were held inside.) While Olivia waited in the kitchen with her Mom, their parish sent up prayers for Bett's safe return and right after that they found her. And the prayers said for Ada's recovery from burns and right after she came home from rehab. "Prayer works and with you praying, God will pay attention, he'd hear us and make the Quar over."

Flattered by her belief and still holding her shoulders he began with a soft reassuring voice, trying to convey the love he had for her... his prized possession. "We've a special place here and yes God has smiled on us, his spirit is in everything we have. You're an important part too, no one understands and represents Lane School and Therapeutic Riding like you do. Your Mom and I are so proud. The town doesn't think the same, so we need to follow their rules ... We need to be compliant and grateful ... Lane School was granted special privileges so we act the part for the time being ... until the whole thing blows itself out. We'll be fine ... see what your Mom wants... remember ....lead by example ... we're all counting on you."

"But Daddy you talk about God but you've canceled Church, we're not a Church family because of you." She bowed her head as he let go of her shoulders and opened the door. She gazed past him reassured by the black book with gold lettering next to his computer. "Bet you pray."

"Absolutely! ...What's for lunch?"

Since twenty-five kids fled their school for his … Lane School was subjected to a curious blend of …**With our authority we will insure the safety of all school aged children** …and… **do anything wrong and you'll feel the weight of the town** …to… **geeze I hope they do something so we can show them who's boss and move into the penalty phase.**

Under the guise of Government control, duplicate state and town officials bravely headed out while the unseen enemy multiplied. Dan and Anne put everything aside to greet the men and women, hand helds at the ready … behind shields and over masks, official eyes gazed into theirs.

Anne found it exciting, Dan remained steady, greeted socially distancing waves with blue gloved acknowledgements, bumping into them in dark corners of **the** mansion … gadgets against walls, flashlights up chimneys. One pretty inspector was proudly shown the facilities. She was impressed … inquired about kindergarten.

While preparations for the enrollment serge continued, Dan was made aware of another request in the area of charter school funding. The Lane school wasn't a charter school but private, still parents who couldn't afford tuition asked the town for their yearly allotment. As town councilor Dan had to recuse himself while enmity deepened. Eventually the town decided the charter school deal had to be settled at the state level… That meant next year! Legislature in full shutdown, Maine was under executive powers, the Governor in control.

During the initial Pandemic pause, shuttering everything in Foster Lake except Supermarkets, pharmacies, public works and code enforcement, Dan gave notice to something else. Marie's Lane wasn't private but town owned. Ever since The Lane School had become an established thorn in the side of Foster Lake, they were the last plowed and out of the numerous dirt roads, the last scrapped. Spring 2020 Dan reminded them twice before it actually happened and then only minuscule effort, Marie's Lane neglected much the same.

Roadside trees likewise were left untended. Foster lake and other towns along Northern Maine's snow-belt took tree set-back seriously as municipal snowplowing needed space. The tree clearing effort, partly funded by CMP, (Central Maine Power), employed a year round guy with his own bucket truck. However, since Lane School's inception, four years ago, Marie's Lane, once tended to like other town roads, was ignored. Dan emailed Public Works about dangerously overhanging tree limbs and smaller ones moving into areas historically kept clear for snow … it got their attention. They sent a flail-mover out and waving it menacingly mowed down a row of rosebushes Nigel planted to attract bees and add beauty.

When Dan without iota of what he was really feeling explained that the roses were 'trimmed' by mistake, would grow back, it was hazard trees that concerned him… They next sent out the bucket truck and removed a beautiful red maple on the edge of their parking lot, holding a sign for The Lane School. It was in the Town's right of way, the man explained. "Ya caan kaeep da pa'eces." he stated blankly, leaving the litter. Their unhappy sign speared into the ground like declaring war on independence.

Nigel saw the downed tree, felt like weeping, covering it with a sheet, the exposed growth rings *innocent victim to man's folly*. He heard Dan's story and although spiky with thoughts of revenge considered **'right-of-way'** and a favorite oak on the corner of his drive and along with Dan chose to grin and bare. Dan let the all female volunteers express opinions in letters to the editor and emails to the town. Later at the suggestion of Public Works Dan and group tagged all encroaching trees, where Marie's Lane bisected a patch of forest and left it at that.

Dan understood the town's enmity came from the fact Foster Lake Regional, hit hard by the lockdown/ghost-town response remained closed into a second month while theirs didn't. Foster Lake began to imagine The Lane School was lying, and sent out a spy to sniff behind the 'false front'. A youngish woman posing as an interested mother of a school aged child. She could only report on air quality issues, (sawdust), noise pollution, (hammering) and mold in the manure pile but it was enough to trigger additional state investigation. During earlier renovations, lead paint, their main concern was neutralized, wiring redone, pulled through the old gas pipe, Dan explained over and over again, wishing to be left alone in his happy struggle with firewood, woodstoves and biomass boiler …making it to the end of another Maine winter.

It only stopped when more state departments were placed in lockdown. Time lapsed in uncertainty then a pair of inspectors arrived in hazmat suits carrying tools of the trade… flashlights and ladders, probes and mirrors, measuring tape and binoculars, documented, photographed, samples collected, it was a smooth operation until they counted bathrooms in the East Wing. So Dan was looking at another outdoor digging project to satisfy their stipulation for a bigger leach field. *The whole state is locked out and they target us for being healthy.*

9
Pandemic

Another shift in consciousness arrived like a silent fart, everyone aware but no one wanted to point out the source. Nigel rubbed his nose and Stan his beard, waiting for it to dissipate while unease hung in the air ... The Woman's Prison.

"Awl da paor baab'y" the birth of his baby son two years ago following the death of his first born, (four years ago) and Rosalie pregnant, adding bedrooms to his new home behind the old granary, beside the disused rail-bed, had him wanting to parent the world.

Had the flu hit Lanzee prison? *Par'fac' plaace fa daath, rea'dy maay'd.*

Dan kept ear to the ground at virtual town meetings, like boring old TV only slower, citizenry zooming in ... hoping someone would call attention to it. It wasn't supposed to exist; the respite care, refugee resettlement program ... whatever it was... and Dan, Stan and Nigel became men who knew too much ... but not enough.

While the state loudly kept score of cases, recoveries and deaths ... location, age and gender, not a peep came out of the deep forest. "No news is good news," said Dan.

"Day awl youn aany-waays,"

"Better immunity, not as suseptable."

Likewise they had suspicions about the flu itself. Viruses generally traveled from the East to some disease infested port city. The usual path being Boston to cities Lowell and Lawrence, up the Merrimac Valley to rat-run Portsmouth, (undoubtedly infested already) crossing into Maine and following the turnpike north to York, Cumberland, Androscoggin, Kennebec, Penobscot, Piscataquis and Aroostook counties. Covid 19, didn't follow the same route, but hit in cluster bombs, spreading south from Canada, east from Vermont, north from Southern New Hampshire and Massachusetts. The Maine CDC silently investigating ... question marks accumulating.

So Dan wasn't that surprised when a Sunday evening in Late March he received a call from the Sergeant Major, "Hello Dan Stevens, how are things going on Marie's Lane?"

"Good,...and you at the base?"

"I'm actually not at the base at the moment but at Portsmouth Naval Shipyard, at a non military conference although all chiefs of staff are present." He let the impression of his importance sink in.

"You're at a meeting?"

"After …In the parking lot, standing under about five cranes, actually."

"An emergency…?" Dan gazed out the window, a beautiful sunny day.

"As you're probably aware this season's flu, COVID-19, Novel Coronavirus turned into a real killer, they're actually considering quarantining south of Portsmouth …not that that would do any good as it's already in Massachusetts and Maine."

"So what's the deal?" Dan needed the purpose for the call. *Blocking the interstate was ridiculous.*

"During the briefing we were examining an incident map and they noticed your school, The Lane School, remained open and virus free. It's usual to find low readings but to come across a public place, special needs kids bused in and numbers of volunteers, plus the workmen totally unaffected. Because of this, it was decided that you were to remain open, granted special dispensation. They and of course your town isn't aware of all intelligence as I work independently and out of a different base."

"Can you please come to your point," Dan wasn't in the mood for 'Congratulations! Everyone's sick and dieing… (actually they weren't that many sick or dieing only a lot of positives), but at your place, no cases what-so-ever.'

"What we have in mind is a visit out to your school to gather cheek swabs, swab various areas, check the place out… catch you doing good. We need a good model to work from, a positive example. If you agree we can be out tomorrow noon. I'll email consent forms … for kids, volunteers and anyone naturally on the premises. Just print out and pass out. …With your OK … permission, I'll get the ball rolling, send them right along."

Dan audibly sighed, *AAUGH another inspection! only this time it ain't facilities.*

The Sergeant Major's voice said, "he who owns the house makes the rules." followed by a patient pause.

Dan's 'ownership' was mired in 501-C3s. He didn't want that pointed out. Then he almost said 'I'll have to ask his wife,' but that was like acknowledging his lack of authority. He disliked the speed of the military, but unlike cops, who show up unannounced … the SGM apparently wasn't interested in catching them off guard.

"Lane School is considered a control in the advancement of science. In order to stay open we need the privilege of granted access."

Dan gazed around his office, congratulatory photos, well wishes of important people, diplomas and Olivia's ribbons decked his walls. He suddenly felt small, a mere speck to be analyzed, in the cause of science … *that threat won't go unchallenged you a-wipe.* "What day are you looking at?"

"We'll need an hour…" The Sergeant breathed excitedly into the phone.

"Yeah, you can, but can you be more exact" He wasn't concerned, Anne was a cleanliness freak, the volunteers picked up the habit, it was like a reverence for her old homestead … Portraits of the great-great-great grands, Marie and Pierre looking out on timeless perfection.

"How 'bout tomorrow, around 1100-1200 hours err… 11:00am to noon. We can be more precise tomorrow."

"Yourself and how many?"

"Myself, driver and two LPNS."

The only preparation needed was mental but after the town and state they'd become accustomed to bee-keeper suits poking around. *But there's always ulterior motives with those guys.* He wasn't going to worry about his wife and the military *Like she'd avail herself in front of everybody.* (as if!) He decided to trust her; believe her.

Leaving his office, through the front hall past the grand staircase, air guns, compressors and other 'men at work' sounds satisfying to the ear. He was especially pleased with the Art/Dance/Play Room and it's balcony, it was a last minute decision made by him to extensively renovate … he imagined big and little girls dancing, boys exercising, preschoolers coloring and music playing in the sun lit space. Anne hadn't seen it yet, he was holding it out as a surprise.

Monday arrived and Dan headed off to work. (The mill reopened in helmets and face shields.) Thinking forward to lunchtime when the home scene would fill up with more inquisitive strangers. *It's the cost of progress, everyone wants a piece of my (ass) success...* Sliding into his 2018 F-250 Super Duty, bought with Lane Farms money, (the old one saved form the scrap heap to haul firewood) the seat cushioned his status, even with all the changes, the deed remained solidly in their name. What was life for? Comfortable seats. He'd figured a way to have it all, donating their space, sharing life and family. Anne had come out of her shell and wanted him to trust her completely. She'd communicated in longing glances thrown at volunteers' cars. But Dan wasn't ready to get her one. *She just refuses to tone it down and she never asked for her own vehicle.* Volunteers lent her theirs, drove her places… one appeared to be left on the farm for that very purpose, to by-pass his control. A little old silver Rabbit. It wasn't a point of contention as she generally told him where she was going, at least when he was home, the security cams did the rest. All he saw was it parked, and his wife tending to her pupils, excited as usual.

Nigel was on hand to socially distant greet the Sergeant Major. (The only male authority figure; Dan was at work, construction guys don't count). Nigel and the Sergeant Major were alike in many ways, the same prepschool charm, no mansplaning or spreading … they bridged more genteel times and were exactly the same height; 6'2", thin, with 'hungry man' traits, an impulse to devour only Nigel was more intellectually curious while the Sergeant cast ravenous eye on anything female. ((*stationed at an all male base.*) Nigel graciously allowed indulgences.) Both were far away from their culture and state of origin and maladaptive to modern times. Nigel; on a precipice of complete disagreement with the century while the Sergeant longed for an earlier time of total submission to authority.

They were told to expect an additional two military, instead they got six, *always the overkill.*

"I brought along extra crew to shorten the stay." The other men in uniform were introduced.

"So you want to see the classroom area first?"

"We need a place to set up…"

Nigel, flanked by two volunteers, led the way to the Kitchen. Anne was seated at the long rough kitchen table, covered over with work-books, tablets, and jars of pens and pencils. Under stained glass windows at two separate tables older children studied on laptops.

Huge, rectangular square with slate floor, vaulted ceiling, exposed beams, tin tile, colored glass, and subterranean stone walls, appeared even further back in time than cirta 1890. Attractive to the military mind was the bunker-like atmosphere.

The space, devoid of the usual classroom clutter and items such as fish tanks or terrariums filled with moss and reptiles, was squeaky clean as if water ran through nightly removing all traces of the previous day. Victorian cabinetry gave the impression of living useable history where scholarship was the norm, it was a room that had long practiced being perfect.

Anne stood, hand on a top button, the other just touching the table top as if to ground out the electrical charge felt from men in uniform entering her space. "Oh," was all she could say.

"This is Mrs. Steven's I believe you meant her earlier at the party."

"Thank-you, Mr. MacPhee," Anne maintained her poise but didn't move forward shake hands, or wave, instead she bowed in recognition of covoid protocol. Beneath face masks, Anne and the other teachers wore name tags to remind them about proper names… that was using sir names. When school first started they called each other by given names and the kids picked it up …so tags were introduced … kept everyone in line. In compliance with town and state and comfort for all Anne and teachers wore facemasks but the children didn't.

After introductions, (the soldiers wore nametags too) they got down to business discovering wellness. Clearing the table, checking permission forms, the Sergeant Major carefully read each one.

"Must be all those tasty energy bars … the ones you gave us at the base," Nigel still had half a dozen boxes in his kitchen and although not devoured, or commented on positively, they were being eaten.

"Could be," The SGM wasn't distracted.

Kids sat at the tables and were interviewed by masked soldiers as to where they spent the last two-three weeks; incubation period for the virus. Their little lives explored, recorded on video devices, scales brought out, height/weight, noted, mouths swabbed, hearts listened to; reflexes, skin, eyes, blood-pressure all jotted down. The room was filled with low murmuring of male voices asking questions and childish voices answering.

They next turned to the volunteers while Anne retreated to her enormous roll-top desk and chair, Nigel stood behind her." It's a military take over," she said.

"Providential Dan isn't here," Nigel held a finger to his mouth, glasses flashing.

"Yeah good thing."

"Augh oh, incoming,"

The SGM made a B-line towards them holding a 'discovery' kit. "If you don't mind," he handed tubes with cheek swabs inside.

"But I never signed a permission slip," Nigel joked.

"Good point," The SGM's eyes got big and he ran to the table, found what he wanted, stapled three pages together and handed over. "Sorry about that, if you'll please answer truthfully it's important for science and we're grateful for this discovery phase, truly thankful that you allowed this to happen… much appreciated." He smiled coolly and left to supervise a table.

It was the standard medical history form, seen in doctor's offices, with an added page inquiring about nights out, exercise ... sleep habits ... "I'm surprised they don't ask how ...many times per week... Leah and I..."

Anne knew what he was referring too but didn't acknowledge. "It's not that bad... and ... if it really will help," her eyes smiling.

"All in the cause of science," Nigel rolled his eyes.

Forms finished up they watched as the SGM moved around to where two other soldiers were 'white gloving' the window sills. The younger children got up so the older kids from the library could sit at the table and get the full inspection.

The SGM strode over, "Your boyfriend's back."

"Oh," Anne looked up from her comp.

"We need, pulse, heart rate, Oxygen saturation ...since you already did the cheek swab. He deftly inspected Nigel, who rolled his eyes as he hated all things medical.

His only distinguishing feature is that stupid uniform Nigel and the SGM were not only the same height but only three years difference in age, the other man being older. Nigel smiled, he didn't question authority, he ignored it. The SGM had his own little federally funded fortress, where he was numero uno but still answering to his superiors. Everything he saw, every tangible item, beneficial or obstructive, placed in his path or glorifying his rise belonged to somebody else, somebody else's game *Take away rank and he's a big fat zero.*

Like many men, Nigel considered the military but thought it a total cop out. A nice place to visit but … it was seductive, ready made slot in society … then you're caught … with each passing year the private sector grows more terrifying.

The SGM's friendly manner was unaffected by Nigel's negative vibe as he clipped a oxygen saturation monitor to his finger, felt pulse, shone light across the eyes. The surprise came when he whipped out a stethoscope and listened to Nigel's heart. This was all done behind Anne's back so she was caught unawares when he asked to listen to hers.

Dan returned home at the usual time, 5:30 ready for a quick tete-a-tete with his wife, followed by daily decompression but instead of normal she ran to him, helping him off with his coat, "Oh Dan," her voice lilted, "have you been up to the new drawing room/ ballroom?" she took his hand turning for a kiss, in homey mask-less intimacy and with light step, belying her weight pulled him out to the main entrance, up the stair, down the hall to the top of the east wing.

They halted in front of double doors; "So how was the Sergeant Major," he wasn't that confused about her excitement.

"Oh them, you know the Military is one big brand name, each and everyone," "I'm a bla la la, like they all wear labels, stuck to …"

Dan examined the floor …

"And then by virtue of sticking around long enough they're put in positions…" she trailed off needing his attention, delighted expression but got the top of his head, … "and totally into product placement, better ones get better rank, move out to the front shelf! Then the old ones who don't move up, get that shopworn look," she slacked her jaw into a hound dog expression… "get thrown in the recycling bin and there they sit in a VA waiting room ….supposedly"…

"Thanks for getting me up to speed on the military." Dan's expression wasn't one of delighted amusement.

"Oh Dan I'm meant for only you," she put her hand over her heart.

He recalled what a Doctor said after listening to it, 'With that heart your wife will live to a hundred!' *She'll out live me! Remarry!* At the moment all Dan could think of wasn't her silly declarations of love but that she, with her black hair, blushing cheeks and high energy would outlive him, take another man to her bed.

She didn't pay attention to the sour looks but flung opened the doors, "Oh Dan come look," she returned to drag him by the hand when all he wanted to-do was his 'home from work' routine, snag a left over nutrition bar, boil water for tea, escape into his office, check out her story on the security cams, go over farm expenses, he needed space, the important recap of electronic messaging, his daily normal.

"Oh look at this room, look at the view, from the balcony …over here, Dan. It's so strange I don't really remember it growing up, the east wing was closed. This was a ballroom. Can you believe it Dan…can't you see the couples dancing! Look at the stage! Where the band used to play… My Parents, and Grandparents celebrated their marriages here … in this room."

He paused waiting for her beautiful lips to become still… "You aren't going to tell me about your day?"

"Only if you dance with me."

"I'm not in a dancing mood, you know that."

"But we used to dance before the twins were born, remember I got so big." she held her hand out to show. "In the kitchen with the radio on. And now we have this room … it's like living in a fairy tale"… she put out her hand, bowed playfully.

Dan felt compromised and unhappy, he'd wanted the room to be a surprise, now she was inviting him in! It was spoiled. "I inspected their work all along, seen to all the improvements from day one … so you discovered it … it's for the school … everything is… I was waiting till it was all done to surprise you … but I don't care … I'm glad you're happy." He lifted her face, kissed her lightly, "I'm really pleased," his voice said while his eyes betrayed anger. "What's for dinner?"

"Oh you know…"

"I'll be in my office," and he left.

She watched the door close and hugged herself and like Julie Andrews wanting to dance all night. She lightly waltzed with an invisible partner, did bread and butter through a stepladder sat briefly on the window sill, remembering just four hours before when the Sergeant Major removed his facemask, bowed before her and asked to dance. The workmen were on lunch break and she was suddenly in his arms and free. Set free from Dan … the school…and pressures of motherhood, her demanding sons that she couldn't relate to no matter how she tried … all her disappointments disappeared, she was in his arms, and he could dance, really bending and swaying playfully. He turned the workman's radio on, found good music, then he tried to remove her mask … asked to kiss her.

"No," she was so suddenly out of his arms that he couldn't hide the crushed feeling.

"I'm sorry, it was only a suggestion."

"Don't be ridiculous, its flu season!" She laughed and wondered why she bothered to fix his hurt … he wasn't supposed to matter. But she was in his arms again, her feet so naturally following his … like they were made to dance together … until the workmen returned.

Surrounded by memorabilia, Dan in his office went over Lane Farm stuff. While he paid Lane School bills Anne presented him, she handled the School's detailed accounting. His job was paying well, consumed most of his time and he felt prospects rising while energy flagged. *Society's sick and they've foisted it off on us.*

Anne on the other hand was full of it. The pregnancy and boys didn't have the desired effect, instead of being over worked like with Olivia, she had volunteers at her beck and call. She'd become the emblematic freed-up female, the temptress.

He considered it dispassionately at dinner, *do I really know this woman?* They were seated at the kitchen table, Anne had sewed two long table clothes together, Olivia set it with fancy china. All the inherited china was fancy, he kept meaning to buy plain but only got around to plastic for the boys.

A volunteer was present with her little boy, about the same age as the twins, she'd taken over the position of nanny …all this was done without asking and it irritated him to have her sitting there chatting with his wife. She was a single parent, lonely and devoted, he'd caught her reading bedtime stories to his boys, thought it was Ann, but when he peeked in the door, expecting a cozy family portrait, and there she was with her son and **his** twins.

Olivia ate quickly and excused herself for her room as Valerie, (the nanny) now helped with the dishes, like she used to and spent the time talking to her Mom also like she used to, so she'd rather not hang around feeling lonely. She might of seen another side of Valerie but Valerie stopped talking when Olivia was present and then Olivia didn't feel like talking with this silent person absorbing everything. Olivia knew from past experience with Leah how impossible it was to shake people off once they attach themselves to her Mom. Better to wait and let it resolve itself.

Olivia was writing a story about 'The North Woods Monster,' and like most kids her age was on social media, but in 'read only' and except for email, no established accounts. Her leaving meant it was the last Dan would see of his daughter until same time tomorrow as he didn't go in her room anymore *the little girl days were over.*

"She's writing this really great story," Valerie spoke, Dan didn't look at her or respond.

"A monster that forms when it's twenty below and dissolves at zero." Anne giggled.

"Takes the guess work out of why no one sees it," said Dan.

"Big Foot," Valerie's son said.

"Clever boy," Dan wished his boys said it, wished Valerie wasn't there. "So what was the deal today, did it get the big delete or was it all dope."

"Daddy day was like dis," his son put his hands in the air to show how tall they were, "an day did," he poked his stomach, "an made me do dis," he looked back and forth. an dis," he placed a pretend stethoscope under his shirt. "He did Mommy too … an she laughed."

Dan put his fork down, he was enraged, looked at Anne, "I see your name tag is missing," he said evenly and watched as her fingers felt her vest pocket. She gave the table a panicked look and ran from the room.

Dan waited for a moment then followed, though the butler's pantry, the dinning room, out into the front hall. He started slowly up the stair. She was about to descend, saw him, thought the better of it, ran to their bedroom and locked the door.

He tried the door… knocked, "Anne you need to let me in," no answer, "Anne you need to tell me what happened."

"Nothing …happened" came through the door.

"Oh ..kay. Then let me in,"

She opened it and quickly sat on the bed and told him about the men, permission forms, the funny things Nigel said, how they white-gloved everything, inspected … and when she was showing off the ballroom …..she must of lost her nametag, that nothing 'happened'."

"He felt you up."

"What are you talking about."

"With a stethoscope … he touched your …"

"He did not!"

"Am I to believe you or my son … at the moment you lose," Dan's rage began to dissipate, he was in control.

"Oh that, he went under the kids shirts but not the volunteers or teachers, to be totally honest they were more careful, had greater interest, spent more time with the kids."

He sat stonily.

"You don't trust me, why don't you"… she started to sob, clutching his clothing, "And I've never done anything, why would I ..I married the man of my dreams."

He remained impassive, "Then why all this… running around … what's the matter with you?"

"I was afraid of a scene in front of Valerie," They looked at each other … she was the reason they left and why they allowed themselves to run out of the kitchen, leaving the four year olds.

Her tears dried and his anger died, they were of like mind, *how much did she See? hear? What was she thinking…*

Later when he tucked his boys in for the night, something she'd stopped doing, they corroborated her story. He wondered if they'd grow up emotionally stunted without their mother's good night kiss. He remembered how she was with Olivia, sleeping in her room, cuddling her to sleep, he did the same some nights with the boys … she's the one who'd changed. He looked through the old window glass and saw his character disintegrate into unbridled hostility, the abominable snowman, fir soaked in blood.

10

Leah MacPhee

Leah was sick in bed, didn't come down to breakfast, aware it was a Saturday, day off from teaching when instead of grabbing nutrition bars, Nigel made French toast, pancakes or waffles. They'd locally processed maple syrup, loved trees even more on that.

She couldn't hear them, the master bedroom tucked away from the rest of the upstairs rooms and free from family noise but not wind. The wind on that strange April morning threw storm litter against windows…pines bent and moaned. She was thirsty, hot, trembling and couldn't stand. *Nigel won't believe me.*

Yesterday morning when he asked her how she slept, she said; "Oh Awful," how she felt, "Terrible" even as she carefully did her hair and choose attire. Ada was away so she decided what to wear, on her own. Appearance related affirmations directed at her full length mirror, "Oh I don't know… what do you think?" and her reflection said, 'You'll get voted off the Island in those … I like you in the new brown corduroys better.' After she went to the trouble of changing her reflection said; 'don't forget you've cleaning to-do,' and she said, "you're right, can the cords for later," and pulled on the old pair of jeans. Friday was a school day she wasn't expected until 10am, so she usually did the house first. Cleaning was her command and control area, but today she flat out didn't care about anything except thirst.

Nigel was just sitting down to his own plate of waffles, reaching for the syrup when the heard a noise. "Must be the wind," He raised a fork full and paused.

"The wind is saying Dad's name," said Jeff.

"There it goes again," said Henry.

"That's not the wind! That's Mom!" Bett yelled and they all ran out of the kitchen.

"Nigel," Leah wailed weakly, dressed in a nightgown she held on for dear life to the top banister. Her family stared up, she always wore bathrobes. Nigel ran up the stair and lifted her off her feet, Bett and the boys stayed below. Some times their Mom didn't act right and they weren't sure about this.

IN THE HEAT OF the day Leah was happy, riding Jack & Jill, she and Anne ambled out of the forest and across their sunny field. Lush warmth after the cool woods had them pausing, mules pulling grass, stomping at flies. They were in conversation about how to do snacks for the Therapeutic Riding kids. Leah wanted to be in on the process as she felt elbowed out by the other volunteers particularly Valerie. Anne agreed Leah was needed in the kitchen too before the conversation turned to Dan. "Can your husband make some picnic tables?"

"Yeah but you know Dan and his workshop, it gets a bit awks ….weeks go by and nothing … . It's like the word PICNIC gets lodged in his brain as a finished product."

"Nigel's all thumbs. He paints." The mules pulled reins loose and wandered in search of better grass. Pair bonded mules meant the women were never far apart.

"I can't remember when Dan actually made anything… all he does is sit in his office and swivel that chair, from comp. to big screen, boys on the couch, its a total man cave … making gaming noises at the TV. I only get spoken to … 'Honey what about those little gooey things, or he wants sparkling ice tea, … real lunch doesn't happen …on weekends."

The memory went foggy … only Anne's voice rang in her head, … suddenly she in the barn, via dream space/time "We don't buy art," Anne explained. Leah was bemoaning the fact that Nigel's paintings piled up unsold as he didn't know how to market them, "It's so messy in there," meaning his studio.

"Dan won't buy anything," Anne stated a fact. "He says that since we take in contributions we need to keep the right impression before the public. That our brand is KISS, Keep It Simple Stupid. He's never bought me anything, only things for the farm." Anne's usually light expression dissolved into tears, she held the back of her donkey for support. "My birthdays come and go and I get aprons, filing cabinets … last birthday it was the water cooler."

Leah didn't know what to say… how to fix it, her friend always had the right words for everyone. Then she laughed, clapped her hands together… "You can have mine! I don't like wearing them …they give me rashes. Nigel and his Mother think I'm a damn Christmas tree." They finished up the barn, and with delighted step, thin Leah and plump Anne, grinning like teenagers ran the mile up to Leah's stately log home.

No one was there. Nigel, still at the mansion, where he had a school comp. for history class. Volunteers and aids had access as well, adding to research, his mind expanded on the input and with Jeff and Henry staying behind working on laptops, the Steven's Library was second home.

Up in their master bedroom, Leah showed off her estate jewelry.

Anne paused, "To be honest, I've estate jewelry too, my Grandmothers… and pieces from Dan's side of the family … I really love it, we've photos of them wearing them …it's just that …" The well of her emotion was about to burst forth again. "Self pity is wrong" she said under her breath.

"No its not. You're married to a cheapskate."

Anne laughed, no had put it that way before but it was true. Dan acted like he owned everything, when it was hers to begin with. But he was better at figuring things out, what direction to take. "The strange thing is … the better we do the worse he gets! I mean … he's always been …so …good…

with." She trailed off, distracted by the shoebox Leah pulled out from under her bed.

"This is my 'gift wear'. Nigel's Mother is the worst; every Birthday there's something sparkly."

"Wow," was all Anne could manage.

"You want this? It's called a tennis bracelet, diamonds as big as tennis balls." She fastened it to Anne's wrist

"What about Nigel?"

"I never wear them so how's he supposed to know. Besides I've two of 'em."

Anne quietly considering the possibility of actually owning one.

"Can you believe they bought me this!" She dove into the shoebox and shook necklaces off a diamond tiara, held it above her head, looked briefly in her vanity mirror, "all wrong." Then she placed it on Anne's head. "OMG's look!"

"Oh!" Anne sat before the mirror, turned her head from side to side, the walls sparkled diamonds, her long fingers tried to remove it but it was caught in her hair.

"Oh wear it… I've a Queen in my bedroom!" Leah clapped her hands together. Anne's shapely white neck, contrasting black hair, high coloring became a portrait in ermine and silk … trumpets heralding, carriages waiting.

"That's all diamonds and platinum. Looks good on you, you want it?"

"No I can't possibly…"

Leah became circumspect, "they think because I grew up poor that naturally I'd want jewelry but I can't wear it. Soooo" She'd never had another woman in her bedroom and was eager to show off and Anne was a queen in a diamond tiara, giving Leah the attention she craved. "But I do love clothes! Look! And she opened her closet doors, turned on the lights.

"Wow," was all Anne could say.

Leah disappeared inside, slid hangers, pulled out dresses, held out to show. "This is what I wear..." she explained the use for each outfit; they went to art openings in Boston, plays in Bangor, concerts in Portland, since the boys were ten and eleven, one of the volunteers became a steady babysitter. "I like everything except the ballet and this... she twirled a bright green beret, "that's going in goodwill," she dropped it in a bag ... "Nigel takes Bett to the ballet ... and Ada to Opera in Portland."

"Opera," Anne sighed.

"We could get tickets for you too ... I'd go, if you went ... and maybe Olivia can come."

"Oh hello, I didn't know you had company," Startled by a male voice and sudden appearance of Nigel, the women became children caught in the act of being feminine. The house rule was sock feet, silent approaches caught everyone off guard and they couldn't hide anything.

"Oh," Anne stood, reached for the crown, it hung snarled embarrassingly in her hair.

"Don't worry about me, I heard voices, had to investigate," he grinned at their silence, obviously waiting for him to leave.... Rubbing hands together ..."I was just going to make tea, can you stay?"

Anne looked at Leah and didn't know what to say. Here she was a grown woman, supposedly able to make up her own mind but all she could think of was Dan returning from work and discovering her gone. "Augh ...augh"

Nigel's ESP bore into the problem, "Dan's home at 5:30? Its 5:15 now, I'll reach him on his cell and see if he wants to join us."

It was so innocent a suggestion, something that shouldn't bother any normal married woman but standing in their master bedroom they felt Dan's control reaching in. "Ok, that would be nice, I'd love too, but isn't it late for tea...."

"We always have a quick cup after climbing the hill for home, staving off starvation before dinner."

"A quick tea would be nice…"

"Good, I'll get the kettle on so when you're ready…"

"Nigel?"

He turned and smiled at his wife, "what?"

"If it's ok with you I'd like to give Anne my extra tennis bracelet."

Anne looked down, embarrassed and called out of her element, contrasted by Leah's closets, her clothes were old and possibly out of style but she never cared until then.

Nigel paused, emotions rising, He knew Anne and his wife were aware of his long standing crush and there she was in his bedroom, standing before him, having sat on his bed, was she real or a spirit out of the past, he almost moved in her direction, wanted to hold her, comfort and call her beautiful, ... steal a kiss ... then imagined himself apologizing, '*sorry! just wanted to see if you were real*' ... Leah was real and he had to be careful, choose the right words, "If she wants it sure!"

"ANNE...ANNE..." Leah said at the blurry outline of a man's head wearing a face mask.
"Not Anne but your husband, Nigel."
'What's going on ... what am I doing here?'
Nigel explained that she was in Foster Lake Regional Hospital, that she had a kidney infection had fainted due to dehydration and would be going home tomorrow.
Leah looked from the end of her bed, to the IV, TV and window ... sunlight seeping in. She had to get home. Even one day away had dire consequences. Somebody else would take over her spot in the mansion, eager faces wanted to become close friends with Anne. Valerie took over the childcare; others were angling for her teaching spot. Leah didn't mind Valerie that much, child care wasn't her forte' showed off her deficits actually but she liked her school and therapeutic riding positions. She was the one who stayed after everyone left, helping Ann. Plus she'd invented a course out of teaching cards and 'off computer' board games; 'now I can play with my Granny at the home,' one kid said. But even with the sarcasm, they liked learning especially gambling;

Texas hold 'em, War, Three Card Stud, it got them thinking in terms of probabilities, becoming mini card sharps, betting toothpicks. She also went over sports rules but they studied better on their own. She tested them on outdoor sports; tennis, golf, hockey, soccer, football and of course, baseball and indoor games; basket and volleyball. Never good at sports she none-the-less liked teaching them ... rules comfortably absolute, like math.

"I have to get home ...Nigel ... oh please take me home," her throat was dry so she sat to drink from a glass, poured herself a second one, felt sick to her stomach, head crashing, "oh my head."

"They're running tests ... you know how they are, guilty until proven innocent."

"But I have to be there, not here ... Anne will get a substitute and ... we've chess and poker tournaments!"

Nigel pulled his mask to his chin. "Calm down ... you'll be home soon enough." He couldn't tell her that her friendship with Anne was bought and paid for years ago when Anne took her riding, taught her how to handle mules, ... or that her teaching position, unlike his own was largely contrived. *It would hurt her feelings terribly.* Besides they never had vindictive words, only surface irritation. Their interactions were the usual calming down of a stressed out female, he was good at it, having eighteen years of experience.

"But why did you bring me here! I'm not sick. I refuse to be treated like a child. Who's the big authority that put me here? This is awful … I want to go home. Anne. Nigel I want Anne. I need her, she'll explain to them I'm needed at the mansion. She'll make them let me go home."

"Careful the walls have ears."

Leah looked frantically around, but when she tried to get up, even sitting was difficult, she lay back, turned to the window, angry at weakness, mad at the world.

"Knock, Knock," a male voice said, "May I come in?" It was the Sergeant Major, in full black uniform, brass insignias, badges, cap, cap device, mask and briefcase. Arriving unannounced and unexpected he paused. Anticipating shocked looks and awkwardness, measured steps brought him bedside.

"Augh …" Leah skillfully dropped her near hysteria and waited.

"I'll only be a moment … I," he paused collected his thoughts, "Came here to see our first casualty," smiling, "how are we feeling today?"

"OK," Leah nodded, felt for her mask in the bedding and put it on.

Nigel stood aside, "Humm," pulled his mask up and looked down.

"You know we're keeping track of this flu pandemic and any information you share with me helps, is vital to the over all picture. Nice to see you again," he nodded at Nigel. "I understand they ran some tests last night and so I'm wondering if, for the cause of science you'd be interested in signing this permission form. It releases information particular to this illness and nothing else … nothing before or after."

His perfect diction and correct pronunciation of all vowels, syllables and consonants, engaging glance, spare form, perfectly pressed uniform, army green facemask, had them agreeing in spite of themselves. They both signed.

Nigel handed the pen back and sprang into verbal action, "You drove the whole way down here? That's a three hour drive."

"My driver did, yes, two hours and fifteen minutes... to be exact. Beautiful weather for it … April."

"You check out all cases?"

"I'm handling the control… the other ones are…"

"Handling the control I see," Nigel touched his moustache, *as if that's new, when control is all they do… control the air, sea, land… now microbes & viruses.*

"The other cases are handled under a different protocol, infectious disease … everything highly professional, a lot protective clothing, cleaning time involved … data entry for covid -19 and non-covid-19 in my test area … and you're in it."

"I hope you find what you're looking for," Leah said miserably *I'm nothing more than a petri dish growing mould.*

The room was silent while the Sergeant Major, rustled papers and placed the permission form in his briefcase and closed it. "Thank you greatly. This will help a lot. I hope you get better and we'll see you soon." He backed up, waving three fingers and left.

"He was pleasant enough." Nigel rather hated him for it, "polished."

The sudden interruption by an authority figure had done its trick; calmed Leah, allowing her to focus. "Anne didn't get the bracelet." Dan came to tea after all and Anne took it off, slipped it in Leah's pocket, giving her sad looks.

"I thought you gave it to her."

"No she wouldn't take it with Dan there."

"Dan…"

Over the past four years Nigel witnessed Dan become deeply entrenched in routine, even as he jumped into their most recent renovation project. Nigel respected him, they were of like mind; keep the mansions beautiful features, while fixing rot, plumbing and bad smells. As an expert in everything old, Nigel's input was welcomed. In all other areas Dan was a one man show. He would choose to announce plans or not and never shared day to day business, Nigel and a chosen few got an 'end of year recap' … Comp. generated beautiful office-pro print out complete with holes punched for safe keeping.

Nigel timed his arrival at the Mansion to facilitate a half hour alone with Anne and their blended family; Olivia, the twins, Bett, Jeff and Henry were set to some task … Anne was generally occupied too but no another adult present meant he could flap open his suit coat, show off impeccable attire, reiterate some silly story and receive delighted blushes and giggles. He always wore suits, three piece in winter, having carefully scraped his face, colored his moustache, reflecting it was perfectly ok to have a female boss, she wasn't a tyrant while Dan was beginning to act like one.

Dan was at work and not missed. Although he once flirted with the idea of teaching woodworking or bird life he'd since received a new position at the mill; he was procurement specialist and now employee liaison. He was paid extra to snoop. His superiors ground him down for details almost everyday. Dan soon learned that he could sway their thinking. He'd report "The men are upset about the waste on the debarker floor' or 'they aren't appreciating the new hearing protection.' When it was Dan who liked his old ones better and had long been after them to save all scraps for the biomass boiler. He was anxious to keep the mill profitable. The personnel angle was an added stress so he expected his wife to keep emotional care of the homefront, let him retire and recharge in his office and she did so with light intelligence and happiness. Dan didn't realize that he'd become completely sidelined as he considered her an extension of him.

"Oh can you please find it? I think it's still in my pants pocket … find it and give it to her."

Nigel looked down at his wife. Here she was hospitalized with what may be a serious illness and all she could think about was Anne. But he understood as he couldn't imagine life without her … teaching was a joy at the mansion. He'd pop in the kitchen unannounced and there she was in a ruffled cowgirl shirt and wool vest, bent over papers at her roll-top desk. The happy smile, obviously glad to see him was precious and Leah when she arrived was given equal dose… and equally enamored.

Anne was able to diagnose any difficulty, lead his thinking, understood his nature; sympathic and kind. The MacPhee's devotion was reflected in daily action, albeit personally hard to verbalize, they never spoke about it to each other … until now.

"You know Dan doesn't buy her anything like that. He's afraid it will hurt their 'brand'. Like televangelists stealing from old people."

"Really?" Nigel was always glad he choose Leah, *at least she's all mine*. Looking down at the angular face he felt misery rising, "Don't worry, Anne won't be so quick to find a replacement … cards aren't exactly core…(Leah turned her face away) "I'll hold down the fort, mention how dedicated you are … besides you'll be home … there's nothing much wrong with you."

"But what if she leaves him? What if she waits 'till Olivia's out of school and leaves him, she might, you know she's not attached to the twins, I mean she's …. and …Dan is just so selfish. He's …"

"Dan's a good man and their well matched, it's not like either one has gone to seed. He's like prize bull and she's a …show… cow."

"The little boy laughed to see such a sport, the cow jumped over the moon."

(Nigel shook his head …)

"It isn't a fairy tail romance. He's such a pig." Leah turned away, she was exhausted, wanted all her worries to end, wanted to be alone .. saw Anne's face giving her a sad glance over the bracelet. "Nigel, lets give her more … you know Dan's taken over all the money and doesn't give her anything, that's why she wears old clothes … we can sneak it to her… she can cash them. You know, sell them on ebay … They let me buy Olivia riding clothes, remember? And Dan takes the twins shopping but Anne doesn't go out, I mean she does but he doesn't take her out … like we go out or give her money."

Through their love for Anne they saw each other in a different light, Leah touchingly devoid of jealousy and he; generous and kind. Suddenly they were holding each other, their own love magnified. "Oh Nigel I hate being here. I want to go home …" she began to weep, "this place is full of sick people … I might catch Covid-19 and… die… never see home again!"

Nigel straightened his back, "You'll be home tomorrow," swept his arm around the room, "It's a private room." The window a gaggle of color in the wall, he wished to escape but didn't want it to show so he patted her arm, kissed her hot forehead, "just one more night and you'll be out.." He left and she turned to the wall like white was her new enemy.

DAN IN HIS OFFICE sorted mail. Anne up visiting Leah freshly home home from the hospital. She didn't have the flu or Covid 19 aka Cornia virus but a simple stomach bug and something else; dehydration and kidney issues. Dan was tickled; it meant his place had some evangelical dispensation, invisible force field, protecting all life with-in, even as he'd moved away from church and prayer ...

It seemed that after their visit to the base, life had changed in an almost imperceptible way. Another power had entered the premises, psychological and physical gate-crashed. *What are we to them? First we go to their house, (the base) and then they come to ours. They sent us home with food bars, they have extensive medical history on all the kids...*

Authority pinged him at work too. The mill ordered everyone to get flu shots, the guys smiled and nodded at one of those meetings where the managers in masks, hard hats and in social distance mode gave orders from the steps. His position as liaison had him finding zero compliance, himself included... of course the report was different.

While believing in divine protection, achieving a great home life wasn't that miraculous. While obese, he prayed hard for a better position at the mill and a beautiful girl friend, while getting drunk every weekend, binge eating and chain smoking. He hadn't given it up for love but for money, he wanted to look the part. Better pay at the old mill lasted only until it was sold and demolished. *Government got involved.* He'd of liked to be able to point at the blue steel building and say; 'I was saw and planner operator …and … (after loosing the weight) Production Supervisor and Procurement Specialist.' Still it was a great seven years, he made himself easy to work with, knew he had it better than even his bosses, their eyes popped out when he invited them over for Superbowl Sunday.

Better pay in the old days was good enough to impress Anne and his engineering mindset knew exactly what to do with her property and how to keep her feeling fulfilled at home. The Donkey and Mule rescue Farm, later therapeutic riding and then The Lane School … Farm and Mansion were in a state of continual change and growth and Anne expanded and grew with it. *She's not the same woman I married.* The increased exposure and activity unwrapped the seductress and everyone was drawn … *moths to a friggin bonfire.* He was the opposite. The more important he became in town politics and his mill position, the more he needed those hours of retreat.

Her love hasn't changed He mulled it over and wondered why, out of the depths of his thinking, male faces popped randomly into his recommended list. She seemed distracted. Security cams showed nothing, he checked them daily. He was waiting to install them in the east wing. *Oh well it's spring and she's getting older.* He kept hoping age would slow her down but so far that hadn't happened. *She smiles and blushes like a teenager and now she wants to take ballroom dance classes when the shutdown ends!* He knew it was all female with the occasional male appearing intermittently, drug under protest by girlfriend or wife. So he didn't object, she'd renewed her license and drove herself in a car one of the wealthier volunteers donated. An old VW Rabbit. *She's like a Rabbit … take one look and its bunnies.*

She's actually costing us money… Dan had long wanted a U-tube channel, up his monetization practices, be in the big league … but he couldn't pull the trigger with her around. She was uploaded and shared by hundreds on FB, the Christmas Party, let loose on social media had everyone wanting to know more, men sending messages, trying to meet her…

SINCE HER HOSPITAL stay Leah was physically healed but psychologically changed. She wondered how she could've fainted, and woken up somewhere else. *It was like teleportation.* She wondered if breaks in consciousness' were spirit leaving and reentering and where she was in the mean time. *If I'm not conscious, not really here than where was I?* She thought about it while brutalizing the vacuum cleaner, incase of contagion, she wanted all particulates gone. They wanted her to stay away from The Lane School for two weeks total and the house was getting on her nerves.

She didn't like the interest of the Sergeant Major or the military. *Can't they mind their own business? People were flat out dieing of opioids and Covid-19 and they're investigating us.*

She also was saddened by the deaths of two hikers. When still in Massachusetts boating deaths by drowning had her thinking for days of ways she could've prevented it, thoughts trespassing into unknown territory, she was constantly bringing it up before her family and wanted to investigate the river, tried to get Nigel out on a boat. Now after two men hiking the Appalachian trail were found dead, in an area between the new underground base and woman's prison she was sure that not only was the base responsible but the trail was dangerous and a highway for the crazy and disenfranchised, but *we'll never know what happened* ... bodies whisked away. She tried again to get Nigel involved and he mumbled something about warning Stan and turkey hunting. *Turkey Hunting! This was serious!*

Leah looked past the timber framed walls of her home to the woods ... trees in new spring leaf. But after months of stark bare branches, green leaf appeared to be hiding something ... bad things happen in summer.

WEARING A LAB coat the Sergeant Major pressed his remote and the 'ant farm room' wall slid aside. With thin smile of appreciation he stepped over the threshold remembering how the boys thought it all CGI, when actually it was a large flat screen behind beveled glass. Inside was bursting with real daylight, magnified by mirrors. *There's no underground facility like it.* He was on board from the beginning, in-putted design layout, now enjoying the actual space, very close to the study models he developed ... only better than ever imagined.

Rows of Pot Plants stopped his mind with the odor of mysterious growth, yellow spore laden buds on a golden mission, reaching for sunlight.... Synthetic marijuana is pooh-poohed by the using community as dangerous *so we'll give 'em the real thing.* Absorbed in thought he reached out to shake hands but the greenery recoiled. *Sensitive...* He found a hand held lamp and blasted them with simulated sun light and heat. Like stop action film the 'herb' leaned towards it and when he turned on the sound system, base violins and dripping water, along with tube-fed irrigation, the plants surrendered, leaves drooping, complete assignation; third generation. Fine, Superfine and Turbo.

Superfine was beginning to form buds, the SGM smiled ... they'd enhanced all properties, *THC has nothing on me... they'll be taking off clothes and licking trees. They want to see spaceships? We can do that too.* An old hallucinogenic Afghanistan strain spliced with Appalachian aphrodisiac... but after the first time, it's all down hill. Paranoia and self hatred set in and they wonder why.

He loved the caverns, tunneling high and safe, *kevzar forever!* LEDs blinking on, *to live always underground only surfacing when we're done.*

Wanting no 'contact high' he accessed a cabinet with moon suits, found one with SGM Insignia ... Fully protected he was ready to enter the flea room. *From pot heads to pet owners.* "How's it going?" He addressed a slight man in a moon suit with a hand held, other lab assistants moved about in silent study, dropping material in various devices.

"The idea of dogs and cats as carriers isn't working see. Come ... I'll show you." He entered a short claustrophobic tunnel, ventilation fans whirring. A second door opened the incinerator.

The SGM needed only a quick glance to get the idea. "That many ... what a shame," face mask moving coldly, behind layers of plastic.

"It looks like rodents are our best bet."

"Rodents are too easily killed." The SGM hid his feelings, actual fondness for the sensitive little creatures. So refined and independent. Really no comparison to house pets.

"Yes but they fit through small spaces and the public won't get it. They'll think it's due to the shutdown, garbage left on sidewalks."

"True and there isn't a home in America that doesn't have a mouse problem."

"Introduce that super carrier, knockout mouse that looks like your average mus muscullus infestation."

"No," The SGM winced at the idea of his precious mice dieing from poisoned bait ... "Dogs and cats welcomed into the home, loved, petted, splayed on furniture, we have a pesticide resistant flea ... adaptive viruses, the hard part's over! This should've been easy. I can't believe they've no anti-bodies or something. I'd rather not use mice, they need to be saved for later."

"Still in the planning stage."

"More than that ... Rodents are restricted because of their value in research. The focus is Domus cattus and canis domum.

"We offer cute little puppies and kittens up for adoption and infected kids sent back home from Lanzee along with free pet food... but no crumb trail," he paused enjoying his own verbiage ... "What will they do? The long lost child returns to kill the genetically inferior and ... and later we can do a trial run with the knock out mouse..."

"You mean the symptom free guy, the one developed not to show ..."

The Sergeant Major paused, the mouse was his baby, bore his name, "needs time. They're not happy about it but ..."

"They know the good you've done."

"They know world runs on physical practicality, the work I've done at their behest reflects a degree of truth. That's the beauty of science, like water it always wins, one is forced to agree. But even if word gets out we can spin it, Op-ed it. Imagine hearing the news, their long lost host carrier ...

kidnapped son or daughter's returning from the grave … whole villages rejoicing over our humanitarianism." Lowering voice to a whisper, "We have to be careful least they fall into the wrong hands … the better looking ones."

A barely discernable wink came through two layers of plastic. "Yeah," the little man grinned, "germ warfare" they were on an A/B system, conversation exclusive.

The SGM smirked at the innuendo, "stolen fruits the sweeter… legal trade in those parts…" They moved away from each other, trying to regroup on task.

The little man turned back, "we'll go in there, offering free shit."

"Not a wiff of true intention."

"A really beautiful virus."

"Yeah and it wasn't that long in development, you saw its potential."

"The synthetically altered transceptor was the kicker."

"You're the one with an understanding of virology's natural evolution.

"We do what the military does; work with a purpose! Only this is a nonviolent …and humane. They want progress … we give them grant-worthy projects, feed the need."

"Indicitive" the little man grinned.

"Exactly, we can't be thought of as inefficient or not with the times. And we do have left over animals." he opened a door to a second lab, turned on the lights, "might as well use them." dogs in individual cages and one long kennel and at least fifty cats in three large cages, … looked up. Dogs barked, whined, he pressed a button, 'dog calmer' device, and got instant quiet, heads on paws, sighing and cats climbed the walls. He returned the calming device to its wall clamp, "Can't use it on the kids."

"Guidelines.".

The SGM paused feeling his self-confidence rise but he still had to be careful with opinion. "Its back to the drawing board, we're almost there, uncompromised by UV-rays, or dry heat. I'd rather not use flies. Fleas form pesticide resistance … not the antibody resistance mutants we're looking for. Imagine a ten year battle with a hundred variants! They'll think they've won and its back-at- cha… *no good deed goes unpunished!*"

"Works for us."

"Use as many test animals as needed. I'll find more … we'll get there," he patted the man's shoulder.

"Population cure."

The SGM paused surprised … that variant was secret. "Are you aware of any hacking attempts against our data base."

"I," … the little man paused, The SGM towered over him, "Not to my knowledge sir."

The SGM paused watching droplets roll down the little mans face. "I wouldn't take it personally." He paused, standing close enough to hear him breathing. "They bred indiscriminately, in that hot climate …."

A reassuring star struck glace came through double layers of plastic. "Won't know what hit em."

Watch them trace it back across Canada to Vancouver. Let's see what stops breeding more … government programs or -----" The SGM paused waiting for the little man to fill in the blank. But he didn't … obviously wasn't in on it. He looked down, anger rising at the small mans physical weakness, how they didn't have a moon suit that fit him … *one punch and he's history.* "This is between us …. keep an ear out … even the slightest reference… needs to be made note of … reported to me."

"Sir!" along with a salute.

Tapping down homicidal rage he continued, "The public is fed on our Social Service but they don't know about this. I'm counting on you."

"Yes sir, you don't have a talker here sir … we'll get her done sir," another salute.

"Thank-you soldier," The SGM saluted, "I'll be back." *No one knows who I'm connected with, this is international. 5 eyes. BIG.*

On his way out the SGM by passed the pesticide room and smiled. Pesticides were brought in as a way of demoralizing the public. The great organic push brought about an abundance of nature and naturally occurring organisms in a self regulating harmonic balance. Insect born illness naturally controlled. Take it all away especially in an urban setting and the area is ripe for endemic desease. The pretext is some annoying pest and we go in and poison every beneficial insect, bird, reptile, small mammal and amphibian. *Guess who's next?* The SGM imagined massive die-off… but not in his life time.

He couldn't resist the scent room and so pushed his remote and entered. His favorite idea, he promoted it vigorously, wrote all the grant proposals himself. He smiled remembering the test studies … *I was numero-uno guinea pig!* They were all set out on tables in color coded aerosol spray bottles so participants recruits didn't know what they were getting.

The appetite stimulant, …. Kids in the nutra-bar room. A second was the opposite, nausea producing saved for a later date. Then they had ten min. duration calming, and longer duration. The ten min. calming happened in the service elevator, one of the men thought we put something in a drink! Then there was the woman's aphrodisiac. Nice big wiff in the girls bathroom and two of 'em made themselves up like whores! And another favorite; the amnesia, only in scientific study… *We'll save it for later.*

Maine women are so unresponsive. He lingered at the scent table, considered the challenges he'd lived through, his loneliness, he hated call girls, *terrible, can't relate … it's so unfair!* And married women, … *Maine married women don't drink or go out unless it's 'all girl'. They form clubs around knitting and childcare … vegetable gardening! They also don't know how to dress.* Good-looking married women of the variety he was most successful with in normal states seemed interested until he popped a good-natured, 'how about a drink after…' and they flee! The only one to take him up on it was sexually ambiguous. When people asked him how he was adapting to Maine life he wanted to Quote, 'women are wicked when you're unwanted.' But didn't … he was a married man.

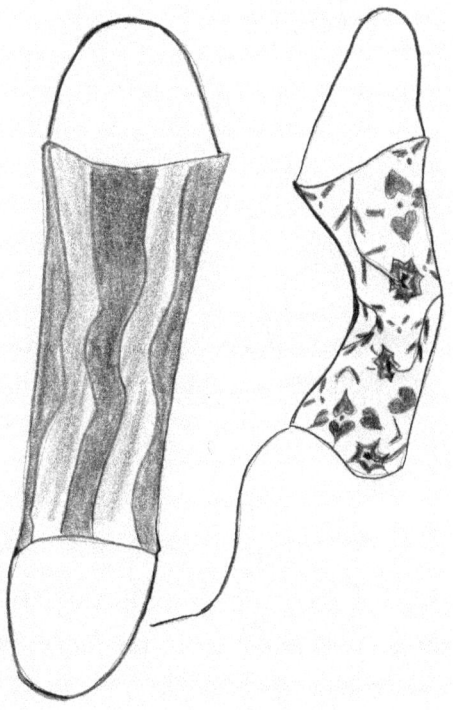

11
Havin' a Ball

No longer in any kind of incubation period and back at her teaching position Leah nervously tried to focus on reality while worries took her to parts unknown; The Appalachian Trail and two dead hikers. It wasn't news that was disturbing it was no news that upset her.

"Try and develop a 'wait and see' attitude," Nigel had his own stones to cast in the great Maine unknowns. *filled with dense material like their minds.* He was sure hundreds of people were involved in a cover-up. *You let people out after the lock-down and look what happens!* Bodies located in an area that on maps looked innocent enough; an unbroken canopy of green. Only he, Stan and Dan and their wives were aware they died between the new underground Naval Base and Lanzee Women's Prison. When people are up to no-good the first requirement is privacy, but to have it undesignated on maps generated a deep paranoia, *the government is out to get us, plus my wife's upset.*

But at least virus and riot free northern Maine was opening up. *Maine doesn't lag, it leads!* Dismayed by riots elsewhere he wondered how looting helped anything 'matter.' Seattle, Washington, NY, NY All the great stores destroyed by who? Colleges students sent home to a society and parents who didn't want them. 'welcome to the unemployment line! So they don't 'matter' either, He remembered taking a semester off from the University of Virginia, how his mother had a fit. His presence interfered with her newfound freedom!

Nigel was irked by schools and government (the law) authorizing the shutdown, while the kids attacked law abiding people like himself. *They attack small business like making a living is a crime. Cops stand down and they get looted. What's their end game? No private property, no marriage, no inheritance, no life?*

Capitalism = inequality …TRUE but it takes a ton of time and work to get ahead. Let the government pick winners and we get windmills, monuments to mal-investment. The little guy entrepreneur is living under a hammer …displays new products and wam-mo … … *Looters think they're destroying the past but actually they're destroying the future.*

RELIEF ARRIVED unexpectedly when Anne asked Leah to accompany her to ballroom dance class as total lockdown had just lifted. Requirements were soft-soled shoes, face masks, gloves and good health. They were on their way to the 'beginners' class that was basically everyone as experts practiced later and on their own. Leah slid happily into the passenger's seat, Anne was at the wheel of the old VW Rabbit excitement leaking out in blushes, glances and sighs.

Like other tax avoiding businesses, dance class was just over the border in the next town, on the top floor of a centuries old woolen mill. Over the long brick structure a clock with missing hands bonged out the hour. Anne and Leah were glad to be early and for the pipe railing guiding them past torrents that once powered the old polluter. Chlorobenzene clean up, huge superfund project, turned dirty water into class-A mist.

From time immemorial they were drawn, not only by signage; dance music trilled… Under the old spillway was a door, they shook off droplets and ran in.

Green and gold arrows led them to a breathtakingly large room with tall windows all around. A single wood desk made up the office where a well put together instructress batted eye shadow, delighted to have them,, knew their names and inquired about dancing skills, (zero). Anne was socially prominent, even if hidden away, she handed over Dan's credit card while Leah had her own. They deposited street shoes and bags in a locker-room containing about forty small lockers.

Minutes early, they walked around the dance-floor. Reflected waves from the millpond rippled across the ceiling and music played "Beautiful room," Anne sat and more women arrived and boys who appeared to be teens to early twenties, but most were women, their age or younger, several seemed retired ballerinas, sinewy and graceful.

They were all in loose fitting pants, floating skirts over leggings or leotards and tank tops. Anne glanced jealously sideways; she was the only one in tight jeans and button down plaid flannel shirts. The colorful clothing had thoughts on cashing in the tennis bracelet at a jewelry shop in Newport, gaining a card in her name, freely shopping on line, packages with smiles arriving while Dan was at work.

"Leah, can you do me a favor and not be mad at me when I ask you?"

"Like it's about to burst and kill us all." Her glance traveled from tailrace to spillway … milldam waters lapping across a new cement top.

Anne stood next to her but without the same alarm, she was focused on pretty tops and tights. "What I mean is can you sell the bracelet? For me? I love it, of course…and I love that you gave it to me … because you're my friend."

"Nigel and I already talked about that. How much do you need?"

Anne was taken aback, played with her top button, it never occurred to her that Nigel and Leah would talk about her, "Whatever you can get is good."

So Leah gave the tennis bracelet to Nigel and he slipped Anne a check for $2,500.00. She didn't need to know the jewelry went back into the shoebox, Nigel didn't feel like driving to Newport.

They'd never participated before and didn't know the class was fairly nontraditional ... starting with country western line dances, clog, stroll and the time honored minuet. It was all done without touching, (covid compliant) if you discount the eyes that told stories of dull female routines that needed a break from virtual reality, everyone loved and hated, their PC corner, cluttered desk and infinite contacts. Life was brought out in the open, women were dancing, in perfect pauses, music cuing, toes pointing.

Anne loved the minuet; Leah the clog. It was twenty women and five boys. Age disparity and social distancing mandate aside they were off to a good start dancing the pandemic away.

Concentration was good for Leah, forced to focus, she 'got' rhythm. At first, she turned the wrong way in the minuet and sat down ashamed but Anne took her by the hand and she was back on the floor, smiling. Her favorite was circle clog dance, making the windows rattle, besides she loved the bluegrass music coming out of the wall speaker, brought back to her family origins; fiddle, banjo, steel guitar and mandolin.

Later they brought Bett and then Olivia. Marie Wiznowski came once but the all girl scene was off-putting.

"It's a crying, dieing, shame without men, Nigel you have to come!" Leah tried to imagine her husband dancing.

"When it reaches 20% adult male, maybe." Nigel knew as the only one he'd be a subject of interest in an area of least proficiency.

Ann anticipated Dan's response but asked him anyway.

"No that's OK you go, enjoy yourself." He was conscious of the new clothes, that she was loosing weight, gaining muscle tone … the all female deal sat well with him.

Since everyone was going, Nigel had them take the Rover, Anne drove with Leah beside her; the girls in the back seat. They were laughing over attempts to find male victims, the girls tried … volunteer's sons and husbands produced no takers.

"I know, let's put the word out to the Base, I mean," Anne blushed, "that's where the boys are."

"That's a terrible idea … "Leah began then stopped conscious she might be hurting her friend's feelings.

"No, not terrible, just something to think about. If we had the Sergeant Major along they'd be good control. I think it would be good for them and they'd have to be on their best behavior… besides many are from WestPoint and know the steps already." Her palms sweating she wiped them together and looked out the window, letting thoughts dissipate.

"Oh no not him! Please don't ask him!" Alarm calls came said from the back seat.

"Whoever do you mean?"

"The Sergeant Major! He's a total creeper!"

"Better skurt it Mom," Olivia, enjoyed the all girl, much less stress.

"The Instructor might not like it," Leah understood the next step.

"Of course I'd get her permission first"

ANNE SAT ALONE in front of her vanity, bowed head of wavy black hair reflected at all angles while she sorted out emotionally charged events and how to proceed. Her chief source of support, Dan wasn't in the picture ... she stood and moved towards a window, trying to manage, arrange events like items on her vanity top... that way she'd know what to-do.

Late Spring became mid summer and the light from the dance studio's windows changed from yellow-green to white. With the influx of soldiers from the base, Virginia reel was dropped in favor of ballroom. Anne mentioned the base to the instructress and sparks produced a bonfire.

They were given special dispensation from Covid 19 rules and were able to drop facemasks and glove requirement. Mandatory cheek swabs produced 100% negative results, the instructress gave the happy news then announced the solders by name and they bowed in turn, including the SGM. Fifteen total, hatless, brass buttons, white belts and navy blue, the atmosphere of feminine froth turned earthly, grounded...real.

She faced the room smiling; "This wonderful opportunity is brought to us by our wonderful Sergeant Major, Bob Mason from Fort Charon. Because of him we can move away from line dance into ballroom. Thank-you so much Sergeant Major for your timely contribution err intervention." She clapped …. they all clapped.

Anne blushed from head to toe at the sight of them and the room murmured in excitement. The Sergeant Major appeared to have left a quantity of his decorations at home, or had a uniform especially made for the occasion, similar to the marines, ID insignia on arms and cuffs.

The SGM bowed double, gave a cold practiced smile, everyone lip-read his mouth repeating; "Thank-you," several times, believing they found HIM exciting and the not the facemask deal.

The instructress waved her hands for them to stop, "we will now move into ballroom dance. Starting with a simple Rumba step."

"A Rumba!" Leah was alarmed. It felt exotic, foreign.

"Don't worry Fox-trot will come later."

"Oh you!" Leah saw her friend had changed, *it's the clothes*. The shoebox filled with jewelry opened Pandora. Anne in tight flower patterned leotard, loose blue skirt, hair up so soft black curls shone with the sweat on her long neck, her stoutness gone to a slim waist, ready for male arms ...*she gorgeous*. Leah was dressed in the same style, but almost entirely in bright green showing off thinness like a bending tree. The girls likewise were a subject of envy, their clothes loving Mom's decking them out thoroughly. But for the moment they were all students watching the instructress sway her hips, arms up to show an invisible partner.

She asked for help and one of the soldiers stood, formally bowed and after she felt his ability, they were all over the floor, Rumba music played, it was sultry, southern, charming.

She thanked him and he sat down, "Form partners please!" The familiar waiting to be asked to dance took moments as the women came with friends … it seemed the cadets, aware of this stampeded loudly across the floor. The Sergeant Major made a B-line for Anne but a blond crewcut, cut him off so the SGM bowed before Leah. Bett and Olivia were partners as the soldiers gave them a wide berth.

Chin held high, he snaked Anne across the room.

"Step, sway, step, sway, one two three four," the instructress had a mic., dancing by herself, then asked one of the young boys standing in the door way. She was a foot taller but he knew how to Rumba, everyone smiled the sight.

The soldier moved Anne away from the crowd, his youth was electric but plugged into the wrong socket, she wanted to learn.

"Talking is permitted you know," he smiled.

"Oh, I'm sorry I don't know how to do this, so I have to watch my feet. You're a very good dancer ... where did you learn?"

"School."

"School?"

"West point."

"Thought so, I mean that's good, a long way for you, do you find it hard?"

"No."

"No? You like it here? Maine, the northern part anyway doesn't strike me as a first pick, for a man with abilities ..." They'd slowed near a window, were looking out at the cascading falls.

"I was chosen ... we're top of class,"

"You must be very bright, ... and get 'hardship pay' ..." Anne smiled, they'd practically stopped dancing.

"I was out to your house, you don't remember."

Anne thought for a moment, "Oh yes, in a blue watch-cap. You were handling paperwork."

"You danced with the Sergeant Major," his voice was matter-a-fact.

Anne stopped... stood motionless... stunned.

"One two three four," he counted out, his white gloved hand tightened on hers, arm around her waist forced her to continue.

"I want to sit down,"

"O-kay," He danced her back to where she'd been sitting.

"Thank-you for the dance," she managed a smile.

He bowed, was going to leave but spotted the SGM heading over and sat next to her instead. Seeing this, the Sergeant veered off.

Anne sighed, the soldier a vision of Dan, young face supplanted by her husbands.

"You like some advice?" He looked sideways at her with ageless intelligence, "Stay away from the Sergeant Major."

The next two classes were more of the same. The soldiers arriving late … oohs and ahhs over their uniforms, blond crew cut monopolizing her. SGM; the elephant in the room. Yet in the middle of a Sway the crew cut said, "The Sergeant Major is key man to the new base and I'm his security. He's an odd guy, we protect him and protect 'others' from him.…"

Anne in his arms tried to hide her thrill at importance of a man she knew was interested in her …. knew he felt it … somehow this wise young guy was killing her, physiologically undressing her. He swayed her down so his head was above hers, "I won't drop you, I'll never let you fall." He brought her up vertical, dancing arms held high.

"What did he do?"

"You understand 'the law of common charter?"

"No, please explain … you must've studied so many things."

"The law of common charter means the accused doesn't have to commit a crime to be charged with one."

"Please give me a better explanation," Anne was alarmed and knew he felt it, awareness reverberated between them.

"The Sergeant Major was deleted out of evidence as being too vital, too big a guy so others were his whipping boy... and now he's got guys like me handling him. It's more common that you think." The cadet's calm face gave way to irritation. This beautiful woman was attracted to a dangerous man, pushing good guys like himself away. *See it all the time, women & the snake ...*

By this time they were sitting next to each other, he was amazed by how lightly she stepped, how he could maneuver her around the room, how responsive she was ... but knew his place, even as he eyed her form. "Take it as advice ... warning, don't go out with him."

"Oh don't be silly, I'm married, ...Do you always give advice to older women? A handsome young guy like you ... and you know so many things ... an intellectual serviceman, I mean so many people don't have that great versatility, I can imagine you're successful with girls too."

"You're missing my point."

"You want me to stay away from the Sergeant Major."

For three classes Leah danced with the Sergeant Major and afterwards, driving home Anne inquired what they talked about.

"You."

"He asked you about me?"

"Except when he wanted to know about weapons, how many guns we owned ... how many your husband had ... where he kept them and if they were properly stored ... if we practiced shooting and where. I said Stan's gun range and he asked your education level," (Anne felt a moment of panic as the topic never came up. Everyone assumed she was credentialed, couldn't imagine otherwise. ... the volunteers thought it modesty, her walls void of framed certificates.)

Leah's honest little voice kept piping along. "I lied, said you had a masters, he asked from where and I said Syracuse." (Anne never lived away from home, never left 3 Marie's Lane, and home-schooled until High School ... only Leah knew the truth, it slipped out while riding when Leah confided she married Nigel before finishing college.

"Thank-you Leah," Anne swallowed aware of the girls in the back seat may think less of her she added, "I'm taking online courses from Syracuse now." It was partly true, because it was Arizona State, a fact both Olivia and Leah were aware of.

Sweat appeared under her hair, ran down her face. She wanted Leah to stop, felt stabbed in the heart as her Head Mistress, physiological arbitrator of truth and grace, her whole Lane School position was called on the red-carpet of reality. *I'm an uneducated fraud... can't help it! Everyone wants me to be a someone for them!* She saw their faces coming towards her with such force she suddenly swerved, *Even Leah doesn't like driving the Rover ... expects me to.*

But Leah, in her socially delayed way kept on, "He asked about other stuff and I lied about everything. So I didn't have to say, "none of your business." He wanted to know income level, how you meant your husband, where he went to school. M.I.T. I said! And how long you were married. I just threw out numbers. But when he asked about birth control I almost said MYOB but instead I told him you were Baptist and didn't believe in birth control."

"He's rather thorough," Anne blushed as she'd recently stopped taking them.

"I told him you wanted another baby."

"You do Mom! That's too high key.

"No … I … we…"

"I made it up ….any way … he's a dirty old man."

"And nosey."

"No new Baby?"

"No."

"You know after a while he smelled kind of funny, I mean so I didn't feel bad about lying. The aftershave wore off and he smelled like burnt paper and dogs," Leah wrinkled her nose.

"Mom you did a good job. I'm glad you lied … he's the Creepiest," Bett said.

"On steroids," said Marie. She'd joined after the boys in blue arrived, even though they didn't dance with them, it was too fun, the girls were laughing until the conversation turned.

"Mom, he's the Joker, you know wearing a mask … I mean a real mask." Olivia shivered, opinion evolving downward, Marie and Bette in full agreement.

The car remained silent absorbing issues, the forest rolled by.

"Degrees in College aren't important," Marie exclaimed, "Just look at my Dad."

"Your Dad really slays," Bett said enthusiastically, "everyone says so. My Dad loves him. I mean… he really slays."

The girls became quiet, embarrassed over the word 'love' and didn't understand why degrees were so important. Believing, knowing Mrs. Stevens didn't need anything to show her value and certificates were better kept in desk drawers.

Anne's sweaty hands slipped on the steering wheel as they turned into Maire's Lane up over the disused rail bed, past the old granary …. reassuring sight of Stan's house, they let Marie go and watched her bounce up wooden steps.

"He also wanted to know if we kept a dog, me or you or if we were planning to get one. Also he asked if the whole place had security cams and I said it was totally covered," and with that Leah was done.

"I WAS WONDERING if you might ask the Sergeant Major for more food bars?" Nigel and Leah were already at work and Nigel missed his midmorning snack and knew his wife had access to the SGM, in fact was her steady dancing partner.

"I'm not dancing with him anymore."

"No?"

"He's dancing with Anne."

Instinctively alarmed, growling stomach overruling higher thought, *humm dancing with Anne…* From the library classroom he made way, out past the main entry and stair through the butlers pantry to the kitchen, found Anne with her roll-top desk open. "Anne, since you in your capacity as head of the school, overseeing all aspects…" he began then cut to the chase, "I was wondering If you might ask the Sergeant Major for a new supply of those food bars…"

Anne's face changed from listening mode to shock, here it was again the perception that people, (the MacPhees'), were talking about her but she managed a smile, kept cool. "Sure Nigel, they are rather good."

No sooner had she left a message on SGM's cell that a cartload arrived, young officers unloading, boxes stacked in the pantry, note read; 'Complements of Marine Base 11B.' She remembered him saying in a call back, "your wish is my desire… but only if you go out for drinks…"

"I don't…"

Next time dance class he wanted the same …."Think of something, somewhere we can continue this conversation … home schooling is of great interest. We've all those kids at Lanzee to educate; your input will help get the ball rolling…"

But mostly they talked about her. He wanted to know everything about her, when she asked him questions he led the conversation back to her. Luckily she'd researched Syracuse and made up stories about roommates, games, outings, music, lectures... their eyes locked and the room disappeared. Sometimes smiling into his eyes, the questions stopped as he regrouped.

He was the perfect gentleman. Once, during a swing move, he dug his fingers in her back and she asked him not to and he stopped.

"We did have a problem child but she was dismissed," the topic had turned back to education, special-ed and problem children.

"Lucky you." they were sitting watching the instructress go over complicated swing moves with her boy partner. Then Olivia and Bett, who learned fast, showed off jitterbug and nitty-gritty. Anne's normal feelings of pride gave way to this man. Her life before he appeared felt distant; unimportant. He always wore the same aftershave and smelling it on other men made her blush. The blond crew cut was absent so they were free and she was helping him... it was delicious helping a powerful man. She'd watched Dan grow into one, but somehow being behind him, watering his seed, was far less thrilling than gaining the interest of mysterious power. Nothing was lost on him, emotion made life wonderful, even her relationship with Dan, always good became more ardent on her part … Dan attributed it to dance class …was glad he allowed it.

"Lucky you," the Sergeant Major repeated when she went over the 'Lucy story' he frowned, "we're stuck. there's no Mama to send them home to, they're a total liability … not only to us … to society … so we're given the problem … stuck with it and …"

"But they're just as important, even if harder … I hated to see Lucy go … Olivia too… wanted desperately to reach her." Anne stopped herself, it felt wrong to ever mention her daughter's name. "We lack facilities but you … you must have…"

"Unfortunately no, that's why they're attached to the women's prison, killing two birds with one stone. Society has a problem but they can't lock them up throw away the key when mans impulse is to cull the herd, … litters have runts." His instructor tone rose to the surface in perfect diction, the voice of authority; commanding…cool.

"But where do they come from?" Anne tried to protest, steer him towards seeing them in a different light.

"Most were over the southern boarder, illegal, we separate the kids and guess who gets what's left behind."

Anne nodded in comprehension.

"Their problems, all the crazies, retards, some with multiple handicaps."

The conversation continued … her compassion turned him into full venting mode, "they give us their problems and we prove ineffective, they expect miracles and complain of time spent, we look for normal but there's no normal there, … what a waste. ..worthless … It's mission impossible with huge price tag. But at least they're letting us do drug studies. We started this year … They're great advances and the kids are perfect for it, in our custody and sick so we've ready made subjects. We're given a complete go-ahead. And if there's any improvement …any show of health regained…. cure …support a claim … there's advancement in that … both ways we're looking good."

"I understand your struggle," Anne quelled alarm bells … she wanted to gently direct … like she did with her husband and Nigel … put him on the right path then help him figure it out for himself. *I can make this man change.*

"No one else does … but you… you … lets get coffee, There's that little place, I don't have anyone to talk to."

"No, I can't, but we can talk here …" he was upset … she couldn't imagine the stress he was under. So much on his shoulders.

"I've a lot to tell you and we can't discuss it here. I really need your help, expertise. It's for the children … please help see me through this. I need your caring, I want to become a caring man… please help me. The children…" his words were meant to disarm … strike home but instead Anne's more discerning/ teaching side came forward.

"I'm afraid that's not possible."

"Do it for the children."

"But we came together, the girls, in Leah's … my friend's car… I suppose I could bring the VW, tell Dan I needed to do some after class shopping."

"Next time."

"Yes."

12
A Major Issue

The Rover bumped along the familiar route up over the disused rail bed, the old granary Stan bought four years ago, his new board and batten sided home expanding with their brood. They let Marie off, ending the backseat giggle fest … one of the soldiers was clumsy, kept stepping on a Mom's shoes, the instructress chose the wrong CD … she had them doing leg-lifts, ballet exercises at the bar before the men arrived…

The girl's mirth was in stark contrast to Anne. Even though on the way to the safety of her ancestral home, the grand Levesque Mansion, cold waves of terror hit her like bumps through the Rover's air shocks, barely discernable but there. … *he'll either scalp me or help me…* she had to tell Dan.

Dan and his Mill job were a world apart. He was fighting proxy wars with his own manipulation and intrigue. He'd prevented a fire, saved a man from pushing the 'on' button too soon, found inaccuracies in scaling that favored harvesters … he enjoyed running around, making mental notes, giving them weekly updates or sooner. Away at conferences they depended on him to run the show. But his real power rested in his mansion home and beautiful family. They'd experienced his life on Super bowl Sunday and his bi-yearly fundraisers. The boys with their cute four year old enthusiasm, beautiful daughter and wife casting adoring glances. He was a whale, ready to emerge from the depths and blow competition out of the water.

Anne was in trouble and she knew it, but there was no one to turn too. They talked in bed and sometimes quietly in the barn while checking animals. But he had a tendency to close himself off in his office and she understood that need. Now she was giving him glances that he failed to read, when before he'd say; "tell me, come here, come to me …"

So she called a conference with Leah and Nigel. Nigel was a man who kept promises and Leah was so ardently loyal in their friendship that occasionally feelings arose over 'giving space'.

In her kitchen, before Dan arrived home she told the whole thing and they believed her. Believed her because of the Sergeant Major's behavior with the sister of a volunteer at the pre Christmas fund raiser.

"What an imbroglio." Nigel held a finger to his mouth. He both sympathized with the man and wanted to deck him.

"And other vocab ... words," Anne sighed, felt it a miserable symptom of her own lack of ability to control emotion, feelings leaked out and she needed help. "I'm sorry about this…"

But Nigel's mind went elsewhere. "This is more…"

"Than I'll dance with you …" Leah held her fists up like a boxer.

"This is about Lanzee, the woman's prison and the strange goings on. I thought the whole thing odd from the get-go. We need to involve Stan. Mesh this thing together, find our own clandestine sources now that we've corroborating witnesses." Nigel checked wall clock and wrist watch. "Ring Stan up, it's 4:30… leave a message with Rosalie."

Unfortunately the drive time for Stan's day job at Bangor Public Works kept him away until 6:45. Nigel suggested they meet at his and Leah's stately log home and they called Stan's wife a second time to see if he'd be free later. After that was settled they checked with Valerie in the Library, attending to their blended family, the Steven's twins, her own boy plus Jeff and Henry MacPhee. "We're headed up to my place for a course review." Nigel explained. Anne ran upstairs to tell

Olivia and Bett and left a note on Dan's computer, knowing Valerie would do dinner and he'd collapse in his office anyway.

Leah and Anne took the Rabbit up, Nigel walked, sensing urgency on that late spring evening with nature tucking in.

Inside the MacPhee's over tea, and 'base bars' Anne forced the news out, glad she wasn't home, Valerie totally out of earshot. Accusations of child abuse left a bitter taste.

"Shocking words, rather indefensible." Nigel though more.

"He was venting." Fear taking over she suddenly stood, paced, played with her earrings. "Do you think I'm paranoid or do you think we need to get the school de-bugged? I mean for computer spy-wear. Things have changed at the mansion, the walls have ears."

"We had to-do that when Leah went on all those websites …" He began but his wife's shocked expression had him qualifying …"she was new to it… debugging is part of running a business …"

"I bet right now they're injecting them with all kinds of crap and he wants you to go along with it," Leah had PSTD from her hospital stay.

"It may be he's looking for someone like you to add credibility to their mission."

"Creeper Cerds! Bett calls him The Creeper." Leah laughed.

"What he told me was largely attitudinal. He needs help. Even top men, men who run things need guidance," Anne sighed.

"It appears he was after more than just the obvious," Nigel stood, finger over his mouth, "there's more to this than meets the eye. If he's after socially prominent accomplice you're dammed both ways … and we don't know if he's telling the truth. He might want you to blow the whistle and when they arrive to investigate ….find happy kids, clean and evidence free. The only way forward is to learn more." Nigel raised his eye brows, rubbed hands together, noticed Anne's sour look, "I mean it would be ill-advised for you to go out with him."

"He's expecting me to next time … I already agreed to it."

"You can have my little Kel-tech," Leah offered.

"This isn't a spy thriller…" Nigel gently admonished.

"But maybe I should wear a wire that way Dan will know I'm telling the truth. He's bound to find out he always does." She winced remembering a harmless flirtation at Church when he'd bundled her off for home. He installed spy-ware on her comp, found a school Dad, put the kibosh on that too.

"He's such a pig, not letting you go out or giving you anything! He's a self-absorbed pig!" Leah blurted.

"Leah honestly do you really think so," tears came to her eyes, "I'm sorry," she said wiping, "this is stressful."

"Look what you did," Nigel again admonished his wife, knowing of the two women Anne was physiologically stronger.

"Well it's the truth but I didn't say he wasn't a good man."

Anne's throat, stiff with emotion barely carried her words, "please don't say negative things about my husband," she stood again and paced, weight loss giving her spring.

"Everyone knows how he's made you suffer." Leah had a habit of not letting things drop.

"And fall into the arms of the Sergeant Major." Words escaped Nigel's lips, he'd meant to give her an excuse … a way out, but it sounded wrong and he couldn't take it back.

Anne grabbed her coat. "We'll discuss this at another time." She felt they were belittling her. All this exposure; *the Sergeant Major manipulating me into destroying my marriage …. and now wounding from Nigel & Leah!*

Nigel stood while she ran to the door and right into Stan. Stan always entered the MacPhee's without knocking … a habit retained from when he slept on their couch during those dark days when his son died and his wife left him.

"OH!" Anne had her head down, didn't see him in the dark entry-way.

"Ohh, waoah, Aanne, aare ya Oh-Kay?"

Head butting his chest released a smell of pine board and gasoline, he reflex-idly caught her by the elbows… solid, comforting … had her longing for male arms… Dan's arms to hold her… "I'm fine Stan, how are you?"

"I'am 'ear fad da paw-woa. Muss bay 'poat'an ef day naed mae."

"So you got my message," Nigel, appeared in the entryway.

"E'd waas lake a caal fom God,"

"Of vital importance," Nigel patted him on the shoulder while the other guided Anne back into the room and removed her coat.

"Oh," Anne hesitated.

"Come on it's not like you're being shown the wall ... we'd never let you go it alone." Tea?" he said to Stan, turned to Anne, "Refill?" rubbing his hands together, he loved playing host for his own little clique.

Stan didn't have to look at their faces, the emotionally charged atmosphere told him more ... they went over what happened giving great care to Anne's feelings.

"I cud flay a dra'own o'va da pra'son, An eye an da skay."

"A little early for flying drones ... we were thinking more in terms of Anne wearing a wire. That way we can safely bring Dan in."

"I'll wear a mask," said Leah.

"They don't make you invisible"

Stan's eyes lit up, "Day 'ave a ladda naw wi-fi cassette. Sha can kaap id in 'er pock-ed book." They left for Nigel's office to order one.

"Sure you don't want to borrow the Kel-tech?" Leah wanted her armed.

Anne smiled 'no.' She was safe ... for the moment there was no avalanche of worries threatening her assent. This was base camp.

BEFORE THE NEXT dance class they'd refined plans. Anne would by no means get into the SGM's car, driver/bodyguard or not. She wasn't supposed to leave food or drink unattended, use facilities after eating, never during. Leah was to drive the girls home in the Rover, then return in her silent ubiquitous e-car and stake out The Pizza Place. After the whole thing was over, Anne in the VW with Leah following in the e-car, would return safely to their respective homes. Leah was to keep her phone close, be in touch with Nigel at any change of plans, if Anne signaled, (she was to take a window seat) …or if something didn't feel right … she was counseled to grab Anne make up a story of a sick kid, abort mission. They'd gone over the script adding and subtracting up until the last minute. Later Nigel scouted out Downtown Foster for an appropriate restaurant and found a small takeout pizza/ coffee shop with people actually sitting inside without masks.

THEY PLUGGED the USB recording device into Nigel's comp and it was inconclusive. The Sergeant Major wasn't interested in talking about the base or himself he was interested in her, wanted to hear about her school, the social-economic demographics of the children and finally about Dan. "Seems like he's using an interrogation technique, asking the same questions but phrased differently."

"Badgering me."

"For the crime of being competent and trying your best," Nigel smiled.

"What about me aren't I trying and ... and good," Leah piped in.

"Oh yes, of course, you've come a long way," *from childish to young adult ... amazing what the right amount of real responsibility brings.....* "and a big help in spy vs spy."

"Nau' din dare," said Stan, "Wad id days nau'din dare..." Stan knew it was a possibility that they were imagining things ... but he was ignored.

"Might realize we're on to him ... nothing there? No we're up against a greater force than we can imagine." *and I'm willing to drop it.* He wanted to add.

"He's trying to get the goods on Anne. Let him try and get anything out of me." Leah made a defensive posture.

"Here we are so far away from civilization and yet under a microscope." Nigel paused stood and paced. The meeting in his own home, his buddies, 'partners in the crime' ... latticed under huge cross beams, his natural superiority in full bloom had him wanting to charge ahead in to places and persons unknown. "You know something else odd, that didn't seem strange at the time... there was this snorkeler at the camp. Used to wave at me while I sat on that bench... and now thinking it over ... his gear did seem rather military in appearance..."

"A snorkeler was interested in you?" Anne welcomed a break.

"I couldn't tell … male or female."

"She didn't mean that." said Leah.

"And then there was 'the case of the disappearing canoeists," Nigel paced finger over his mouth, "You know weird things happen around military bases. This new instillation has state-of-the-art stuff."

"Disappearing canoeists?"

"Yes I was on a solitary adventure, paddling along solo, when I came across fellow canoeists, but they kept their distance, moving west towards the sun and then poof gone."

"Mysterious," said Anne.

"Quite."

"What do you mean, 'poof gone'?" Leah said.

"They were clearly visible one moment; gone the next, I kept trying to catch up. It was very strange." *Also strange was that Dan is insecure and takes it out on Anne.* Nigel was under the impression handsome competent types were all womanizers like the Sergeant Major, while wives of nail biting miscomputes had safer marriages. "There's an unseen hand guiding this … anything's possible in this international, global environment."

"I dan lake da zap-dive, lat ma gat some dan wid a ca'ma."

"Yeah, lets try again," Leah clapped her hands."

"I'm on board," said Anne.

"James O'Keefe," Nigel smiled, "miss me yet?"

IN THE BEGINNING everything went as planned. Anne danced with the Sergeant Major, blushingly changed into street shoes, securing key in hand bag while at the same time pressing the camera's 'on' button. Anne and the Major left in separate cars for their prearranged rendezvoused at The Pizza Place.

Leah ran the girls home in the Rover at top speed, bumping over the disused rail bed, kicking up clouds of dust, the girls were dropped off together at the mansion, she switched to her e-car, conveniently waiting in the school parking lot.

She raced back to the restaurant wearing a baseball cap over her short think hair, a distinguishing feature best hidden. With a novel bookmarked halfway through, cell phone handy she waited behind Anne's VW, thought the better of it and took up position across the street.

Very little was happening, two old store fronts displayed second hand goods, a Laundromat in-between, a tiny travel agency, plastic cruise ship sailing optimistically over glass and a hardware store. *Totally decrepit.*

Customers actually frequented the hardware store, came out carrying purchases. Leah's glance traveled from the silhouetted Anne and SGM, to the road, millpond, shops and back to her book. The novel taking her up to the scene of the crime, perpetrator hiding in the attic, dogs sniffing … something clicked, she dragged her eyes away … a man was watching her.

Acknowledging her glance with a nod he turned and crossed the street to The Pizza Place. Leah's eyes followed him and watched him and enter. *Bet he's his driver. Anne and SGM, sipping from styrofoam hadn't moved from their table seat.*

She looked down at her book again, it was chilling, the murderer in the attic watching from a window for the cops to leave. They didn't know who he was or where he was or that he had a unique power that fogged the cops reasoning ability but not dogs. The dogs kept barking at the house, until the protesting animals were dragged back to their cages, closed in …whining. Leah was terrified for the family. They were on their way home unawares of a killer in the attic. The cops called them on their cells and reassured it was 'all Clear!'

She glanced up and the hair under her baseball cap stood on end. *Anne's car was gone!* "Oh no Anne," she fired up the e-car and silently zoomed around the corner to the parking lot, but sadly there was no VW or limo, (the Major's ride) only an old RV half obscured by bushes. She rounded the lot a second time then the block, checked the lot a third time, then up over the bridge, back around the other way, doubled back twice, turned, went down a side street … then she thought a car was following her, went around the block again trying to lose him, then slowed, his face in her mirror… the same man looking at her earlier. He was too well dressed, fit, groomed to be from here. Trying to get a better look at him, while trying to lose him was impossible so in a panic she took the Lake Road out of town, turned off a side street, gasping for air.

Consciousness returned with the wind, blowing trees in shadow blotches across the e-cars hood. "That's better," she said out loud, heart back to normal.

Foster's thin blue line on leisurely patrol, turned down the street, paused backed, motioning with his hand to roll down her window. "Everything OK Mam?

"Fine, Fine." Leah, smiled girlishly and held up her paperback. He saluted. She saluted back and her grin disappeared as paranoia pried open the gates of hell. She practiced square breathing, *in through the mouth, out through the nose… in…oh good cockamamie-ville's leaving….* The cops red tail lights turned safely out of the picture … she followed … but there he was on The Lake Rd. …

The E-Car's electricity in her … she turned, didn't look back, drove in the opposite direction the whole way out to Foster Lake State Park, only then did she look…no cop on her tail she rolled the windows down feeling the breeze, caught a glimpse of metallic blue mountains poking out of mist, … forgetting her mission, the day so bright … feeling that she should get out more often, really get away, tired of online shopping she wanted to be in a city again, take the 'T' to North Station get off at alewife station, walk around Cambridge looking in store windows, up the escalator to the second floor of the Harvard Co-Op, load up on novels, sit on a bark bench ... *Why am I here? I was always a city girl. Oh right Nigel.*

She decided to head home, *Anne was probably there by now,* but her jaunt up to the lake left her disoriented so she stopped for coffee at The Pizza Place, ordered inside, sat in a booth. The stark bitter taste made her stomach lurch, so she got a bagel and cream cheese, but she felt awkward alone by the window and wanted her book but didn't want to leave the food unattended and didn't want to lose her window table so she left and got back into the e-car, resting her book on the steering wheel she looked up to see the same man staring, sunglasses reflecting her.

He nodded bent forward, gave a little wave, through the window, she felt a slight mist ... he smiled, his finger tips reached over the glass and a second spray dampened her face...

Hands trembling, keylessly starting the electric motor, U-turned up over the curb, he jumped back and laughed, her novel, bagel and coffee, not residing in their respective holders she lurched down the street, correcting things.

Suddenly she didn't know where she was, everything appeared foreign. She grabbed her cell, reached Nigel on speed dial.

"The Lane School, Nigel MacPhee speaking."

But the *where am I* continued. "Nigel ...I..." She tried to get her bearing.

"Where are you?"

"Who are you ..." she wanted to say, but didn't have to...

Nigel instantly understanding the issue, had her pull into a dirt lot that was used by float pilots, several planes tethered in the millpond bobbed on a breeze of unseen wealth and adventure. She waited and Nigel drove down to collect.

Usually when Nigel, Bett, Jeff and Henry arrived home it was too a flurry of activity. Having waited till the last minute, grabbing as much time with Anne as possible, Leah would zoom home just barely ahead of them and be madly correcting things, wiping down, getting dinner, straightening shoes in the entryway. To see her motionless in front of the fire, feet planted in a foot bath, hair in front of her face like a child they weren't certain of how to react. The foot bath was Nigel's discovery. *Grounds her back into reality.*

After awhile he thought of something else and left for the kitchen leaving the door open. He never gathered spent plates for the dishwasher, but once Leah had packed it, he liked to rearrange. The clink, clank of his rearrangements had the desired effect. She leapt to her feet, "What are you doing … stop it right now!"

"How are you feeling?" Leah had slept peacefully through the night.

"Awful"

"But how did you sleep?"

"Terrible."

Obviously she was feeling better so Nigel left her alone.

Back at the school Leah remembered the business with the Major but failed to recall other parts of the day before. The VW was parked in its usual spot, Anne still under the spell of various sprays, was at her roll-top desk, dressed in bright new clothes, glamorous and poised she greeted Leah.

"Looks like you got home OK," Leah managed to say.

"Yes, oh Leah I'm looking to change the curriculum for next year to include more science… look at these great references … ebooks … really exciting," glowing with enthusiasm she smiled at Leah.

Leah jumped back, Anne was different.

The Sergeant Major was tickled, not for obvious reasons but because both of his aerosols worked; the amnesia and heavy hormone. He'd used the light hormone during dance class to prep her body and heavy during their previous coffee … but she remained cool. The last time was a huge success, the one hour amnesia worked wonderfully and the collection was beautiful. He had two lovely eggs to add to his study. He used her signature from the health forms, for the egg donation consent forms and registration card. This was the second time he'd pulled it off. The other one was a congressman's wife. Both 'proven winners'. Other Silly women were flattered at the suggestion, his catalogue contained great beauties … he loved examining the cylinders, close to fifty … and now he'd pinned the butterfly … the high energy Anne.

13
Undocumented Time

After a week of attending to Lane School Anne, Leah, Nigel and Stan found themselves back at the MacPhees waiting for the spy-cam's zip-drive to download on Nigel's comp. Anne was eager to listen, recollections of that afternoon remained sketchy.

As with the previous audio, the Sergeant Major kept the conversation focused on her, going over her days, students and curriculum. He also inquired as to their health and how they liked the nutrition bars he'd sent over.

"They loved them."

It was then that he started to stress science. The nutrition bars were scientifically formulated and the future will be filled with scientifically engineered nutritional formulations. In response to her 'Why' he said; "Why not eat perfect food? Perfectly formulated to your gene code and blood type. Think of it as preventative medicine. Remembering that science in it's pure form is a quest for perfection … man always seeks it, … the perfect car … house, job … social life … wife … breeding… tweaking nature to achieve the model in mind … and … then when we find it we always guild the lily."

"Yes that's true but isn't it also a matter of opinion?" Anne's voice was louder than his, she reached inside her purse for a tissue and directed the lens upward, capturing his jaw and mouth.

"No, perfect health isn't a matter of opinion… and perfect health is beautiful … Perfect health can only arrive when society agrees to certain things … optimal nutrition, fitness, cleanliness and by following new parameters derived from the study of genetics. Take you for example, you and your beautiful skin and high energy. Your genes naturally 'knocking out' undesirable traits. Your daughter inherited the same features and you had twins, two for the price of one … and what did you say their combined birth weights were … somewhere around Fourteen pounds!"

"Olivia was nine, nine pound, four ounces." Anne said with pride.

"And no problems having them?"

Anne blushed as her voice said; "No, All natural … I had a good Doctor, lined the twins up perfectly, no problem."

During a pause you could almost hear the SMG/ MD/ PHD … smacking his lips. "In a genetically controlled environment women like you would be allowed to breed indiscriminately, donate as necessary, help prefect the gene pool." He paused ... Stan and Nigel exchanged glances.

"My skin burns... I get wicked sunburn," Anne's voice came across as making light of the topic.

"Wicked? A Maine colloquialism, amusing but unexpected from a woman of your standing."

"Wicked sorry," she laughed.

"A beautiful woman with a sense of humor, I like it."

"You were saying about science?"

"Yes we no longer have natural selection, weeding out the inferior ... the desease ridden, immune compromised ... imagine no disabled children ... instead society coddles the deficient, makes excuses for the low IQ masses and lets them breed indiscriminately. Man's instinct is to cull the herd, drown the imperfect puppy but society won't go along with it and knowing human nature ... killing would get out of hand ... think French revolution and the Nazis ... for the sake of progress, science must start with genetic testing of all couples." He took a sip of coffee, turned his head sideways, in the window's glare the fleshless face cut into triangles.

"You study a lot."

"Yes and people, even well taught women like yourself, don't fully grasp history," he glanced out the window, "we live in a period of abundance, a golden age ... except for small pockets of dearth, we've conquered hunger, the oil crisis? ... a thing of the past, ordinary people with simple ideas, like overnight shipping, become very rich, violent crime is down … but imagine all this extravagance taken away. Imagine a pandemic of proportions far greater than 1918 … than Covid-19. Once people feel the pinch, once society runs out of vital resources do you think they'll coddle the autistic child? Send them to special schools? It really is a fight against time."

"You're burdened with a lot."

"Yes it's uniquely frustrating but on occasion there's a beautiful woman sitting across from me and … you dance … so well.

"So do you.".

"Smooth," said Nigel.

"Daan'gar'us," said Stan.

"Creepy," said Leah.

The recording continued with Anne's voice … "I haven't talked it over yet with my husband or our advisory board but …"

"Yes?"

"I was thinking therapeutic riding might be offered to the respite care kids at Lanzee. They might…"

"Absolutely out of the question."

"You don't think?" Anne's voice betrayed her … she was hurt.

"No I don't think … we could never consider it besides the kids are in quarantine for all sorts of diseases. Some have polio and small-pox antibodies and some are plague survivors…

"Oh I didn't know your job involved that much danger, I hope everyone stays safe."

"I'm a person who's always gone towards dangerous situations if I think it will benefit man-kind. With the understanding that science must be believed in as only science can save us. To not believe is turning your back on truth, believing lies, like there's no such thing as climate change… it shows a willingness to destroy humanity. Saving humanity as a cause must then be international, across all classes …ethnicities.

Silence continued, then Anne's voice, "Are the kid's OK? It must be terrible to be so young and sick and far away from home."

"They're well cared for and most don't really care … only a few … nurses and inmates play surrogate Mom."

"Well if there's anything you need in terms of schooling…"

"Schooling?

"It was something we spoke about earlier … you needed … help. In any case I'm willing to do whatever we can. We've plenty of volunteers who'd jump at the chance as a résumé enhancer … and one, Valerie Martin is somehow connected with the place, although not forthcoming… but you know how it is with ex-cons. But she's ok, really good with young children … I trust her completely and the twins love her."

Another spot of silence … that continued for awhile….
"Oh yes, yes I did ask you! We meant and came to the conclusion they're fine and in an adjustment period … and

in the grand scheme of things you must realize ... far better treated than say Mexico or Guyana or the Amazon basin or what ever shit-hole... Some would've starved to death at birth but now we have them ... our country is burdened with them, streaming across alone or in the case of the sick and disabled... their' parents' used them then left them, that's how it worked ... how it's done... no one in their right mind would take them in ... but we do with the understanding that they don't really matter, the advancement of scientific knowledge does." He kept turning his head, looking out the window as if he was waiting for some signal. He paused, imperceptibly nodded. His tongue hang out like a barely under control animal ready to devour a peace of meat. *Operation Plush-bottom on track!*

"Lets meet again ... these discussions are what the future depends on ... imagine science progressing so there's no more genetically transmitted desease. Only beautiful intelligent women like you allowed for breeding..."

"It's getting late..."

"Yes, there's next week... same time, same place..." They got up, helped her with her jacket, through the restaurant door, the camera pointed at the floor. "I'll walk you to your car."

There was a long quiet walking sequence, admiring the warm summer weather, the rushing river, until the car opened and it appeared the camera was shut inside something ... it played on in darkness.

"I forgot to turn it off," said Anne …. waiting. They stood, Nigel went to a window, Stan's eyes got big and Leah paced … while an hour or so of darkness continued.

"WHAT NO MORE dance class?" Dan, dubious at first …later all for it, his wife regaining shape, returning home amorous … "Worked out OK."

"Well, you know … classes run eight weeks and then … it's summer vacation and we've doing all that hosting." she sighed, muffling excited bells. "And they said something about shutting down nonessential services again. Therapy yes; dance; no."

After the shutdown and continuing riots, everyone needed therapy. Although untarnished by the horrors endured in other states, murder etc., the shutdown's psychological trauma had couples opening up on each other.

A volunteer's husband, a psychologist wanted to host couples weekends in the newly renovated east wing. It meant they had to haul all the furniture back up from the basement, purchase mattresses and bedding.

The new accommodations had the old servant's quarters opened with their secret back staircase that ended in the library. The servants quarters, cut up small rooms, many with gables, were set aside for couples who weren't at the point of reconciling their differences with a shared room. Opening up the secret back stair was exciting, as its existence was known only virtually in old architectural drawings. It ran straight down, bypassing the middle floor and ended in a narrow door, set to appear like part of the Library's paneling and was privy to only Dan, Anne and Olivia.

The secret lasted until Ada came home and Olivia showed it to her and Bett. Ada imagined the master of the house and tip-toeing, trysts with pretty servant girls. The other 'servants' stair was well-known, connected their bedrooms to the kitchen; the secret stair served the other side, that in Victorian times it was a man hangout, for smoking, reading and drinking sherry and cognac.

Olivia asked him about other hidden passageways, trap doors … imagination sparked by Ada. Dan smiled and changed the subject. He added fire doors to both stairs and they were code. He wasn't looking for more.

He wanted to sit in on group counseling, see if his own issues, Anne's flirtatious nature, was a universal problem in other marriages. But with dance class Anne passed the test. He knew about soldiers from the base and saw her thinking only of him … As a consequence he'd allow more liberties, even though she seemed to revert back to her old self, left new clothing hanging in her closet, wore less make-up. So he encouraged, telling her how he liked seeing her in new things … "they bring out the woman in you."

Anne winced, choked up and said, "Oh Dan I love you," closing her eyes to shut out the world and memory, scary flashbacks and was ready to burn everything associated with dance class. Instead she boiled them on the stove when Dan was at town meeting. Some items suffered, others not so much. After boiling they were pinned to the line and left out in sun, wind and rain. Nigel reminded her to bring them in. "It's not your fault, he drugged you," he whispered and she ignored him. "Really, Anne."

"It's not just that, I can heal, it's the kids, those poor kids, my stupidity has let them down … he probably recorded it … will use it …if we try and help them … we're up against something far bigger. He watched everything … pegged Dan, pegged me … I let it put me in danger … thought I was in control … now he can destroy us."

"Pegged Dan as controlling … Pegged you as…"

"Susceptible … and Dan has always know this about me … sought to shelter me … knew what was best for me … everyone thinks he's selfish but it's not true!" She suddenly stopped … Valerie had walked into the kitchen.

That night she had a dream that she was part of a team of scientists. In the deep sediment of Lake Champlain, bones were discovered and everyone agreed it was a short nosed bear, extinct 11,000 years ago. But the DNA samples found it a beluga whale from 5000 AD. Their cloud recomputed, they redrew the borders so Lake Champlain went to the sea. Anne woke feeling a great Northern sea of DNA had enveloped her. Out of the muck a sonar message, a dolphin smiled knowingly …

It didn't really fit with a previous dream. In it she was picking her way along a muddy roadside, only she was wearing clothes out of the mid 18th century, a coach stopped and a gentleman alighted offering assistance. She assented, and was handed in. A second gentleman was seated and as the carriage rolled she recognized the Sergeant Major ... felt right to be with him. They crested a hill, down to a port city ... Suddenly she was dressed in new clothes, traveling attire, boxed belongings, bustled off on a long adventure ... a new world.

She remembered dreams yet couldn't concentrate; lift the veil on that second afternoon she had coffee with SGM (*I was reluctant but had to do it for the kids at Lanzee*) When it came time to leave she'd gotten in the old rabbit, turned key and drove away, feeling happy, contented... even though the sun was at an odd angle, not a late spring sun blazing at her windshield; but lower, behind trees. Then as she went over the disused rail bed, passing the old granary and Stan's place, feelings of gratification left ... instead it was odd, like her shoes were on the wrong foot or she'd misplaced something.

The yard, barn, mansion, everything appeared normal, ... *oh look at the time* ... Dan wasn't home, the kitchen clock said 6:15. Valerie was with the kids, *I need to thank her more.* She used to feel Valerie was a sponge soaking up her energy but now was grateful ...she could go on adventures, dance with thrilling men, be admired. She was attracted to the Sergeant Major ... *who wouldn't be* ... but nothing happened.

Valerie appeared with the lockdown, she came from Washington needing shelter in Piscataquis county, found a small apartment living with her son, until the pandemic ran out. Her child was very bright and Valerie very quiet and needy, Anne sensed it and paid attention as needed, used to wants and needs …

Weeks past and Anne began having nightmares of men wearing surgical masks. She tried to scream … something sprayed her face. She sat up in bed gasping while Dan slept like an angel. She came close soothed by his mind, wishing all the stories in his head were hers and they were someplace else.

But the anxiety wouldn't dissipate, dismayed by how wrong she was … under Dan's warmth she'd grown sure of herself, she'd taken on the Sergeant Major. Nigel, Leah and Stan supported but … what did they know, *they're innocent…* can't imagine evil, understand its existence in modern society… Evil had passed into history … it was Hitler, Mussolini. Anne understood … today's evil's attractive, seductive, *brought me in close* … a desirable moment … Evil was the devouring wolf … confront it, try and retrieve pieces of selfhood and it bites again and again.

The original thought was to include Dan … now that was impossible. *Nigel, Leah & Stan thought he raped me.* … Wouldn't let her continue their little spy adventure. She kept the experience compartmentalized; the story of a strange woman.

14
Couplings + Other Problems

Couplings, they called them, like the immature version of couples. Nigel and Leah; Dan and Anne weren't acting superior, they were just having fun in an atmosphere of brevity, it was impossible to be heavy. The couples came weekends and were gone, even Dan wore a smile. Weekdays were spent in anticipation of the next group. Arriving Friday afternoon, leaving Sunday meant Saturday was the only truly hectic day.

Tuesday was briefing day, four to five couples. The Psychologist, (Couples Councilor) was an overweight bald headed man who sat like a round granite marker, anchoring the room while everyone became little boats tethered to his vision, … except Dan. Dan in his office was happy to wait for Anne's perceptions. Anne filtered them into hilarity; Dan held her while effervescent giggles popped. "They've spend half their lives in therapy!" Dan hated the thought of wasted money except for the weekends …. that was well spent. Dan received no profit, only depreciation … but made sure all their volunteers, employed as wait-staff, kitchen help, chamber-maids and gardeners were justly compensated.

COUPLES RECOVERY SUMMER
Friday
1:00-2:30pm arrival time.
room assignments
3:00pm orientation in the Library and mansion tour
4:00pm tea in the dining room
4:30pm walking meditation, (no speaking) up
Maries Lane to the Piscatagua River.
Tour of the MacPhee's residence a classic Maine log home.
6:30pm Dinner in the dinning room.
(most everyone dressed for it.)
8:00pm Dancing in the ballroom
They were taught the Minuet, Stroll
and Virginia reel by Anne
Done to a superb sound system
ending at 10:30pm

Saturday
Buffet Breakfast from 8:00am to 9:30am
10:00am to 12:00 noon Group Therapy. in the Library.

Couples individually say what they wish to accomplish over the weekend. and anything else they want help with.

12:00 noon buffet lunch

2:00pm to 5:30pm trip out to Foster Lake.

Tea served at 4:00pm at picnic tables under the shade of towering spruce trees.

6:30-7:00pm Dinner

8:00pm un-psycho-drama. They acted parts in Pygmalion, (or My Fair Lady) The Taming of the Shrew, Who's Afraid of Virginia Wolf and Long Days Journey into Night. Given scripts earlier at Group Therapy, rehearsed at the beach, lines read out loud and practiced ahead of time.

Sunday

Buffet Breakfast from 8:00am to 9:30am

10:00am to 12:00 noon Group Therapy. in the Library Couples individually say what they felt they'd accomplished over the weekend. and anything else they need help with going forward.

12:00 noon light buffet lunch

1:00pm to 2:00pm departure time.

One might imagine Anne's energy stretched to the limits … Dan's wise oversight retreating to his office and the buoyant atmosphere surrounding three Marie's Lane brought to a halt. But for greater angels that might be the case, Ada, our greatest angel was home for the rest of summer. All other prep-school students were sent home previously, with the exception of the tutored, they stayed the term.

Ada arrived at the barn like a large green well had opened in the floor and everyone's sorrows and cares instantly vanished. Every good thought was supported, every happy face acknowledged and time adjusted itself to a slower pace. Beauty untarnished she delighted everyone with stories of dorm life and dumb courses. In her heart of hearts she didn't want to go back there, it was so void of life and going forward she saw herself skipping undergraduate work, heading straight to law school. The idea was to make everything right for everybody and take the quickest path possible.

Ada's presence put a stop to Nigel and Stan nagging Anne about calling the authorities on the Sergeant Major. Nigel, in his desire to protect Ada from evil dropped the subject.

Ada did the trick by merely showing up while Anne had tried everything to make him stop mentioning it, "It is bigger than just that … It's about the Lanzee kids … not me."

"We need law enforcement! You're right it's not about you but to serve justice… what about other women … he's done it before and will do it again! There's a rapist at the new base!"

Then to protect her from stray gossip he went ahead and told Ada as much as he knew and supposed.

"Dad you can't make accusations without evidence and you don't have any." Ada knocked him off his justice seeking horse.

Anne held conference with Bett and Olivia in Olivia's room. When they found out Dance class was given the green light to continue without face masks no less, (again the Sergeant Major). Olivia and Bett were excited and wanted to go and Anne had to break the news. She knew better than to insult Olivia's intelligence with a made up story, the bargain was; some of the truth for all of Olivia's confidence.

Anne started with Stan's discovery, their hope it was nothing but respite care, the Sergeant Major's creepy claims for the advancement of science, and how she was trying to get information out of him.

"Oh Mom, can I help? I'd like to get information out of him."

"That would go over real well with your Dad."

"But if we aren't even going to dance class anymore he's totally deleted," Bett didn't get the attraction.

"After a break we can see about it."

"He might be gone by then." Olivia was intrigued by the idea of using her feminine wiles to trick the SGM into divulging the truth, the thought of rescuing kids in trouble made something deep inside burn. She stared dreamily into space.

"I don't know about signing up for fall classes, they might clamp down again. Insist on facemasks all the time… but they'll be time for dancing … next year… oh and not a word about this to your father … otherwise he might pull the plug … and never let us go, ever."

"Oh Mom we get the whole thing already! I'd never tell Dad. But Mom we thought you were dancing with the Sergeant Major 'cause he's a good dancer and knew the steps already … like he was your teacher. We never thought it was that tight. Now we know what's happening …. we'd never tell Dad! He's too strict. Bett's Dad isn't like him."

Anne smiled, heart beating in love and fear imagining disaster. "And not a word to Valerie."

"Why would we tell her? Mom I don't like her here all the time!"

"The boys like her and I like her and she needs the structure of a normal family to help her heal."

Olivia wanted to scream, 'Mom! Make her go away!' Her mind challenged behind red cheeks. "But everywhere I go there she is watching, like a spy …*Gobbling up Mom's attention,* "why can't she just hop off!"

"She's a shy person who wants to be liked."

Olivia stared at nothing … futility setting in… "Her boy doesn't even look like her, when did she have him … when she was like twelve."

"Sixteen … Olivia show some compassion, empathy."

But no one has compassion/empathy for me! I hate her and Mom doesn't care! She said nothing but gave her a stare until Anne looked down.

"Olivia, we have everything we need when a lot of people don't. Think of the kids at Lanzee Prison. The have no parents or home or toys of their own, only a borrowed bed to sleep in."

"Yeah okay so what about them…"

Anne paused, paced. "There's a lot we don't know … only … assume they're ok. It's a women's prison and that means visitors, families on the outside, a lot of communication, cell phoning… And you know women can be wicked, when it comes to protecting kids …I just can't believe they'd let him get away with anything. But you know some of the old institutions for children in Maine were found out and I believe the State's still paying … Like the scandal at Baxter School for the Deaf. The State was sued and lost … and took time paying so the story didn't go away but was talked about decades later."

The girls sat quietly. They knew the world was dangerous, they were always on the internet Mail-on-line, Utube … "Don't the kids matter? I mean …"

"I'm going to try and find out and I'll let you know," Anne paused, Olivia doesn't know the real world of right and wrong. "Some of the stuff's OK, like when they came here trying to find out why we're so healthy … and some… but if you see anything, hear anything …please come to me first, not your Father, you know how he is. He'll lock us up and throw away the key!"

"What can we see from here… I mean we don't know anyone there." Bett said.

"Yeah, Mom the prison's miles away and there's no connection."

Anne paused pacing, "You're right," *but the Base is closer than you think!* Oh well, I've work to-do ... we'll talk some more later and remember a lot is happening this summer with the couples so stay on your toes!"

Anne closed the door to her daughters room. The space stayed in her mind, tin tile ceiling embossed with stars, window seats and dark wainscoting reminded her of the past, it was her room as a child.

She paused on the landing by a favorite stained glass window, and through the clear side panel viewed warm sun gracing meadow grass, morning haze lifted... suddenly it dawned on her why they were healthier... it was the sun, the doses of sunshine in and around the barn... the new indoor riding arena had fiberglass skylights and kids went on nature walks. They lacked a gym but did cross-country running and skiing.

She recalled something else; a conversation with Valerie concerning Lanzee prison. Valerie said it was a two way street, the inmates were better behaved due to playing big sister and providing child care, how women's prison systems were evolving, she knew someone there, ... she then made an observation about cleanliness and space and how well the kids were treated. Anne inquired if their special needs were adequately addressed and Valerie gave her a curious look, "Special needs, " she repeated. When Anne questioned her more about it, she turned evasive. Anne tried a second time, offering to go with her on a visit, she clammed up.

Conversations with Valerie were often short and surrounding childcare.

Anne paused again in thought. Valerie had an odd defensiveness that made her at times appear tough. It wouldn't be hard to imagine her as an inmate, 'in the system' That's it! and now she's atoning, serves and expects nothing in return, background checked so she can't find real work. She had a sponsor, a mentor sent along with résumé and references. Maybe the sponsor was her parole officer. *She eats most meals with us, saves on that.* Anne's last fear was Valerie in some fit of do-gooding would spill the beans about the SGM to the police, bring the school into the inquiry, interview kids about the base tour and pandemic screening. *Thank-goodness the girls were sworn to secrecy.*

Anne wanted to love her sons but couldn't and didn't know why. Only occasionally on Mother's Day, Valentines or Christmas when presented with a scribbled card, did she respond. She needed help from the beginning and with so many women lending a hand she'd failed to bond, felt her sons watching her, waiting for her to come around. They'd fall, hurt themselves and a volunteer came running. Because they were fussy eaters lunch was prepared by Valerie and dinner when Dan attended town meeting was scheduled for early bedtime.

Years of motherhood and Anne forgot their food preferences. Valerie had it down to a science, she was often in their room putting toys away, remembering stuffed animal's names... Anne rarely visited their room, never got into a bedtime routine, was too busy with school. Dan picked up the slack, rubbing heads and hugging, feigning interest in fire trucks and comp. games, reading them to sleep at night.

"Spend more time with the boys," He admonished.

"I would, but you're better at it."

Dan wouldn't let it go, dug deeper and discovered it was because she was an only child that she thought in terms of singleness and was just twenty-two when Olivia was born.

Olivia was a miracle; the boys a disfiguring burden, she didn't respond to them as infants and didn't like the noises they made as toddlers. She never confided in anyone, felt they did fine without her and it was good for Dan, they buddied up right from the beginning. She didn't acknowledge the issue and because of the sycophantic crowd surrounding them, no one dared challenge the lack of love.

Anne felt safe, thrown back into her element, protected from what she wanted and didn't want, mind busy with details. The journey out into the big world was a disaster, a little murder she couldn't avenge. She reverted into letting people come to her...on her own turf. ...and only sometimes danced alone in the ballroom with an invisible partner, while Valerie read to the boys.

SEVENTEEN YEAR OLD Ada MacPhee knew something was amiss but couldn't put her finger on it. She could feel aggression in the air. Jeff and Henry, her lively ten and eleven year old brothers, still at sports camp, Bett's best friend status with Olivia was on a forever trajectory, while Mom Leah, lived for Anne and last but not least, Dad; Nigel, found solace in his porch studio piling up canvases.

Their stately log home echoed with emptiness and Nigel flourished? The Cornavirus hit his investment portfolios, like he'd turned his back on a toddler and found it drowned in red ink, when he was a mature investor, knew better … massaged his head looking for soft spots.

He was homesick for his old balance, substantial bite out of the ol' pie chart, he'd held through down drafts before… but this was different, the market a zig-zagging Zeus. *May I too be saved from Saturn?* He felt his chin and gazed out across the Piscatiquis, the spring; cold and damp; summer cool and cloudy, his old Boston friends; a fading memory. But somehow in the midst of it he'd found comfort in just being himself and wandered around in sandals, old cotton shirts covered in paint, beard in various stages of bright red growth, humming tunes out of the eighty's. Ada was sure he was developing early onset dementia. "Do you really want to hurt me… do you really want to make me cry." He sang to himself, hands covered in paint.

"Dad you know Boy George is gay," Ada's scornful glance reminded him of his formerly upright, exemplary citizen, conscientious parent image.

"Maybe I'm a bit gay myself," he smiled hugely.

"I don't believe it."

"Ah well … come and see my paintings," Nigel led her to his life's calling, he was all in, pleased to have finally freed himself from reality, he propped his newest works in a row, they went from easily recognizable to a sort of abstract expressionism.

"They're really nice Dad," she shook her head, backing up … "I mean it must be hard to get the paint to stick like that and not fall off …but I gotta go." She grabbed her tab, water bottle, readied her ponytail and ran to the Steven's.

Barn Scheduling had special needs kids, Moms, carers and teachers leaving at the same time as couples arrived.

The week passed without injury or disagreement and the volunteers wanted to bask in a golden glow of accomplishment. Feeling this Therapeutic riding contingences never wanted to leave and just hanging around the barn became a part of Friday afternoons … less impaired kids happily bugging volunteers for chores, donkey cart rides and other amusements.

The first group of couples changed that to parking lot chaos. Slamming car doors, they were excessively polite or came in separate vehicles. In no time it was a mad scramble to see the riders off and adjust frame of mind.

Anne ran to greet them, the sight of her blushing excitement, produced a contrasting calming effect … in unison they turned from this bouncy voluptuous woman's over eagerness for their problems. Anne cooled her jets with formal welcoming, introducing, social distancing out of habit, some wore masks, some didn't, they weren't instructed either way, having all tested negative for anti-bodies they followed Anne down the well worn path to the mansion, and over the threshold were confronted with everyone in masks and a box of free ones on the umbrella stand.

Ada, Olivia and Bett looked on from cracked barn door. It never occurred to anyone involved in the formation of couples weekends that marriages in need of intervention might've an injurious effect on the girls future … luckily matrimony was the farthest thing from their minds … they were living the life of smart-phone espionage.

While the entire mansion became a nest of voyeurism; Anne and the paid volunteers, therapist and his aids had no idea there was an understudy…The girls were supposed to be helping out in the barn.

One by one they slipped away, Saturday morning sometime before 9:30am, Olivia said goodbye to her riding class, turning them over to capable volunteers and followed.

They meant in the third floor servants quarters, whispering and giggling. The new back stair fire escape walls were covered in a special fireproof plaster-board ie sound-proofing, the girls tested it out earlier, squeaky treads bore making tape and avoided. Murderously steep, they descended in delighted step, cracking the door, smart-phones positioned earlier along the library walls, recording what eyes and ears missed.

The first Saturday yielded four couples. The girls attached nicknames from the barn door; 'beige to off-white', 'hound dogs', 'fashion-fire', and 'Awks -combo'. Judging from the cars they were all rich in a crashy angry kind of way …

"WE'RE HERE to regain joy of life. And to-do so requires adjustments, agreements, compromises… and forgiveness. The lockdown had us face ourselves and many faced a two way mirror, one reflecting, the other absorbing in an unhealthy way." Pause, big baldheaded smile, "first of all I'd like to start with the idea of having fun in the moment, stop for a moment …. breathe in … and …enjoy this beautiful house and sunny fields. Taking this weekend as an opportunity to heal and reclaimed couple-hood. No one is expected to give up anything or be forced into anything. What is expected is that people feel love in this natural setting, in this room that during the school year is a classroom, imagine the openness of children and recall feelings of love … for friends, family, associates, teachers… remember people who liked you, times you had together with loved ones, and build on the feeling."

The girls exchanged glances, not breathing, through the cracked door a sliver of events played, the room vapidly mediating on love … encouraging words followed.

"Well since you all know each other, this in some way, is a continuation of the talks we had already. It's good to get space from Bangor… Now try and imagine where you want to be in ten years … ten years from now."

Silence followed. Chairs brought in from the dining room were set up so couples sat about a foot apart and six feet from other couples. The girls poked and pointed at their unhappy expressions at not being able to move away. 'Social distancing' prevented it.

"Well not here," a woman's voice said, "he tricked me said it was a weekend in the country …"

"You knew …" …a man cleared his throat.

"I always come out of these meetings with a long list of things to work on and he does the checking," another woman said.

"Let me step in a redirect you back to the idea of progress … because in a ten year timeframe a lot can be accomplished and here we might sow seeds for that future."

"But I can't imagine a future without my daughter and … I don't know what's being asked of me … I'll never see her again!" a different woman wailed.

"We shouldn't be doing this," Ada clutched her throat, "I can't watch this," and she put her head down covered her ears…. But they were trapped on the stairs, with the door ajar… afraid to make a sound.

"I'm here for you, everyone in the room is" …a woman's voice.

"You don't have to go it alone," another woman's voice.

"Yes and we aren't going it alone either. My brilliant husband thought we'd heal better with his kid brother staying … and there he sits in front of his computer day after day."

"At least he's safe."

"Like a parasite."

"What do you want another death in the family? I had to take him … he was kicked out of our parents …and it's not so bad… he does everything we ask him."

"Except get a job … he thinks because our daughter's gone that he can stay indefinitely and I don't want to hear his problems!" She put her hands over her ears. "I refuse to worry about his problems if I do his problems become my problem!"

"Worked out real well with …"

"Oh shut up!"

"We thought she had the virus and it turned out … she was suffering from the symptoms of withdrawal," her husband filled in.

"She went out with friends, came home feeling better… and … and the next morning she was blue! I walked to the top of the stair… opened the door to her room…"

"I have to go," Ada stood gasping for air and lightly ran up the stairs, Bett and Olivia followed.

Away from the scene, Ada recovered, they returned to the barn, busied themselves with the odd chore, finishing up therapeutic riding until lunchtime gave them the 'all clear' for retrieving their cells.

Cells hidden in pockets they waited till the kids were picked up, equines brushed and out to pasture, (helping with that) The adult barn volunteers, aware of their disappearing act and resulting giggled whispers thought **Teenagers!**

The safest place for downloads was Ada's comp. Ada hoped for emotional distance from the couples problems, cell phone recordings had wonderfully dispassionate flavor and might translate into an interesting vlog. kept private and unshared of course … technology conquers! Only in this case there was no advantage, no safe two way mirror, Ada felt it went one way, straight at her, reflecting her old problem like a puddle at the bottom of a black pit she saw her face from four years ago, ashen, tragic and still there inside her waiting for pills. She pulled back, paced and gazed out a window.

The idea of testing out a new video app brought her back in focus … each tape ran simultaneously, on different portions of the room. Propped on the floor, tilted up, giant in focus feet, the rest smaller, with a blobby talking head and very poor audio. So instead heart-wrenching it had a cobbled together affect with the physiologist's voice intoning directions. The husband sitting closest had an affair about six years ago and his wife kept bringing it up… then he called her a lesbian. Their problems all had lengthy histories, baggage that only the therapist understood. His aid was also taping, (2020 nothing went unrecorded).

The couples ideas of what a therapy session was supposed to be like diverged greatly from the therapist. He lost control, stopped bringing them back to a ten year goal plan. The chaos of the moment made ten years hence unattainable. *We won't be free.* The words popped into Bett's head, she shook them out ... they didn't mean anything.

From ponytail to riding boots, Ada was happy. Bett and Olivia behind her, giggling and touching her shoulder, erased the sorrow of being away. She'd stayed at school after the shut down, cramming for the CAT, suffering in facemasks and single rooms, returning home a week before Jeff and Henry arrived back from sports camp. Particularly painful was how much bigger and smarter they'd become. All the screen time, messaging didn't translate the same as a hug, feeling their strong health, grown just fine without her, she felt compromised, unneeded... sad. It was like she'd died and come back from the dead, the way they'd quickly adapted to life without her, but here she was again, hoping to pickup where they left off, resume her old place as tutor, mentor, protector and looked askance at their achievements, as they breezed through reams of material on their smart phones, no longer needing her.

What she didn't know was five week 'Sports Camp' didn't really happen. Kids from other states and countries were Quarantined out ... it was only ten Maine covid-tested kids in one cabin. Just enough for vestigial baseball, double up soccer and pick up basketball. After about a week of that they switched to mountain climbing, killing days in the New Hampshire's White Mountains, bagging peaks, soaked to the skin. Time proved that boring so they assembled in the huge kitchen for cooking classes. A couple days and knife wounds later it was back to sports and computer games, they also went social distancing sightseeing in Bangor and had a miserable five day hike on the Appalachian Trail.

The last two weeks were spent learning carpentry, basic plumbing and how to lift a camp. They mixed concrete, poured posts and rounded it out with a couple days of ground maintenance. Later it was learning how to humanely trap and relocate of groundhogs. They placed mothballs under beds, removed screens, bordered up windows and doors, cleaned security cams, latrines, winterized plumbing, ratcheted dock systems onto the field, rolled the float ashore … lowered the American Flag … had a grand 'ol time.

So they were a little quiet about their time away. Mom and Dad were in their own worlds and Ada didn't question their accomplishments. Instead she questioned academics in general … Why judge growing kids? Give them marks, test and cubby-hole in terms of achievement, athletic ability … rules learned and followed from a hundred years of establishment. *No wonder boys want to break them … they're like little donkeys kicking the stall door!* She wasn't far off. Jeff and Henry had developed a taste for the real world and real work and just being away, turning into competent youth;

Jeff, junior high age, Henry right behind and far ahead of their piers in regular school. They were dying to leave the area ….boarding school….. anything.

Ada didn't miss anyone from school. All she saw was a variety of facemasks coming at her. She threw herself into work, test prep, college level courses, walked with her head down, didn't join any group, spent social time on her comp, checking on family and the barn. She felt the greater world was responsible for her past addiction to pills … age thirteen, *when I was supposed to be happy!*

Even though it happened in Bangor, consequential to burns from that beautiful and terrible summer of 2016 … In the aftermath all she wanted was to leave … Foster Lake in particular, it was so dumb … where people struggled to do good then bad takes it all away, *it's like falling from the top over and over no matter how careful the climb.*

She'd wanted desperately to get away … but when she got away …it was the institutional similarity between people in the hospital that said, "here take this, it helps with pain," and her teachers saying; Government mandates, prerequisites, SAT< SAT< PSAT < CAT, 600, 700, 500. In her single dorm room, she closed and locked the door.

It felt like rehab, established, authoritative, like standard medical practice to control pain. *They'd find out I'm stupid, unworthy and do it again.* Find some reason; make her an addict, dependent on methadone hand-outs or worse. No one knew how frightened she was of re-addicting. So she ran to her comp hoping for messages, living for her brother's funny smart phone comments and faces, she was miserable when days went by and they didn't show, her greatest fear was being forgotten by family. *They must never know.*

Giggles sweet music to her ears, Bett and Olivia eased her broken heart. She put off thinking of next year and college; she wanted the summer to go on forever. She wore shorts again, her burns long healed, skin perfect, she was ready for attention, a sense of control over her own life dominated ….other people's struggles eased her own.

She'd read a story about a girl who fell in love with her rapist and saw a connection to her burn injury. The accident was like rape and now she was owned by where it happened, the burning field, behind their stately log home. She fell, a Cop found her carried her to safety … events played in bittersweet flashbacks. But she didn't want a boyfriend, she wanted to be somebody first.

Listening to the couples, Olivia wondered how two people could ever get along. It seemed to her that they became frustrated and irrational when they couldn't change the person they married … the man wanted his wife to be someone else. Aside from the couple who lost their daughter, (the hound dogs) the rest were unhappy about everything and blamed their spouse for their own unhappiness. It was all they did; Blame. From the girls perspective they saw no way out … it was hopeless. *Why can't he just give her the money when she asks for it.* She tried for a solution. *Obviously he's got piles. Is money more important than love?* Money was like food. In her heart she felt love for the donkeys and mules, loved the activity they shared especially riding with Bett … but without money they wouldn't be fed, all the love in the world wouldn't do that.

Fashion Fire was further along in their marriage. She had a spending habit that her husband tried to curtail. "Why doesn't she get a job and spend her own money."

"He won't let her because then she'd leave him. He's like a frog."

"She's taller."

"Like a bowling ball and pin."

"She could push him off a cliff."

"Don't say that!"

"Insure him for a million."

"Stop it!"

"Or he might get cancer."

"That's not funny."

"Beige and white have it already."

The learning experience of editing three smart phones into one vlog … was great but over and Ada was desperate to fill her day. Reclaiming her position of 'Barn Queen' proved problematic. The whole structure had changed, instead of ruling the roost she was psychologically shut outside scratching at crumbs.

Next morning Ada, arrived at the barn power dressed in riding boots like she was still in control. ... It was a weekday and scheduling had changed, the sounds she expected to hear kids arriving, van doors sliding shut, excited voices ...were absent ... therapeutic riding was now relegated to afternoons. Mornings were 100% Olivia's ... she was Head Teacher, center of learning; the hub, ... Olivia had taken over.

Many Autistic kids 'graduated' from therapeutic riding so it was decided that before noon, (brains at optimal functioning), was the best time for regular riding classes. Seated on huge mules, mammoth donkeys and other biggest, the children learned walk, trot and canter. Blushing, long black hair in a bow, she demonstrated, the children were in rapturous awe ... she was their 'Miss Olivia'.

Ada watched, so completely displaced she struggled for breath and hid behind bales of straw. Afraid hatred would light them on fire, she left by the sliding door.

"Ada!" Olivia in pure excitement rushed at her, "Come and watch my class! No one believed they could be taught to ride without special-ed saddles but look! Oh please come see."

"Okay," stiffly allowing herself to be pulled back, face pale, heart like leather, leaning her arms on the top rail, waiting out the appropriate minutes. The kids smiles were sweetest as they rode past, but they didn't reach her heart, even the little girl with broken teeth … she couldn't return joy, her mind went dark. Then understanding the threat of exposure, she tapped it down, put on her best smile.

Olivia, five foot seven strong and shapely … *but completely stupid, hovering up my place! Look at her, her clothes… way too tight and no makeup.*

Like a devoted nurse who poisons her patient, she had to get close, close enough to inflict pain, but she had to be subtle and wait. Ada recalled when her own Mom bought all the gear and outfits. The Steven's were afraid of spending money on themselves and Olivia didn't have nice riding clothes for horseshows so Ada and Bett's Mom Leah bought for her and continued to do so as she grew… every year aged nine-thirteen, her last growth spurt took everyone by surprise… Anne was only five foot five.

Olivia set her class at a walk and smilingly came to see Ada. "Aren't they great? Some are naturals … look at her seat." she pointed at the little girl with broken teeth. "She can't talk but she's riding!"

"Good job," Ada looked down afraid a direct glance would betray her jealousy. "Your clothes are too tight … want me to put in a word so my Mom can get you new ones? Since your Dad's so stingy…I mean they really look small like low…low-key… and if you need help with makeup,." Ada flicked her braid and smiled.

"Yeah, ok," Olivia's walk back to her class lacked her previous confidant spring, then she seemed to regain her footing, adjusted a kids stirrup and another's girth before announcing a trot.

Ada watched the kids, four girls and three boys concentrate on posting. Focused on the center, Olivia smiled nodding encouragement, not one gave Ada a smile or even a second glance and she recognized all but two. They used to call her Miss Ada when she stood in the center.

She'd had enough and was leaving when Olivia ran over, her class practicing standing still. "Ada! Ada!" All blushes and beautiful girlish figure bounced up, "You want me to teach you riding, I bet you'd be a natural … then we can all go, the Mammoth's are really gentle! We'd go on trails… you, me and Bett!"

"I already know." Ada turned and left. It was another sore point as Ada didn't want to expose her lack of riding skills and no one dared mention it before when she was in charge.

At home Ada sat before her comp. but didn't turn it on, instead she descended to the first floor. The house was empty but for her Dad, covered in paint and humming to himself, "Some enchanted evening … you … may hummm." He squinted and dabbed.

She walked by invisible …life had taken on a vacant stare, found a couple Foster Lake Gazettes and was returning to her room…

"Ada, do you know anything about shoplifting?"

"What?"

"You know…" Nigel was in the doorway of his porch studio, bright as a lion in Africa, bouquet of color and odor.

"I don't do it …"

"Sooo… would you know what happens when one gets caught?"

Ada wore a puzzled expression.

"Hypothetically of course."

"I don't go into stores … I shop on line…" She backed up for the stair and the safety of her room. *Dad's totally sus.*

Nigel's hope of leaping the gap and having a conversation with Ada about guilt, (his own) … ran away, while confusion expanded and contracted with each breath. *Should I go to the store confess my crime, ask for mercy, … take whatever justice was due? Or should I continue on like this; a guilty man, ….unconfessed, confused and lonely…*Nigel had accidentally made off with multiple items from the supermarket … 100% for Leah.

Gum was part of Leah's everyday and he didn't mind her habit, *she chews instead of chewing me out … besides it sooths her tummy.* The gum packets, nail files, tampax, bath-gel and antacids were small and wrapped in slippery cellophane. How was he to know they'd fallen from the cart's baby-seat and disappeared between the huge package of toilet paper and carriage back. And since he wanded the toilet paper they remained undetected while he finished up at the self check-out.

Innocence lost when he noticed them peaking out while loading the Rover. In momentary frustration over the day, Leah, so occupied at the barn he ended up shopping and every unpaid item was exclusively, (unforgettably) hers and even after Augusta lifted bans on hoarding, she was the one who insisted on stocking up on toilet paper. Why can't she return her own stuff, confess the crime… but ….*My husband accidentally stole these and was too embarrassed to return them so asked me to-do it for him…* he could see it now, her affinity with truth and his picture in the Gazette…front page headline, GUILTY! WEALTHY MAN CONFESSESSES TO THEFT OF WOMAN'S TOILETERIES.

He sweated driving home. The forests, a great green love turned claustrophobic, the day was stifling and he was stuck… No help coming down from the sky.

Except maybe he could one day … impeccably dressed per usual for an anytime stroll away from Marie's Lane, with slight traces of oil paint under the nails, a faint whiff of the same, he might take the ram by the horns ... sidle up to one of the heavily made-up middle aged women behind the service desk and confess. But what if he fumbled it? What if they didn't understand? Disregarded his innocence.... mistook him for a shoplifter caught in ceiling cams, dimed out wirelessly, security on their way, cops, handcuffs, booked, printed, flashbulb... pic. in the paper.

The terrible scenario was suddenly pierced by new realizations ... *Wait a minute was I robbed?* Holding up the receipt for a little lampshade he bought at Goodwill. Leah was always sorting out the kids clothes and so handed him two bags, these he dropped off and on the way out snagged the most perfect and perfectly new lampshade. After inserting his card the cashier said, "minble mum one?"

"Hugh?"

The face mask moved again, "mumble min one?"

"Sure!" Having no idea what he'd just agreed to. He stood under the pantry's LED, read the tape and sighed. *Only a dollar.*

As he unpacked his thinking eased into a routine, "I remember you .... You're the one who made... humm two kisses ago" He filled the fridge and put Leah's contraband in a bag next to her comp... "and when my life is through and the angels...humm humm" Sighing... life wasn't so bad up here in the internet connected virus free second district. The stock market rocketing into darkness, Northern Maine's star filled sky might net it, bring it home to earthly hoarding;

reams of toilet paper, cans of tomatoes and beans as if they actually liked beans, everything on March's restrictive list was acquired in over-drive.

Tossing his purchases hand to hand he mused on the passage of time. *Dear Time with your inspiration and grace … please take us away from the next crushing blow …* he was sure of it, prophetic cans filling the already packed pantry. He carefully turned the labels out, some expensive …. *One can't live on potatoes alone!* Potatoes remained plentiful and un-rationed; the MacPhee family put peddle to the metal on spuds, March had them devouring like a post Irish apocalypse, to save electricity, in a dutch oven placed inside the great-room's fireplace …authentic taste had them reverting back to their Scots-Irish roots. Fiercely loyal to the apple of the ground, giving thanks for the abundance while doubly thankful hunger wasn't driving them out of Northern Maine. *We were desperate … looking for answers. Now its summer and still no answers.*

ON THE OTHER hand Ada found what she was looking for …a way out! A small theater group was happening in Foster Lake. They seemed to form and disband every summer, vowing never to do it again only to be drawn in like a Pavlovian response to high sun. This year, owing to coronavirus some positions were missing… they needed a directors understudy to help with scheduling, costumes, set design, etc etc. And it was supposed to be audience free. Ada filled out the online form and didn't wait but borrowed her Mother Leah's e-car and headed out. She found the theater in an old firehouse, got out and paced. Water rushing behind, Maples in front had her clasping her hands together with excitement. She could see herself, tab in hand…helping …supporting…directing. She'd found it… she'd arrived… and Bett loved the stage … she might entice her away from Olivia. *Let her find out what it feels like to be displaced and lonely.*

Ada waited to be excepted …brilliant, beautiful and five foot nine and a half were obvious plusses albeit the real world considered the practicality of her families wealth, not paying her way through college as primary advantage over other applicants. The time lapse she experienced was their hope for someone of similar 'background' but with experience.

15

Saving the World

The Sergeant Major was given the go ahead with the new anti virus/vaccine lab. He didn't have to twist many arms and it was too beautiful, … unsaid words and large expense account matched imaginings. The pretext was the China threat, developing quantities and the need to defend with ample ordnance before time ran out.

It was exhilarating, life underground! No untrustworthy women (or indiscriminate breeding)… The men weren't totally cognizant of what they were handling, white moon suits floated about in silence, only dripping water and electric fans. Everything asked for they got, experiments with plenty of space and light.

Underground visions grew, lived and moved. Beneath the hollowed out mountain, magnificent forty foot ceiling, Kevzar's unique properties breathed through crystal. Like minute sparks bouncing off facets, his thinking advanced; crystallized to greater world vision. The humane separation of healthy producers from disease ridden masses. *We'll eat perfect food, live in clean beautiful cities, advancing knowledge... then recreate, attend healthy amusements... Once science reigns, freedom will ring!*

Like great artists, visionary scientists work best out of sight, masterpiece hidden behind a curtain, in the depts. of an old volcano waiting for that right moment to pull the cord. Earthly issues didn't exist in his underground world. Above man changes with the tides like seaweed. Some underling lab assistant proposed a system of shoots, harvesting test subjects from above. "People disappear all the time." He laughed.

"Logistics," said The SGM. "We'd need a decontamination area, quarantine barracks… but worth considering."

"Quarantines?" the Army Specialist made a face through reflecting plastic layers, lousy voice quality … "quarantines are a bad word, synonymous with (mumbled word)… like mask-wearing … like freedom's a disease."

"True," The SGM agreed then countered "But, with the two parties battling for control, science works away unchecked and always wins. And mask wearing helps erase the idea we're individuals, instead of faces they see masses with 'certain unalienable rights'. And wearing a mask isn't racist, right or left leaning, but the sensible thing to-do so you didn't give it to Grandma, but Grandma gets it and dies anyway."

Several lab workers put their tests down and gathered round intrigued and ready for a break. Seeing this the SGM adopted teaching diction, communication skills at the ready, suit's microphone turned up. He looked and sounded like a robot that needed a card replaced. "To understand their true mission, their real goals you must understand that time and resources are running out. A society used to abundance like ours won't necessarily behave itself under dearth or even the threat of say… rationing. Imagine no internet! They'll call it something cute like 'power pauses, or 'comp respit' do PSAs, save your files, freezers full of jell-packs, whirring generators, gasoline EBTs, same as grocery EBTs for everybody! But I digress.

"Along with understanding the threats coming out of foreign labs we need to move forward with our own storehouses of viruses. This has been a calling of mine, the vast unseen world of the microbe. Before they find the perfect bio-weapon, we must have vaccines at the ready.

"The virus is to achieve several things… like mumps rendering men sterile, spliced to increase virulence … spread… It's that close… Then we're ready for a test run. Placed in aerosol and sprayed where the homeless congregate, low smudges in Phily, DC, NYC and Maryland … Atlanta… Detroit … they'll be thanking us … think of the decrease in drug use, crime … and it will go unreported as they won't be missed, morgue employees in full hazmat managing remains, cremation the end game.

"You see how I've gotten into the mind of the bad guy... Ha, I had you going ... some of you. ..When reports finally surface ... spreading from homeless encampments into God knows ... force will be applied but by then no one will care. The frightened middleclass will thank us for clearing the streets. You understand. Pity is given to the homeless as long as we stay safe, take away that and its every man for themselves. The fear is foreign labs will do this to us ... create chaos in our society. So we need to be ready or we'll become test subjects, like rabbits with color coded dots on our backsides.

"Imagine them developing different strains for different ethnic groups. No out of the realm of possibility. Prospects for spreading contagions on a grand scale are limited. They tried infiltrating Jehovah's Witnesses and Mormons, (door to door) but it didn't pan out ... too many moving parts and unscientific pyramid scheme hierarchy.

"That's the advantage of ice-cream. Picture a summer fair filled with happy crowds, a booth set up with organic ice-cream samples, couples; $1 dollar, singles the same and $2 dollars for families. Children with robust immunities won't succumb, while genetically inferior Moms and Dad's might. Hand out forms indicating flavor; chocolate, raspberry, mint, (virus, microorganism or bacteria), on the grading sheet they write down age/gender of participant. One to two month incubation period, good cover, fairs over, forgotten.

"Aerosol anthrax in the petting zoo was discarded as too risky, too old school. That's another reason for opening up the country ... harder to spread pathogens in a shutdown.

"Let me reiterate we're getting into the mind of the assassin here. Take this wall for example," he waved a hand towards a long cabinet, tiny bottles glowed in back lit glass partitions. "Umpteen viles of water born illnesses, legionnaires, listeria, Giardia, Cyclosporiasis, Amoebiasis, perfect killing machines...", he paused.

Suited for safety, the men shuffled, uncertain. A man raised a huge contamination suit finger. "I'll take questions later as this meeting was impromptu ... or better yet submit it in writing." He paused enjoying their unease... "Dismissed." The SGM turned on his heal, left them hanging. The men staggered back ... *The best of the best!* Not sure what they just heard.

The SGM smiled, an optimist at heart, with a progressive understanding of common good. *They won't get it until their shut up in cubicles, ...clutching ration cards!*

Rationing, waiting lists, no gasoline and other wonderful imaginings blossomed into reality when he came to the rat room, his card making entry. *This is happening, they're part human.* Sound deadening tile decreased the level to classroom noise, tolerable to the human ear. The lovely awareness of being alone with his favorite creature.

They were docile, the right size to pick up. Though double layers of nitrile was a beating heart. Inquisitive noses, sensitive whiskers, eyes that couldn't see but found what was desired, always on the hunt; food, mates and genetic imperative to start new colonies. Rats were the most perfect vecter/spreader.

He found the new cages. In the middle, a tiny operating table, two years of work injected into tiny rat brains. The added component? Long term memory. He wasn't privy to the exact discovery, a rat brain evidentially tested positive for human like cells, they'd knocked out rat genes and replaced ours. Rats with emotional reactions, understooding photographs, followed directions, used symbols. Jackson Lab look out, there's a new guy in town.

He turned black lights on their last exquisite venture. It was a huge achievement, lifetime accomplishment to design and oversee.

The installation was immensely expensive. A three hundred thousand gallon saltwater tank, a hundred and twenty foot deep and miles from the ocean. Borestone made it possible, the insides of ten million millennium year old volcano replicated deep water pressure. 'Fracking' out the tank and simultaneous growing of the Kevzar dome took three years, so there wasn't out-ranking hysteria over time spent.

There was a slight problem with noise. Like a throat with a perpetually stuck bone, the work rattled on day and night only stopping in high winds. Then like the giant finally cleared it's windpipe it celebrated with air-raid sirens. The valley was subjected to non stop wailing, stronger in gales, that only stopped when rattling began again.. The tiny forested towns became obsessed with thoughts of war and engrossed in bomb shelter designs … and contacted Maine state reps. … Eventually the military owed up but sounds persisted even as concern abated.

The Vampire squid, Vampyroteuthis Infernalis the ocean's garbage disposal, cuddling and destroying, now adapted to all ocean temperatures and depts., was the reason. The idea came out of a Washington think-tank. (no pun intended). He was called to a meeting, introduced to great men. The discussion was deep-ocean … a new frontier in GMO technology. Imagine a creature with insatiable appetite for garbage. Human refuse devoured. The Pacific garbage patch in the history books along with their names.

The trouble was it didn't like plastic but iron and steel. It preferred living deep but would actually patrol the surface ISO ships … replicas, his men floated. Feeding was entertaining, like 'battleship.'

Would their attributes, penetrating suction, great staying power ….be enough to scuttle opposing foreign powers? The small, gray Squid, innocent beanie baby and the Russian navy full of holes, our hulls safely clad in protective coating. The new genetic model almost ready for primetime.

He tapped the glass ... nothing, then like live sediment rising from muck, one after another, they appeared, put on a light show, eyes red to blue and back again... *"We better not show our hands just yet"*, he said out loud, looked around ashamed at his carelessness. *My creature, my Vampy .... The grant proposal thinks you're garbage disposal! Modified to rid the oceans of plastic!* The squid paused glowing magic colors ready to-do science's bidding, eyes communicating world to world, the unseen depths of time, oceans immortal ... The SGM projected powerful images ... control the oceans -- control the world.

A single Vampyroteuthis stuck to the glass silently waving a long delicate arm then gone. *We're alike you and I ... I'm super human and you're not a squid but an octopus, synonymous with ultimate power, eight arms; the states, judiciary, all departments, executive branch, federal reserve, media, armed forces, corporations...all pulling towards the center.*

The SGM shrank back, Fukushima, atomic isotopes, in their digestive systems... *I'll get the most sensitive instruments, rid you of poison...* The creatures returned, delicate undulations, tiny suction cups, *we'll live on you and I; in purpose if not in flesh.*

For all his happy thoughts of the future he was in a bad mood. He'd had unpleasant row with his wife. She came up from their home in Maryland and although parts of the off base vacation were good ... It was her discovery woman's names and addresses… when his second cell rang from a dresser drawer. He'd stepped out to contact the base on the other. "No you can't talk to 'Bob' who is this?" After that she probed his menus and found the list. Women's names and attributes created a fury he wasn't used to. Life underground was all nods, hushed words and text messages. She was screaming at him in the close space of their little resort cabin. He wanted to take her out back and put her down like a rabid animal.

"I know what you're up to over there, using innocent little kids for your Nazi experiments!"

"You're perceptions are a clear misunderstanding of our mission. We don't want to hurt anybody. Everything done at cellular level. We're working for the people to ease suffering!" He couldn't alter the hate filled looks. *I don't like problems either. I like solutions. The future is at stake.*

Anne Steven's understood his stress. How he'd resisted temptation, been a model soldier. Listened without passing judgment. Plus he'd already earned double advanced degrees before enlisting… and was a practicing MD, didn't expect reimbursement for medical school and excepted their meager sign on bonus… doesn't that count for anything? He'd endured incredible hardship, in service, sacrifice for their future and not his own. *I was always above average, stronger than others, physically and mentally more fit, more readiness. Lucky them, I'm on their side.*

Excepting a single lab worker, his 'little man' friend, everyone else at work lacked a full understanding of his mission. *Man needs a trusted friend to see him through.* Unified in thought and action they failed to find one thing to guilt over. It was a perk, ranking and still compassionate, the privilege of his leadership position …vision and stamina.

Besides, he had to gain access to the egg donor's health histories, intelligence and other attributes to complete genetic profiles and that often meant their homes … and the women expected it! Most were married, middle class, looking for excitement, some needed a little something to calm them down so they could be brought to the mobile lab, his pride and joy genetic extraction theater. Disguised as an old camper-trailer, he kept it parked in plain sight at the base. Only two hand-picked specialists knew of its existence.

He'd perfected the hunt, could go from taping women on the street, … then discovery phase; kids photos, family health, net worth, social status … to egg collection and in as little as three weeks.

The wife suggested they go in for counseling, "No," he said, "but you can go."

"How can I go to a couple's group alone."

"Couples group?"

16
Ada's New Job

As expected Ada was hired on the spot, all other candidates hit the dust bin. The impression of complex intellectual depth, vulnerable beauty and physical strength won them over. Because of the pandemic they'd failed to meet recruitment for full length plays and so scrapped the idea for judged skits. "This will bring more young people in," the seventy-five year old director was optimistic in his flimsy blue mask.

The old Fire House 'theater' building wasn't owned by the company, it was a shared space. The tenets each had their own locked storage room in the basement and even though the theater dominated with their own stairway to the stage and makeup area, there was a sense of others, a confusing lack of ownership, of having to put everything away following rehearsal, of rules set down by an authority that wasn't their won.

Ancient wiring; one long bank of toggle switches with a dimmer on the end, rickety track lighting, vague dangling curtain pulls … Ada cautiously patrolled getting a feel for problems before asserting authority. She wasn't sure how far she could go with no budget. But one thing was certain with no other able-bodied person present she sweetly obliged, taking over many tasks, feeling good, moving furniture, placing heavy tables and chairs. She immediately grasped electronic issues, confiscating cordless mikes prone to feedback she gave full attention to lighting, sound and making magic.

In a month's time she'd taken over, memorizing banks of switches in the light and projector room, understanding the needs of the judges, encouraging, remembering, controlling. She opened doors and windows letting musty air out, made a rope clothesline by the river to hang costumes on. "Look at them sparkle," she smiled at the director.

"We need young bodies to fill them," he gazed wistfully at her like a timeless goddess had arrived from outer space to rescue them. Contemporaries, competition didn't exist in her new self engineered reality. Nothing was pricking her bubble of running an older set of once brainy, capable people, who due to forgetfulness, lack of strength and other physical and mental issues were in a state of complete assignation, she was their rescuer and she loved it…. (taking Bett away from Olivia was still on her summer agenda.)

They'd broken down into three groups of five, for one act plays, skits judged each Friday. That way their small audience was given the task of helping judge and social distancing not a problem. All the prep work was completed site, the Hall only theirs Fridays from 4pm till closing. Ada's brain storm was to champion one group per week, invite them to the mansion, practice on the ballroom stage, Bett becoming part or not, Ada wanted to compete and win.

Under her revolving guidance, she picked up multiple successes, no matter the people or talent. She was open to involving Mrs. Stevens and even Olivia … together they'd dominate, star and pile up little plastic trophies.

Olivia and Bett saw the old people and weren't interested. They couldn't imagine the light fandango, effortless mirth … frumpy, curmudgeonly acting in a time warp, like young people playing old; happiness over wrinkles. Ada's project was 'beauty inside' and from the moment she arrived they were beautiful and young … her vision resurrecting former selves.

Old righteous perspective knew good when they saw it, understood her need to dominate and transform and gave her complete control.

Bett and Olivia's rejection hurt, but Ada wasn't dismayed long, instead she posted advertisements around Foster Lake to attract new members and to her excitement and amazement got several fifty year olds. Thespians from their college years paid dues and delighted everyone with relatively youthful energy and able bodies for moving props. They also brought furniture and costumes from home. The storage room was bursting at the seams.

Every Friday they presented three skits, ten minutes to a quarter hour, most short Saturday Night Live style comedies, self isolating together, Ada helped write and direct. The Democratic Candidates debates were rather funny, candidates wearing cover-all facemasks pointing out words set to music, follow the bouncing ball as no one could understand a word they were saying.

Coronavirus became the corn-virus, a huge ear of corn, wearing ten face masks chased screaming people around then showed up in the park, sat quietly next to an old-lady who turned into an angel. The last was the facemasked ball. Using every period costume at their disposal, facemasks decorated to the max, they danced to Karma-Chameleon like it was yesterday.

After the audience voted, judges made decisions, with Ada gently instructing about not breathing into the microphones, and other 'feed-back' etiquettes.

Everyone stayed milling, some in costume minus make-up and masks gathering around the refreshment table chatting, enjoying fellowship without audience, like *what pandemic.*

One day while in the darkened theater, practicing dancing and rehearsing a skit about Trump's triumphalism, love of parades, golf, gilded palaces and winning, ... Ada heard a faint background noise. It turned out a mic was left on and a nearby stack of styrofoam cups toppled, draft from the door left open, they fell one by one onto the floor, sounding like Plinko on the Price is Right Ada ran to fix and ran into the Sergeant Major.

17

The Vampire Squid

"Guess who's coming to Couple's group?" Dan was securely in his office chair while Anne hovered in a dubious state of mixed emotion.

An earlier couples group uncovered an embarrassing flaw, one woman had a peanut allergy, others allergic to gluten and they'd only accommodated vegetarian meal preferences. Dan insisted on couple's names, food and other allergies. Next week's list had a surprise guest.

"The Sergeant Major and his wife."

"Oh right, the creep who came to our Christmas party … and,"

Dan's own mental tape played out his old time dulled accusation … the issue was settled … past.

Anne's relief was so apparent she was glad to be behind him, just above the growing bald spot. Her reflection on his screen spoke, "well hopefully he has a problem we can fix."

"I've a problem only you can fix and he spun around, grabbed at her but she sprung away, thought the better of it and came into his arms for a hug.

Over his shoulder was father time, the ancestral grandfather clock ticking out impartially as Dan held her tight like he'd never let her go. She was stifled, exasperated … it wasn't like dancing it was like being possessed, owned like he'd taken over everything but … the longer he held her the more she recognized how used to everything she was at thirty-six she'd never give it up … she felt old tender love for him but needed to be let go of. "Dan, honey, I've got to get ready … there's so much to do…"

"I know." He squoze tighter, feeling her ribs.

"I love you honey, but come-on, I've tons on my mind." She wanted to confide in him like they used to but he'd changed, didn't see the entertainment value of the couples … like it was unmanly, he'd lost his sense of humor… and the Sergeant Major hung in the air … a gap impossible to bridge. Above everything she desired a return to like-mindedness and would've told him a partial tale, a cleaned version, but it was too risky. The secret stayed inside, he sensed deception and it was killing her.

He abruptly let go and turned to his research, not looking as she left.

Ada wasn't there for the couples arrival Friday afternoon nor did she help serve dinner, or watch the dance, she was officiating her own group or going though the motions her mind that distracted.

Besides the Sergeant Major and wife, three other couples signed up. State government workers, lifers, inhaling the great indoors, pulled out of old filing cabinets, covered in Augusta dust.

The girls assigned boomer nicks; Roadrunner & Wile e. Coyote; Morticia & Gomez, Homer & Marge; SGM, (Sergeant Major) & SGMW (Sergeant Major's wife). She actually looked like him, in a tall fair dried out way…but she was more closed off, emotionally unavailable while he surreptitiously checked out the merchandise.

In their forties and fifties, rugged bureaucrats that even Lane Farm air couldn't cure facemask claustrophobia or erase the aura of palace intrigue, deep money, post it notes and family photos, truth hidden behind smiles … for the time being.

One couple drove a red 1969 GTO and the men just had to see the engine, check mileage, go under the hood, open the trunk etc.

The women were above average; better dressed, made up and accessorized, glittering in the high summer sun, chatting in springy walks. Anne was tickled, back in her 'plain janes' she still turned heads and briefly acknowledged the Sergeant Major … sunglasses nodded. and smiled.

WITHOUT ADA'S interest, the ballroom session was left alone. Bett and Olivia spent the evening hours in Olivia's room, searching stuff on line, watching Utube … dance tunes wafting in the open window. Couples discord out of sight and mind, the melodies were dreamy… romantic.

"They're trying to make them not mad at each other," Olivia sighed.

Wish my Mom & Dad had couple's group, Bett thought, having watched with interest how the groups changed, came with ugly expressions, left at peace. "You know my Mom's emo. She was a hater except your Mom changed that." Bett had never put it into words what a bad scene her Mom was before Mrs. Steven's.

Olivia paused, didn't want to go into details … her past feelings were those of a little girl … the older smarter Olivia knew better, *I used to hate her like poison!* "I like your Mom, she helps my Mom a lot, my Mom can tell her to-do anything and she does it and …my Mom works really hard and my Dad doesn't see it …and like it's a sus party of her of being with other men, they go in his office and shut the door, I mean it's not like I don't know what they're talking about, I don't have to hear it."

"My Mom yells and Dad calms her down and they chill on the couch, have a snack, watch a program." Bett confided, "She gets hangry making dinner, when they skip tea. It's like she's younger than us… doesn't get that she needs to eat. That's why your Mom has her all the time, cause your

Mom knows about food. She knows about different foods and mood."

"My Dad's always in his office, he's probably there now and Mom's out helping. He's in there thinking Mom's smashing some man. But you know..." Olivia paused she'd never told anyone only watched it get worse. *Dad's put her so high on a pedestal that the fall will really hurt ... if I tell Bette maybe it will help.* "He's right. I mean she's not... you know but you should see her at church, coffee hour is so embarrassing. I tried to get Dad to go but it's not like I'm going to tell him why. And I know she talks on her cell in the butler's pantry, and shuts herself up in the downstairs powder-room. And remember her and the Sergeant Major? First the Soldier and then him at dance class. Dad doesn't know about that but at the same time he does. So we're V dumb on the subject.

"My Dad takes Mom places, she gets dressed up and they go to Portland sometimes."

"Yeah the bling! I used to think your Mom was a noob but she gave my Mom enough bling to like last for ever! We still have some of it. My dad knows about it but he doesn't care."

"I like your Dad, I mean he's gotten kind a quiet, doesn't hang out at the barn like he used to."

"That's 'cause of my brothers, he has to baby-sit, Mom's busy teaching and Valerie's takes care of them at the preschool table, with her boy ... but when Dad's home he has them twenty-four seven .. I mean all weekend. But Valerie doesn't leave! She stays around anyway and helps Mom clean like I used to."

"Yeah, she's always here."

"Dad doesn't like Valerie, he doesn't say but he wants to cancel the whole thing … and she's kind of crashy, I mean she's always hanging around in our stuff and she's like this blob, like she's absorbing and so weird, quiet like she's afraid we won't like her, when we already don't, only Mom does, cause Mom likes it when people have problems and talk to her and then they won't leave her alone! They totally glom on! And Valerie's not straight … I mean she's not totally bi but Dad thinks she is. Mom called her a 'treasure' that made Dad mad, he kept repeating 'treasure' to himself. He's always throwing shade but she doesn't care. Mom makes him get it and she stays. It's not like normal with her and her kid at dinner every night. It's not like it used to be, like we can talk about stuff."

The girls were quiet, music wafted through the window, South Pacific filled the air with romantic images.

"Imagine people falling in love and then a couple years later falling out," Bett said.

"Yeah it's like my Mom fell in Love with Valerie. Dad won't let her be around men so she found another way.

"That's crazy."

"Oh yeah and she knows how Dad and I feel and she still won't stop having her here. It wouldn't be so bad but it's all the time. But Dad drew the line, … if Mom asks him if

Valerie can live here, stay in one of the guest rooms he told me he's going say 'no'. And Dad spends all his weekend, you know, spare time with the boys …he actually shut his office door in her face.

"Wow."

"Wish I could've seen it, he told me about it afterwards. Poor Dad, he's never mean to anyone ever but he knows something's not right. I mean Mom's good and I love her … but…"

"If only she wasn't here."

"Yeah that would be better."

"I know, lets tell Ada, she'll figure out how to get rid of her."

Olivia thought back to riding class. "She might not be in the mood. You remember Lucy and her Mom? Dad never liked Lucy's Mom, he was so happy when they left. We knew Lucy didn't do it, she wasn't strong enough. They got the idea from when Lucy cut her hair off. …Mom really liked Lucy's Mom too. Cried when she left."

"Then we'll do it. We'll plant something on her like my Mom's jewelry, err your Mom's jewelry," Bett was ready.

Olivia smiled at the thought, then imagined being caught in a lie, both parents looking at her, she blushed, the scales of justice tipping over … *But its right to get rid of her!*. "It's unfair… we can't get rid of her … it's just so unfair," Tears welled up and she wiped her face, knowing better than to cry in front of Bett.

"Valerie's unfair… and your Dad will be glad, like he was about Lucy only … what happened to Lucy was wrong but what will happen to Valerie will be right."

"Yeah Dad will be glad… why did we have to live with her around for so long. It's like Mom likes her better … than Dad or me" more tears escaped.

"We… we could make it look like that's why she's so nice to your Mom, like she's a thief you know 'casing the joint'." Bett giggled.

"Yes but," *Dad would be furious if he found out.*

"Can't you see, it's you… us … or her."

"Yeah YOLO," and my parents won't call the police, 'cause my Dad will 'handle it internally.' You know like he did with Lucy."

Olivia felt better while they went over plans and quietly crept into her parents room and her Mom's vanity drawer. They had to make a trip up to the MacPhee's stately log home to retrieve Bett's Mom's shoebox from under the bed and added Leah's diamonds to the pile as Anne had sold most of hers. The combined diamonds were placed in a zippered bag used to house pantyhose and hid in the bottom of Valerie's back-pack under a change of cloths.

"WELL…WHAT DO you expect me to think," Morticia gesticulating "first we have a plague of Locust in West Africa, then Ebola and while focused on that, their problems … what to do to help them… way over there … we become part of a world wide pandemic! How am I to distance myself from that!" …

The girls held breath on the incredibly steep Victorian stair, feet braced against molding, hoping their cells picked it up, they glanced at each other in half lit suspense.

Chairs, set up as before; couples side by side, six feet from other couples, but the whole lot was moved down to the other end of the Library, under tall windows. The discovery of the chair change came too late for the girls to rearrange. They couldn't see any people except of course each other. Glances between girls supported intelligence, whispered labels confirming.

"Ok so doomsday isn't the issue anymore, but what about all the funerals, before the quarantine you went and some of them pretty distant, …people we barely knew… what a waste … all that time … and they die anyway."

"I go where I'm needed."

"But not entirely expected."

"It destroyed so many peoples lives," a different mans voice intoned and they weren't certain who it was… "Not the virus but the lockdown and market crash and its just beginning, the economy crushed … we don't feel it, working our government jobs, sitting out the hours … face it, we're not exactly indispensable …"

"Yeah no need for back up."

"Won't work and can't be fired." A man got some giggles.

"Well now we can't, work that is and without us they won't get approvals. Won't get their projects approved" a woman's voice piped in.

"Yeah it's pretty much a paint by numbers deal, I mean… our opinions don't matter, we're just smiley-faces … I mean," the deep voice paused, "at the department … we can get tough, get real and we get some real, A-holes.. I mean we've the courts, … police… so what can they do? I mean who wants that added expense… it's go along to get along, done before they start …

He paused, encouraged by their quiet went on. "We're shut down so we can't shut anyone down… and that's what they want … and we have to-do it, to show our departments' strength, goals, augh … progress. You know carrying out important stuff, environmental stuff, you know run a tight ship…" The man shut up although the room was hanging on his words and wanted more. (*We have no friends on the outside.*)

"We're the bureaucracy." The same woman said with unexpected humility. "I mean that's good, we handle a lot but honestly not the same amount … at least for the time being … and its lasted a while. There's a lot of agencies that do more policing than us."

"Yeah," a male voice paused, "all these little authority figures popping up, petty tyrants and Karens,…keep a six foot distance… like six foot under.""

The room paused waiting for the Dr. to intervene; redirect. He didn't and the man continued… "Lets be honest at least our jobs are secure, we're part of it … write the rules. My poor brother, my best friend lived for his investments, he was over leveraged … then came the margin calls, had to sell out positions and it was like death around his house. We had to hide weapons. He was devastated, hollowed out, moaning and this is when he saved seventy-five% of value, got out too soon ….a good man."

"Animal spirits tore him apart?" An empathy lacking woman made light.

"That's tough"… her husband covered.

"Yeah, all good intention, working for the family … gone …"

"Lots of people weren't reading it correctly," the counselor said.

"Served up a great big flip-side," a third man said.

The Sergeant Major's voice was yet to be heard.

"Yeah the feeling of unreality won't go away."

"Feelings are real, in this case … we're forced to look at ourselves," the councilor redirected… "and take positive steps."

"Yeah," the man who's brother lost money in the market continued, "he was always his own man, wouldn't except help … I mean he wanted hugs but when I tried to get him to-do the obvious… take a shower, change his clothes … he refused. Then he let the outside of the house go, it had been a pride factor, 'meticulously kept lawn.'

"Now it's like abandoned, like urban explorers, waking up, like devil worshipers chanting…" his wife said.

"Tough," the other man said.

"Yeah and he was always the go-to-guy."

"The whole sheltering-in-place deal was hard on all of us … people like are a social disease."

"And my brother kept repeating headlines, "'It's over … I failed… I'm a looser … should've known, should've gone short!… I was buying long positions! Long positions in a collapsing market!' And then the opposite happened. The market recovered. He sold at a low."

"Let me remind you it's over now … summers here." the councilor notified.

"In Maine social distance comes natural," a woman said.

"Yeah and everything outside the home feels unreal," another woman said.

The Sergeant Major took a breath in, longing for his timeless space deep underground. With no circadian rhythm he found long bouts of daylight disturbing. Looking straight ahead he took in the room peripheral vision unimpaired … and began to well up with homicidal rage at the ridiculous women and retarded men. *Jellyfish.*

Spreading his fingers he pinched the webs, a habit he picked up from military time; hurry up and wait. Masochism makes time go and being in the home of Anne, his 'lady friend' helped ... but she was absent.

Impatience surged through his veins. He was in a race against time. *What if half of all women took testosterone, became men, married fertile women, had families via random sperm donors, produced genetically compromised offspring .... held the world hostage in their gender neutral utopia!*

In a model universe, where I'm the man in the clouds, High Priest of sex, with access to all genetic data, after the great reset, there'd be no suffering, no disease and my girls in an extra special, breeding pool, plus surrogates, pampered, not have to work, with privileges ... he almost spoke out loud to an invisible adversary "*my life goals are different from yours. Yours will die ...mine will live forever...*

He slumped, closed his eyes in thought. *My connections will be international, sperm will end war! There will be no want, no families, nations, borders; selected sperm donors will stop all reason for conflict ... everyone will be related! Imagine women having donor parties, sibs all over the world speaking different languages or better yet English!*

He smiled to himself from the middle of a sperm cloud, until reality came calling and he listened. The fat man's advice wasn't about action, plans or even well said. It was a lot of squishiness; unmanly, stupid. The room was interesting enough; he probed and rested, the tall windows, dark beams, huge fireplace; sheltered, airy, ancestral. He'd been in homes of the very wealthy before. Fortresses against poverty, danger locked outside, but here the public was invited in... for what? To make us more acceptable? Our feelings all the same? Turn perfectly good problems into loving couples. Don't they understand people love to fight. *Only I know how to fix it... forget repairing marriages live in Donor Groups! Life will be one endless girl party.*

He reality scanned, smelling. Uninteresting lot, compared with the owners ...all second rate. And too well groomed and accessorized. 'News-flash,' it doesn't make you better looking! Men in important watches, women with silly bracelets and earrings. The women he could understand. *Poor dears can't flip a switch on ageing, so it's off to the Mall.*

Out of the primitive part of his brain a deep hatred rose towards the men, a desire to tear them apart, ... *in the blink of an eye I'd spill blood. Think, man ... Concentrate on Anne's plush-bottom sitting upright at dance class. It's somewhere in the building right now moving energetically around. She'd never manage 1 &1/2 hours of this.*

But his wife could and did. He glanced sideways, the once pretty woman ... a brittle stick! They'd gone over ...little speeches to give ahead of time. Given her recent outburst he wasn't positive she'd stay on script.

"I get so lonely when he's away. There's no married couples quarters on the base and I miss him. Am lost without him" Her raspy, once sweet voice managed.

She did hooray! "Now dear," he patted her hand, "I've already put in for more time and requested off site housing for our brides." The room rolled eyes. at the old misogynistic term.

"Yes but you didn't at first ... at first you said, "we'll have to live with the space."

"Yes dear," in tones of theatric sweetness, "we're fixing that! We're moving on, we're talking month's not years."

"What happens over at the base if you don't mind my asking," a man's voice cut in.

"It's 90% nutritional studies. Creating the perfect food bar."

"And the private sector can't?"

"Not with our degree of certainty."

"You make nutrition bars and …"

"We're working on military grade mirage, building materials, G-force shoes and moving platforms. We're also looking into CO_2 trapping, actually Liquefied CO_2 held in tanks like LNG. Just in case it gets cold, then we can pump it into the atmosphere, warm it up again."

"You're joking," The deep 'smiley face' voice said.

"Your tax dollars at work…"

"So … military grade mirage, building materials, G-force shoes, platforms and CO_2 trapping." Deep voice again.

"Correct. … Everything in the field of health and savings, finding ways to cut back on expensive diseases… Building a better world."

"Underground?"

"The building materials are meant for underground, it makes for better experimentation, we aren't building replicas…" his voice trailed off.

"It's dark as a dungeon, damp as the dew, dangers are double and pleasures are few," a female voice quoted.

"Ok lets get back to the original question. Where do you want to-be in ten years?"

"As far away from her family as possible!" a man's voice blurted.

"Can you elaborate?"

In the darkened stair well the girls went from rapt attention to completely cramped, their eyes lost brightness, air left the room as she reiterated her tale of furniture, wills, trusts, then her voice changed to anguished sorrow and a long list of family cruelties followed.

"You're an adult and not dependent on them right? You get along fine without them. Your life is your own." Tried and true from the psychologist.

Her husbands voice, "we had a death in the family … finally lifted the lockdown and had to go. Hanging out with them destroyed my faith in humanity…"

"It did not."

"They wanted to hug my wife goodbye."

"They're good, and they're like me… we're clutter bugs …and"

"…I dragged her away… Corona virus was the excuse but … who knows the cruelty gene might hop off, … she'd change … become destructive … you know," he did a man spreader "flip a switch and she'd act subconsciously and sabotage everything that's good in our lives. We'd become like them, pathological hoarders. She has the hoarding gene but we keep it under control. But they hoard way more than stuff. They hoard emotional abuse… like inflicting pain, enjoy suffering, my wife their favorite target."

"Talk about flipping a switch! He flipped, went nuts! Gave my brother a shove, reached in and dragged me away," she cheerfully bragged over his protectiveness.

"Surprised you hugh?" (The counselors voice.)

"Yes. I mean he doesn't lose his cool …eve'a"

"The healthy functioning adult male brain works on a system of control similar to a circuit breaker. When challenged by irritation, small annoyances, disagreements, kids, he keeps his cool… deflects with humor. But when he experiences a real feeling of loss, say at a funeral, his wiring is more loaded and although he'll respond in a gentlemanly manner, he feels the blocked charges to his system. Under normal circumstances, say a family picnic he might've handled it differently but the stark reality of death overloads the system. Everyone comes from somewhere, has past family experiences. Seeing his wife touched by 'the enemy' tripped his breaker." The Psychologist obviously delighted in a deep discussion of gender.

"But I didn't feel threatened."

"Women respond differently to threats. Women will disperse signals, distract themselves in small caring gestures, when that fails they weep. Male rage is characterized by a sudden loss of control."

"Women rage too," a female voice added languidly.

"A woman's anger is often for many things; they feel deprived of attention, they're bored, lonely, unappreciated. Woman use energy in a generalized way, while men direct it. They play a sport, attend a meeting with a goal in mind. Women desire many things while male desire is directed, needs results, he desires power, control and gets it by being a man."

Silence followed. A complete lack of disagreement to his authority wasn't exactly submissive by the female component … rather it had a patronizing flavor. The girls on the stairwell got it, eyeing each other in agreement, ready to manage future men with love and flattery, that way they'd be protected from all threats; physical and psychological.

"It's not like it used to be," the instantly recognizable raspy voice of the Sergeant Major's wife paused, "now with the pandemic everybody wants to control us and I'm so lost and lonely. It was different when we were together …. and at first living separate was ok but I just can't stand it anymore!"

"We're working on it."

"I might as well go home, leave Maine, live in Baltimore."

Silence followed, waiting for the Sergeant Major to speak.

"And he bought himself a travel-trailer but does he take me camping? No! … Says he's doing wildlife research. But that's all he tells me. I don't know what's going on over there."

More silence, *I'd like to wring her neck*, the Sergeant stared straight ahead, knew better than to dignify her statement with a comment. "Lets go apartment hunting right away…

after we're done here … lets!" It sounded un-spontaneous … studied.

There was a pause and the room suddenly clapped, first a splattering than longer, louder ending with the sound of her blowing her nose. "Where Bangor?" came out in anguished cry.

"We can start in Foster… and use Dover-Foxcroft as a fall back."

"Oh," the raspy teary voice cried.

"Then Dover-Foxcroft it is," tones of theatrical sweetness gave way to sounds of chairs moving back and hugging… long happening hug.

"Wonderful a real break through …we're all so happy for you," applause continued for awhile. They wanted it all; pats on the back, arm punches … hugs erupted spontaneously like paying tribute to the newly resurrected God of social entanglement, physical interaction expanded … love and acceptance filled the room. *She's forty-two … post menopausal see what a great guy I am…*

Session not over they sat back down.

The occupants of the stairwell waited for various articles of dirty laundry to get a full airing before the boomer memes, SGM & SGMW and the esteemed boat anchor, finally collected themselves and left the room.

They peaked around the corner, breathlessly quiet, then burst in for their cells … but to their astonishment the Library door opened and the Sergeant Major appeared. They gasped, Olivia frozen at the secret door, Bett in mid-stride and Ada reaching for her phone… everyone stopped breathing.

"Well, well, well, what do we have here," The Sergeant in his earlier inspection of the room noticed the open panel but thought it a cabinet. He saw one of the cells but thought it was the older Steven's recording, for no other reason than to satisfy voyeurism.

"Oh please don't tell our parents," Ada distracted him while motioning Bett and Olivia to leave. "They can't know about this…" Ada paled.

The Styrofoam cup visitor,' Creeper from dance class, rehearsal gate-crasher etc, etc tilted his head and smiled, "no need to worry." He retrieved his own cell from where he left it on a chair and silently approached her, "No," he repeated, gentlemanly, soave, like it was 'situation familiar' the trapped apologetic female in a bind pleading for assistance. "you don't have to worry…"

Ada gasped for air, he took a step forward, she took a step back, seeing this he stopped. She was ready to run but at the same time curious about him, his manners, incredible looks, married to a wizened wife, not much there … Ada in her superior way felt sorry for him. "I'm sorry, we're wrong, but if they don't know, no one will be hurt and oh please don't tell anyone."

"No, you're safe, I'm not that kind of guy, trust me and…" he took a step forward and she took a step back, … chin up watching him. "My name is Andrew Dempsey, (gave his real name, not good), my friends call me Andy," he put a hand out for her to shake.

She took it and he covered it with his other hand and tried to draw her towards him, she resisted and he let her go. "In any case we need to be friends you need my friendship, help and I need yours, you saw my wife, nothing to fall in love with …but you…you… you could at least agree to meet me, say at the stables at 1:30, I'll slip out for a butt. My wife is used to that, my after dinner smoke, I'll be on the far side of the barn, don't be late, you see we need each other…I can help you … do we have an agreement?"

"I…I" she stared at him in astonishment, knew what he was after but the bluntness of his behavior said many things.

"You won't be risking a thing, I'm after information, the same as you, it's not what you think. You weren't here for the original study. I'll bring forms… Ada," he smiled took a step forward, she took a step back so she was almost at her escape, "This is your CYA moment …" and she was gone running up the passage, just as Valerie stepped in the room.

Valerie, wearing a bandanna, from working in the kitchen, brought with her a whiff of lunch menu. "It's all set…" she whispered, then in normal tones, "the buffet's ready,"

"Operation love bird." he whispered back.

She nodded.

THE GIRLS IN their own territory weren't afraid. In fact they delighted in the prospect of watching the Sergeant Major from tack room windows and set up behind a piece of cardboard, a cell in the corner of each pane, westerly sun shining on dirt, they were invisible from the outside.

The dining room and kitchen, crowded with volunteers, eager for a paying job, full of mirth and understanding, devolving periodically into giggle-fests didn't notice the girls had slipped away, they simply took over their tasks, more help than work on that ebullient Saturday afternoon.

They took position behind the window and waited. To their suppressed excitement the SGM appeared around the corner, tacking back and forth he lit a butt, actually looked at his watch, moved away from the wall, stretched and returned so suddenly facing them they ducked. When they dared look he wasn't alone. Valerie was showing him a paper. They were so close to the glass the girls could see it was a diagram. She waited and he photographed it with his cell, took a puff off his cigarette and walked quickly away. She left in the opposite direction.

The girls considered the scene, staying behind cardboard, Ada shivered, chilled to the bone. The absence of life, when in her real sphere it teamed plus the contrast of the SGM to her Dad's high-mindedness, Mr. Steven's deep warmth, Stan's happy ways and practically ever other man on earth; from schoolboys to old guys in her theater group added up to an ordinary masculine vibe, same male scale … but this person was caged and even though neatly dressed looked unclean... "We can't deal with him!" Bottled up feelings vented in a gust of expression. "We can't be near him... or even at a distance!"

"He was dancing with my Mom. She was trying to get information from him ...but we don't know what...and then ...and then she washed all her new clothes, some she burned."

"The Creeper."

"A guy from the base told Mom not to dance with him but she... she"

Ada's imagination needed containment. "Lets go to my room ...just get out of here. He won't try anything with all the men around and they're at the beach this afternoon. There's the State Park Service ...you know Game Wardens, they've got guns, like Park Police, Oh my God," adrenaline ran her cold.

Bett felt it close to the bone, "What should we do?"

They were legging it up to Ada's and Bett's stately log home and stopped on the road ... looking at Ada for direction, her mind went back to the mansion, the busy kitchen, surrounded by high windows and stone fortification, couples wandering towards lawn furniture, or up in their rooms happily getting ready for their excursion to Foster Lake. Into this atmosphere of afternoon calm, after lunch flavor, resting off too good a meal, overindulgences settling in the well-intentioned government workers trying to improve their marriages, looking for turning-points while wishing they'd consumed less lunch … into all that Ada injected terrifying images … a predator on the loose ready to single out and destroy, circling prey, looking for weakness, some poor woman would disappear, later found in pieces.

"What do we do now?"

"Tell Mr. Stevens."

"My Dad can't know my Mom danced with him!" Olivia almost shouted.

"We don't have to tell him that."

"We can tell him there's something weird about him."

"I'll tell him he propositioned me." Ada was ready to sacrifice.

"But you're seventeen already" Bett and Olivia waited.

"Tell him he propositioned you!" She meant Olivia.

"And you heard him, like I was the one caught in the Library and you were watching from the stair."

A splinter of competitive anger almost derailed Ada, *it wasn't about you!* But she got a grip, looking down the road at the mansion, barn, cars, Stan wandering around with tools.

Olivia watched her face change. … "and that Valerie, she's totally sus, tries to get in tight … but Mom … why did we let her in! She's like his accomplice."

"Creeper accomplice.

"Finds women, girls for him…"

"We have to-do this he's like a serial killer."

"Bodies buried all over Maine."

"New Hampshire! With heads missing!"

Sure it was Ted Bundy reincarnate about to pop in at any moment, with some sympathetic line, like he needed help with something and helping him was the last thing they did.

The girls returned to the mansion to warn the others.

By the time they saw Dan he was at the kitchen table, napkin tucked in chin, enjoying leftover buffet, Anne serving him tea, volunteers loading a restaurant style portable dishwasher, others covering dishes ... it was a peaceful domestic scene of clattering harmony that quelled anxiety ... like nothing bad could happen as long as Dad was fed and Mom was beautiful.

"Valerie had to go home," a volunteer was at the door with the twins. The girls looked at each other.

"Oh can you find them something from the buffet? Plates are still out there," Anne delegated, not comprehending or feeling the change in atmosphere yet.

"Sure," she left, twins following.

"Have you eaten yet?" Anne addressed the girls. But they were too excited. Anne saw this, looking into each of their faces, Ada's fair skin and huge green eyes, her daughter's porcelain features and Bett's rosy tan, seemed to allege some unspoken anxiety so she put work aside and followed them into the butler's pantry.

"What's wrong?"

"He propositioned Ada!" Bett and Olivia blurted together.

"Who?"

"The Creeper! Sergeant Major"

"Wanted her to meet him behind the barn! We went out there and hid in the tack room, he couldn't see us but we could see him. But he meant Valerie …what's she doing with him! What's she doing here? I mean she's … she's always with the twins… what if she took them."

Some instinct deep buried woke in Anne. They wanted her strength, her calm, her slow deconstruction of their problems instead she swooned, almost collapsed, had to clutch the counter. Ada caught her. "What happened to you!"

"Mom! Big yikes!" Olivia's voice rose.

"Shush!" Anne motioned her head to the dining-room door just as it opened and the boys paraded through, like miniature men, proudly balancing their own plates. The volunteer smiled, made clucking noises.

They waited till it was safe and spoke in loud whispers; "Mom what if something happened to them! What if Valerie took them and we never saw them again."

"Valerie would never harm anybody."

"She was with the Sergeant Major." The girls stared at Anne. *She wasn't defending the boys!*

"Mom he did something to you… he did something and you're under his spell!"

"It's not that … let's not get ahead of ourselves." *how can I tell them … they're babies.* "Nothing happened."

"Nothing happened? You were dancing with him … drove us home, went back! Mom!"

Female power, sisterhood of understanding gave her strength and she softly went on… "I don't know what happened, it may be, he took DNA for one of those ancestry studies, …I'm 100% French Canadian … and he kept calling me good breeding stock," she burst into giggles looking at their expressions.

"Why are you laughing … it's not funny!"

"I'm not laughing … it's just so … to be a good business lady one has to hob-knob with crooks," more giggles.

"Mom! What are you talking about!"

"The dark side … the abyss," she sighed, finally admitting what she felt along, *he's one evil dude.*

"How can we stop him if you won't tell us."

"I'm … I can't remember."

"Try."

"But he drugged me … drugged Leah. She was supposed to follow me and she can't remember a thing. Your poor Mom was so panicked. And couldn't give any information, evidence … she's still having PTSD flashes… I'm so sorry, It was all my fault, thought I had control, like I do here, and I do love you all …and wanted to bury it… forget, was afraid Leah would've a nervous break-down…. I had to get on with my life. I have no evidence … it wasn't anything. I wanted the whole thing to pass. Then he shows up here again. That's the fourth time; the Christmas Party, Pandemic forms, the Base tour, and now couples group…"

"Dance class, Mom! You forgot already."

"Dance class," Anne repeated, forehead struck with pain.

"Sounds like a stalker, like he's stalking you," Ada became circumspect, *stalking me...*

"Mom he's a stalker! Mom you have to tell Dad … We have facts."

"For real," said Bett.

"Dad will know what to-do."

"We've got the receipts."

"He came to one of our rehearsals, in the ballroom" Ada began… "you remember?" She gazed down at Anne where she sat on a small window seat under the butler's pantry window.

Anne nodded.

"You let my theater group practice on the ballroom stage. He came to a performance at the old Firehouse, kind of appeared … I mean he's not your basic visitor, like a husband or someone who has an interest in acting. It was weird to have someone with so much clout just show up. But then he liked the performance … the skits …fist-pumped, clapped. Then he asked about where we rehearsed, like he already knew it was here." Ada paused, "So he came, but he was ok, adulted around with the old people, danced with a couple women. I didn't tell anyone about that, he was here and gone and only stayed about forty minutes, maybe an hour.… and only once… and ghosted … like he knew I didn't like … him.

"It didn't seem important and augh … the women were flattered by his attention, you know…cause I didn't go to dance class … didn't see him like you … not in the same way."

"Mom, he was in the Ballroom! Checked in here too!"

"Yeah… strange him showing up here … but I thought it was okayed,"

Anne bowed her head.

"But how did he get here? It's so extra," Olivia said.

"I know it was like he CGI'd."

"You know when the military's around," Anne said softly.

"Yeah convoys and top guys roll in Escalades."

"Nothing that extra here."

"Changed into a bat and flew down the chimney!" Bett giggled.

"He may of gotten a ride with someone from the group or, I don't know." Ada thought for a moment, "Before Stan built his house, people used to park at the old granary and that's not that far. So he comes in, looks around, wearing a facemask … he wasn't in uniform like couples group, but I knew who he was, he seemed alright, wasn't shy at all, walked up to me asked if he could observe. Then we had the dance sequence he asked me to dance." Ada looked down with confusion and regret … "but I didn't dance with him, honestly Mrs. Steven's I'd of put him 'on read' long ago, social distanced to the max … but he's a good dancer and I wanted too but he's … anyway I … was going to, he bowed you know … I didn't like his hands, they should be quarantined. But the women were lining up, so I said, 'they're waiting,' and he got the message and actually helped teach … you know the old extras were swooning, hypnotized."

Ads's voice was soothing … everything was ok. It's all talk and talk's good, dancing, swooning, hypnotized is good … Anne closed her eyes and went momentarily to her garden. Planned from the beginning of January on through the shutdown she bought seeds, read journals… dreamed and it was like a dream, time going by, sun giving life, growing things. She kept purslane from taking over, *Man-spreader!* Talked to veggies… "I made space for you to be yourselves…" Calling them by name; "cutie cucumbers … lettuce be lovers" and they spoke back, *'wait till after the rain…' we'll be ready for the table then'*. Their taste a thrill; sharing, healing, like thoughts of a perfect growing season, bathed in green, mind absorbing, learning new love. ... the bottom dropped out, she dove into darkness, dream people beckoned, almost crossed over ... her eyes opened, the girls staring at her, "oh right, that," she played absent mindedly with her hair, "Humm maybe we should just skip it."

"I'll tell Dad myself." Her daughter's voice popped up like weeds in her back yard except Olivia wasn't to be yanked out.

"No I'll do it." Anne's normal excitement missing, she was drained, defeated, *I've lost my head,* in the faint light of the butler's pantry, holding her own hands in submission. They couldn't possibly know what she was going through, how much she missed him. Dance music in her head, ear parasite sucking her life forever. The room was a blur, they moved so fast, lightly holding his shoulder, arm barely touching her waist, a light caress. She told him of so many things, personal and important, giving life examples to guide him, while he expertly glided her across the floor. He loved playing with her and she loved it too, wings on her feet, hope in her heart... All the responsibility, the boys she couldn't find joy in, her husband holding her captive ... the volunteers demanding attention and Olivia, Daddy's girl, believed in Dan, loved him more, she was certain. She was an accessory to him and a servant to her and had no mother's love for the boys. *There is no such thing as true love,* she kept hoping to find, in the next new person, that spark ... fire. How she wanted to leave with the Sergeant; travel ... yes! ... See the world, hoping he'd suggest it, that one day he'd confess his love and beg her to leave with him, buy her bobbles, make bold promises … it had to be all or nothing… now she knew it was pure fantasy, a goose egg … she wasn't anything… to him.

"We'll come with you." Ada didn't believe Anne would say anything … especially something upsetting to Dan.

"We got to stop the Creeper… Mom! What if he's a serial rapist … I bet he's a total rapist and then he kills them. Oh Mom … like … you were ready to chill with him … he might of killed my Mom!"

"No … you don't understand… it was my fault. And I was never in that perilous a situation …was … in control… like here but, … and it wasn't only me but Nigel, Leah and Stan as back up."

"You had them as back-up! Mom!"

"I was the only one who knew him well enough to-do it and so naturally we eventually agreed it had to be me. Nigel bought a voice recorder, like a thumb drive … only…"

"OMG, Mom"

"…with a camera. Stan was lost, you remember? That night last Fall he stumbled upon kids and young women in cots in a dorm like situation at the woman's prison. And then at the Christmas party Nigel overheard the Sergeant … you know the rest … but if your Dad knows about me and the Sergeant, that I went out with him … even if it was only coffee in the daytime at The Pizza Place … It would just kill him."

"Oh yeah great, my Mom, head of Lane School, playing detective with the History teacher and handyman, Big yikes, Mom"

"Fantasy football," Bett giggled.

"This is serious," Ada waited for Anne's ok.

"Mom we have to tell Dad, you tried but failed, totally bombed, It was like your mission,… now it can be our's … Mission Creeper."

"Creeper Stomper," Bett giggled.

"I don't know… I,"

"Mom you don't have to come with us. We'll do it. It can be about Ada … say he tried to-do something to her and that he tried to-do something to me." Olivia wanted justice.

"Ok, but you have to sound matter of fact, no emotional outbursts, if your Dad sees tears he'll kill him. I'm serious … Your Dad will kill the Sergeant Major…. Oh my dears," she reached for them in a general hug, "I'll be in the kitchen, your Dad's in his office… good-luck but please nothing about me….We've got to get back … they'll be wondering what we're up to."

Anne wandered towards the kitchen in state of non-feeling. It was highly personal stuff, best kept private, she moaned, buried her head in her hands … *stripped of decency and dignity in front of children* … her only confidante was Dan. Now the closeness was gone and she had no-one, … *Olivia's overbearing … the volunteers don't know me …* Then she remembered prayer, *Dear God protect me from what I want...*

Dan felt the roar of his F-250's eight cylinders, racing through town, slowing to not appear homicidal. No person on earth deserved it more ... *Hey Battle Rattle, Bob Mason... Got something for ya!* But he couldn't walk right up and shoot him, with the wife present. Couple's therapy was very popular. Shutdown allowing, more signed up, virus testing, Fall was looking good, who knows ...it may extend it into winter. What's the worst that could happen? Host Shoots Customer ...

He'd gotten truth out of the girls after promising to simply call the police, he ushered them out and went to his gun-safe. Oil smell filled his head with power enough to kill a man. All he could see was his wife violated by that arrogant prick. He chose a handgun, perfectly weighted, tossed and caught it, tried the clip, grabbed another and came apart, tears falling on loaded slugs, wiping his face on anything, he couldn't go on ...then into his pocket. He gently closed and locked the safe, like the last good thing he'd do on earth ... targeted the grandfather clock. *I'm done.*

Everyone left for the Lake but the residue of adults, sweat, perfume, aftershave, and not the familiar scent of children, hung in the hallway lowering his mind. He was certain, had the means ... But a longing to see her one more time had him peeking in the kitchen door. The volunteers looked up, questioning, instinctively avoiding him… "Where's my wife?"

"Upstairs."

Back through the butlers pantry he went and stood at the bottom of the main stair. She was in their bedroom, felt her there, *my ground zero,* … came into his life after losing a hundred pounds he wanted a hundred women then saw only her … nothing darkened his heart, until now.

Gazing up the stair, their bedroom door shut, he sensed her sleeping head on a pillow, didn't want to wake her, didn't want her to know what he knew, *she'd try and stop me.* Then without thinking, his feet started to climb, tiptoeing to their door.

He heard sobbing, unmistakable, "Anne you ok?" The door was locked. "Anne let me in," rattling the knob, "Anne…"

"I - I can't … I need to be alone. I, I'm sorry Dan, please…"

He felt the gun, rage blinded, pointed it at the knob, then paused. It was one of those replacement knobs he paid $50. bucks for… he turned and tiptoed back, no one saw him leave.

But she's responsible. There was something going on and not like the girls said. Sky, road, trees …signs magnified, coming at him. I'm on the money on this! Dance class over and she wasn't last to know.

They'll take me down, take all my money, destroy my life … it's all her fault … I've tried … every day I think of ways to help her with her problem ... she'll never change! Tears formed ... she's driving me to-do this ...

Lusting after violence, getting the drop on him... the men's room, following him in, or a group hike, wait and separate him out, beat him to death with a branch ... push a dead tree on him or off a cliff ...a hole in the middle of the forehead, surprised look on his face.

On the familiar winding road, shadows played, blood drained from his head, *what am I doing.* It was ridiculous... he needed a brick wall, love's comforting spirit ... a happy-ever-after at the mansion, where everyone came to him.

Snorting like a mule, long mental run, head un-swelling... *Every man for himself.* It was the atmosphere of the times. Authority stood down, watched business burn to the ground, whole communities wiped to ashes. He had to do his part and stop the madness. *I'm an ordinary law abiding, tax paying citizen, jumping through all their hoops and this is what they hand me?*

A government stalking horse ... targeting me... good guy... family man. ... Tears fell ... crazy vibrations interrupted by flashes of reality... the running joke at work about his wife ... invisible woman not allowed out ... the nagging truth ...

They want me to commit murder over that? And she's none the worse! He saw the guys at work shaking their heads.., *Dan, smart- guy, top-notch ... fell in a trap* ...And the mill making bank right now. He was over due.

A fatter paycheck and Anne's excited hug of approval, *I'm the one that made it happen,* ... *Their future falling into place.*

The girls trusting faces, standing in his office, Oilvia, Bette and Ada, all looking at him, he had to do right.

Ada suggested starting rumors, elderly thespians on board, "their anagnorisis moment," she said. Plastering light poles with the SGM's face ... DO YOU KNOW THE RAPIST??.... She laughed, "What could they do ... arrest my old people?"

How upset they'd be and he couldn't calm them, ... let alone protect them, his virgins ... approve of their boyfriends... husbands ... locked up somewhere, awaiting trial ... Anne managing on her own, hiring men ... divorcing him. *Would she?* And what about everyone else he desired to protect, shepherd through life... his big guy ambitions for the Blaine House, *I've got the women.* Life in Augusta surrounded by female aids ... came towards him once he dropped ... the gun, the G-19 ... he had to get it out of reach.

A state cop appeared behind him, way quicker than the Foster norm. He was speeding, Cop on his tail, tagging him in, lurched, screeched around lights and sirens, just as an ambulance came wailing the other way, forcing the trooper back behind. Both pulled over, rolling rough, straddling the shoulder, sensing the world had collapsed in an instant, the Statey drove close, paused, nodded... sped off.

Dan slowed to give him space, pulled the G-19 from his pocket, hid it in his glove compartment, ruffling it under the usual litter; manual, ins. forms ... registrations, gas receipts ...

himself … that low key patient guy people turned to, *my problems don't make anything better…*

Pulling into the Lake's parking lot, it appeared evil was on lock-down, Foster's three squad cars, state police, municipal fire and forest ranger trucks swarmed. His couples huddled on the side, Dan arrived to help.

Epilogue

Valerie stood by the window of her Washington apartment. It was three weeks to the day that she'd fulfilled her mission and left Maine for DC.

First it was surveillance, arriving at Foster Lake in February with her nephew, before the pandemic was news, his doctor parents panicked and parked their five year old with Aunty in the safe haven of Foster Lake, Piscataquis county Maine. They'd arranged a position for her to volunteer at the donkey rescue mission, enrolled the kid in preschool there.

She was supposed to teach a class in marksmanship at the new base, but put it off indefinitely … responding to the Sergeant Majors pleas with 'soon'. She had more important things to-do. Living two thirds of her day at the Mansion, in the quiet atmosphere of love and devotion, a pleasure dome of simple family life … she'd never been happier or more secure.

At only twenty-.one she was, (unofficially), top markswoman in the Army. She toyed with her award pin, thought of her commanding officers pleased expression, in the dark room with only aids for witnesses. He saluted, shook her hand, the aids likewise with deep admiration ... a clean head shot, bolt from the blue, 400 yards. She'd scaled a 'decommissioned' wind tower, the stationary blades kept her in shadow... but now she was broken.

The full extent and flexibility of her mission was confidential only to herself, one handler in Bangor and commanding officer who eyed her with new respect. The thing had gotten out of hand, the SGM under global influence, too much outside intelligence.

There was hesitation over the obviousness, it would look like a hit, but form the rife-range, the cover-story was a discharge, stray bullet, someone fooling around, no corroborating evidence ... leave it at that. Close file, cremate, console the widow with a box of ashes, nice pension, allow spasms of grief and relief ... SGM Blabbermouth deleted. An MP lab assistant dimed him out, digitally enhanced audio, the wife corroborating. They were horrified. All that grant money gone to waste.

When the word came to take him out ... *operation lovebird*... she did the set up. SGM thought she was arranging a hit on his wife and reluctantly gave trajectories, preferring some other way.

They told the wife he was being reassigned; told the SGM his wife was a critical security risk. Separately sworn to secrecy, the Dempseys resigned themselves to governmental fate. They were to sit on a park bench, using a picnic table as angle reference, Valerie couldn't miss.

Valerie promised the wife no violence, she might react by holding him, making a second shot impossible, (actually she ran away.)

But now she was wounded, shot through the heart. *I will always love that woman there's no one on earth like her... so womanly... like a goddess..* She saw Anne's face and wanted to confess her devotion and knew Anne would take it in stride, love her back, show sympathy make more time for her ... but it never happened. Her unrequited love was pure... she didn't expect anything but to be near ... help her and receive acknowledgement of her work... she'd hung on Anne's every word, nod, smile. *To spend the rest of my life with her.* She sobbed. Then from her tiny cluttered room, she felt love leave her heart, bounce off capital dome and down to Anne in far off Maine.

It was like living a fairy tale, a delicious castle, cute kids, beautiful princess, glamorous King and Queen. She had to close cover and be strong.

She was soon off on another mission. This time Los Alamos. In a zippered compartment in the bottom of her bag she discovered jewelry. Held it up to the window, Anne's diamonds, lots of them. She clutched them to her heart ... WHY OH WHY? *Her parting gift? Anne my Anne, wanted me to have them ... diamonds are forever.*

IN LIFE THE Sergeant Major thought of himself as a brilliant social engineer, ahead of his time but after arranging his own dispatch, he was thought of very little. He had no children and his wife married her lover a year later. That's what happens to people who think they're number one and it turns out not to be. However he did take to his grave the reason why Foster Lake at three hundred-fifty feet deep is warm. Meanwhile in global oceans, reports came of carrier hulls disintegrating, likewise submarines full of holes like something was eating them.

A PERSON REMBEMBERED and never fully recovered. *Part of me died with him ...* No one suspected the reason for sorrow and she learned to live with it. *Without the hurt, I'm not myself...* expanding into all things, *life is supposed to be painful ... with no girl, no Valerie to help me.* Dan was tickled to have both the SGM and Valerie gone, didn't enquire as to what, where and how afraid truth would cause a reappearance of Valerie. *Don't look a gift horse in the mouth.*

He liked the new solemn Anne, *just like the woman I married!* Their wedding day three months after her parents died. So he started taking her out, enjoyed the tears, thought they were for him and bought her things.

Chains of sorrow bound her for three years until God unlocked her heart and love flowed once again.. She never told anyone about her feelings or about the missing diamonds and Leah didn't notice either.

THE GIRLS LOOKED at each other in amazement. The two people they wanted gone; suddenly were. Olivia and Bett thought they had special powers. If they wished for something strong enough it would happen. So they wished and prayed for all autistic kids to heal.

Ada thought the death of the SGM and the sudden departure of Valerie were connected, but how, she wasn't sure. Theator group ended with the summer and the Pandemic closed Carlisle Academy to everything except on-line learning. She started helping out at The Lane School, took over Valerie's position, loved having two little boys to influence again.

NIGLE SAT IN BED not sure of anything, throat burning, head throbbing, body aching he lay back down... He wasn't old, despondent, given up on life, projecting pain on unsuspecting Earth, NO! ... he only wanted to let go and had beautiful dream.

He was handed a huge metal bowl full of molten gold. Beautiful music came from within, wrapping the air in new arrangements, classical instruments only finer, *This is how music is made ... it all comes out of this bowl..* In a state of bliss he prayed, "Dear God thank-you for my beautiful children, devoted wife … Lane School … my life on earth is better than ever imagined, hoped for … it's just that I'd rather stay with you!

Out of heavenly blue a finger pointed downwards, "You need to finish the job" then hand, finger, and emotion disappeared. Set free from edict, clouds became music … resting in peace, not caring if he woke. *I do hope they still support windows 7 in heaven.*

STAN PULLED the clutch on the dozer piling fill up the side of an already substantial berm. The dozer was his, he'd moved out of Nigel's garage into his own repair shop, under the disused rail bed, behind the old granary, far away from the MacPhee boys and anxiety over injury. *Loosin' un baoy as affof.*

Back and forth he rumbled, his twelve years of loyal membership to the range was reason enough. *I done ba'lave id* They put two and two together and swarmed his favorite haunt. *Day done naw wad dare dankin'. Id warn't na stray bullad.* Stan knew better than question them but he also wanted to make sure they'd never think it again. They wanted twenty feet they'd get twenty feet.

An day nava' took a look a' Val'laa'ie. Day din wander why sha laf.

Valerie was suddenly gone that same Saturday their world fell down. A note taped to the Steven's frig. read; "I'm sorry to leave, my Mother has taken ill and I have to go. Please tell the boys bye for me," *Valerie*

Papercuts

He walked down the long corridor, shelving rose on either side, not distracted by the lift back-up beep, whir of warehouse life, shadowless lighting. He was in perfect shape, as expected for a guy in his early twenties, everything worked, he could hold pee for 4 hours, there's a great advantage to that. He hadn't eaten much breakfast, apartment-mate sleeping, he desired efficiency and that meant no cooking. He'd grabbed a nutri-bar, provided by work, tailor made to his needs, perfect combination of fish & coconut oils, gluten-free grains, just sweet enough and took the electric tram over, wistfully watching the green blur of trees happily anticipating a long awaited break, shop-made camping trip. They used to swipe badges, now their helmets IDed them, visor flipping down, telling him where to go. Along the way he was reassured by the play list, coming up as he passed, *his favorite animal, the horse in a sunny field pulling grass. Then came an image of his grandmother wishing him a good morning,* "Good morning, Wesley dear," *no one else could see her, it was that precise. Other workers had exchanges with their own relatives, not cyborgs or real, but imaged algorithms, relatives brought to life, immortal spirits. Central has it down... this compassionate mental support thing.*

Overdue at the packing train, he was there to watch key components and load when needed, another guy was attending already. Images played on his visor along with conversation hints. He found this very helpful as he was naturally a quiet guy. *Central is turning me into the man I want to be*. But sometimes the hints were passé, no one goes to games anymore, it's more entertaining here, games are 'fleshy', *we're cerebral*, although he sometimes watched old video to remember his Dad, the smell of hotdogs, that no one in their right mind ate now.

"Ola, Wesley," he returned a friendly wave, visor produced one-eyed smile, "get your snow machine back?"

"Not yet." They'd taken his away a month previous for service.

"Seasons over anyway."

"Yup."

"Won't be doin' much ridin' now."

"Unless we get a UCS." (UCS; uncontrolled storm)

"Can't predict," Wesley had run out of small talk, when his visor prompted him, *Ask how his wife's doing …* along with an image of her in hospital. "How's your wife"… awh, the name 'Janet' flashed, "Janet?"

"Better, got a live update just a minute ago, specs looking good."

"Yeah, well that's good news." Wesley tried sounding enthused.

"It's been a tough week but we finally rounded the corner, she's off the ventilator and they're talking rehab."

"What was the matter?" Wesley's visor was blank of info, but he didn't feel abandoned, there's a message in silence.

"Flesh eating bacteria. It started with a pimple then she …"

"Yeah," Wesley winced looking for a way out he desperately eyed his visor, the last thing he wanted to hear was fingers dropping off.

"Wesley Herd, wanted in receiving, Wesley…" Saved by Central yet again. Classic cloud rescue.

"Scuse me," Wesley nodded politely. His helmet was upgraded last April. He wasn't supposed to let co-workers know. The improvements came gradually, memory prompts, mechanical answers, he was enhanced, supported, directed, had the edge and he loved it.

At Receiving he got that much needed breath of fresh air, his visor told of extremely low emission levels, he believed in a future of zero, next year was 2031, *about time.*

Instead of actually reporting to a new space, he veered to the left, the small door meeting room, ducking to enter, it immediately covered up with shelving. Inside was a different mode, these people were his colleagues, on the same wave length.

"Wesley, you came without problem," the men smiled, used to his efficiency but not taking it for granted … things change. "You know we put you in charge of the camping trip up at the companies RV park, we've decided on late June, Wake Mountain, trails will be good that time of year, lake water warm. We expect you to manage all aspects for a group of say Eighteen to twent co-workers, for three days two nights of semi-wilderness adventure. You'll notice many on the list aren't in tip-top shape, not feeling well, depressed and this will come as a welcome break, short recreation, time to talk it out, share and feel safe. Once we have your input everything will be waiting, all food, equipment, transport; everything … prepackaged, ready for use, just add water and stir … no, just kidding. Here's the list of names, you're already familiar with most.

Wesley silently read the company's tablet, it synced with his visor, even so he didn't exactly remember, details escaped him, but when his eyebrows became question marks his upgraded visor did. "You think Arbitame can handle it … he's 56 and was down with", *pneumonia* said his visor, pneumonia."

"Possibly," The man said, "but he's an avid outdoors guy and will be an asset." They watched Wesley's face flush with pleasure, he'd found the name.

Sandra's coming, oh man oh thank-you, he'd wanted to meet her for a long time but the right opportunity hadn't come up, he wasn't a real forward guy, already had a girlfriend … He smiled and they smiled back.

Sandra belonged to them, a long standing part of the team but Wesley didn't know that and they knew he didn't know, they also knew he was looking for someone new, wasn't in a totally committed relationship and thought her 'girlfriend' material. They'd kept tabs on him for a long time, watching him watch her. He had an interesting quality of self-reliance, intelligence and distance, *a lot of guys his age don't like working on their own.*

"You'll have your own RV of course, with kitchen, map and material storage. Married couples will share and the rest will go into single sized pods."

Love in the storage room he forgot himself for a moment, gazed wistfully into nothing.

"Make personal contact with each individual, you'll find an itemized personal list, you'll notice they're expected to bring an item for the pot, 'Stone Soup' is always a high point. The food item is supposed to represent some bad behavior or feeling they want to shed."

Wesley overlooked the weirdness ... *trying a bit too hard...* and focused on Sandra, she'd been on his radar since he was a new hire ... a little over a year. She appeared unattached and she was beautiful, really stunning body and friendly helpful smile.

"Mr. Hurd,...oh Wesley."

"Stone Soup, sounds medieval."

"Medieval, ha excellent observation! Medieval, we love it," Don't we?" The other four men nod in agreement. "Thank-you for your in-put on the attendees ahead of time, we look forward to your findings."

"Sure no problem, are we to meet again ... here?"

"Won't be necessary, just interview within 5 miles of the shop, G-6 will pick it up."

Under the visor his head left the meeting room with body attached. Calming he went over the list, did a mentally enhanced check list as to unit location, the 'shop' was three square miles! He considered taking a PFD, (personal floor device) but he was actually quicker, limbs longing for automation, human machine craving it.

He completed the task, enjoying how it mirrored psychology courses ... plus he was an EMT for a year, leaving it for mechanics, nana technology, *machines make it happen!*

The men in the room, CERTS, (short for Certified Electronic Technicians) were correct, all the people on the list needed a break. He heard, "My dog died last Tuesday; My daughter moved out of state; I've got arthritis; This job sucks; Life's not what it used to be and other sounds of depression, auditable despair; sighs, groans, shuffling gait, heads down ... the shop was that compassionate, lifting the low down, alleviating human suffering. All but Sandra, her eagerness knocked him off his feet, but he wasn't eighteen ... could pull himself together and wait, *there's danger in them there arms!*

THE SHOP HAD it's own fleet of service busses and gave him a good one. He stood tall, checking every person, the only two under fifty were Sandra and another young woman. They were friends requested a double pod, when they found out they'd be in singles but said they didn't care either way, "we're accommodating," giggling the whole way up, as single young women do, in tight shorts and bulky sweatshirts hiding curves, *this is going to be interesting.*

"Make sure you get their measurements." the tablet said.

Wesley read it several times before comprehending. "What measurements?"

"For new uniforms, complete extensive measurements are necessary. You'll find instructions in your RV."

The place was remote but not terrifying. Tall ancient black and white spruce, pine and hemlock darkened the ground, as the bus drove conversations slowed to mummers of exclamation, the canopy opened, lake appeared and a large flat area. In a semi-circle were the pods, cute bubbles with plexi-glass tops and fiberglass sides, the RV's were larger of course, his stood at the end with a wooden deck surrounding giving off an air of permanence and authority, *image is everything*.

With a rush of air-conditioned energy, heat and humidity was about to destroy, they attempted to unload cargo. "Golf carts over there." The driver pointed. So Wesley brought it over and left to access his RV. It turned out he didn't need to, all info; diagram of the park, area amenities were already pictured on his tablet. He allowed himself a brief look in then closed the door and locked it.

He returned to find the golf cart empty and sleeping arrangements already assigned. He walked around the park looking in pods hearing happy exclamations at the interiors, drawers opened, clothing hung … each pod had a chair and sink… small pods on each end held bathroom facilities, married couple's and to their delight the two girls, had tiny RVs with their own showers.

The Driver turned the bus around and left, Wesley watched it leave with dismay, his escape route gone in a cloud of dust. Sandra took his arm and squeezed, "They always leave us here, like we're kids about to be homesick, running after, 'I wanna go home' but you're not homesick are you Wesley?"

"I … I"

She abruptly dropped his arm and ran to the middle of the Pods, shrieking "Who wants to go swimming?"

The lake was calm and beaconing, air; hot and humid after the air-conditioned bus ride had them longing to jump in. Wesley excused himself to the old people, who'd turned to Sandra for direction anyway and returned to his trailer. He'd brought Speedos, but decided on trunks … his tablet flashed; 'pick up the tablet on the counter,' it commanded. He found it and the first tablet went dead but not before emitting a tiny electrical charge, stinging his hand enough so he almost dropped it on the floor.

"Thanks a lot," Wesley got no response while the second tab. came alive. On it he saw the girls undressing, he looked around his RV for spy cams certain he was being watched too but didn't want to miss it, transfixed, everything played out, they poured their bodies into relatively modest 1-piece's, brushed hair, ate snacks, checked nails, did teeth. They exited their RV as he did, towel over his shoulder, new tab that was giving directions as he walked. He was ordered to have each person stand in their bathing suits and be photographed. "Explain to them it's for their new uniforms," the tab said.

"It's for your new uniforms." He had them stand so their backdrop was blue lake water, the women giggled, the men struck poses, he captured all 20. *The shop is a caring place! But wow some of them are in tough shape.* Instead of gawking he checked the images, front and back he didn't have to key in names, the tab knew. *Jeeze, they need a lot of help, all of them.* Four were morbidly obese. One man covered in skin tags, a woman had horrible varicose veins, a younger one with a vacant stare. He ran through them pretty quick until he came to Sandra and friend. *Oh man.*

"Like my picture?..." she said in his ear, smelling of sun block.

"Sure," he looked away, *not now girl*, then got up, keeping his distance… "Going for a swim?" he asked coldly.

"We'll catch some rays first," she did a playful walk back to her friend and lay on her towel, moving provocatively, turning to watch him.

He found his sunglasses, attached grippers, made for the waves, feeling the water, the soothing effect on his libido, the gentle sounds of old people venturing in then laughing, splashing, *Just what they needed.* The shop a distant second, reality now was nature, sun, fun … summer. he swam towards the center, turned on his back, eyeing the beach between his feet ... *Cripes I hope they don't expect me to life-guard!* Breast-stroked back just-in-case.

He sat for a moment on the sand, feet in the water, sun on his back, "You might want this," Sandra held the tab in front of his face, legs touching his back.

"What are you doing with that? You aren't supposed to touch it!" Voice elevated, it was the last thing he wanted to have happen.

"Sorry, don't be a grouch, it's just that it was beeping while you were out," she said not the least bit concerned with his temper.

"What?"

"Over there on your blanket. Beep, beep, beep."

"Alright in the future, leave it alone ... it's a security minded outfit ...we work for."

"Sure," showed her tongue, pulled at her suit and went tail wagging, sat back whispering to her friend. He retrieved his towel and left for the picnic table, he'd gain space and could still play lifeguard.

"Time to get dinner underway, you'll find everything in the RV." the tab texted "Have the girls help, that's what their there for. They've done it before." *Done what befor?* The tab went blank. He climbed the steps, shut the door and peaked out a window, the girls were in the water. *Good.* Changed out of his wet suit, got into long pants, *more authority*, and a blue tee-shirt, he wore a belt, sandals, lightly groomed.

Still he had a problem and opened the storage containers looking for clues. *Looks like Mac&cheese for dinner .... where is everything.* He went to the tab and it flashed the last message, at the same time there was a knock on his door. "Hi Wesley, we're going back to change and will be right over, don't worry bout a thing" they left before he had a chance to respond.

The girls were great, found every-damn-thing for the barbeque, knew where seat cushions, utensils, the grill, everything was. Found the freezer, masquerading as a bench, it ran on LNG, held several whole meals and then some.

He was ready to play chef but the girls tasked a big fat man, who was actually better at it, having multiple experiences, he flipped, joked and carried the day, giving Wesley space to observe the crowd, take in the scene, make mental notes, that corresponded with his visor, he was in sync.

Grilled entrees laid out on the picnic table in a civilized buffet, the girls made little signs, proclaiming vegetarian and non, gluten, salt or sugar free, there were several salads, organic grilled squash, potatoes, peppers, onions and tomatoes, it smelled heavenly. The old people were happy, reminded him of his Dad, before he passed, his image waved from the visor, appearing in good form, rosy red cheeks, full of it.

Piles of nutrition bars in separate bowls were for desert, with lists of names, so they wouldn't accidentally eat the wrong one. Wesley's appetite left him, watching the old people eat turned his stomach, he grabbed a half dozen bars, pocketing some for later, and moved away, claiming a rock near the water, he unpackaged dinner, watching sun and waves.

"That all you're havin'? Hey move over," It was Sandra, plate piled high, large drink in one hand, he'd forgotten to get one for himself, "You need a drink? Want me to get you one…" She'd put down her plate, smells from it filled his head, he was missing out, "grape or cranberry?"

"You choose," he smiled and she acted affected by it.

"Back in a flash," She returned along with her friend and he found himself sighing with relief. But there she was, way too close, he couldn't move away, her friend was on the other side.

"Oh I'm sooo hungry, you don't mind if I eat up,"

"Sandra doesn't do small talk," her friend said. "Sandra's a PHD."

"Yeah right. .. a PHD in food," She devoured her plate, veggie burger guts spilling out, she ate with her hands then ran to the lake to wash, washed her face, shook the droplets off,. "Don't tell the EPA," giggling like nature's child. "I love these breaks, don't you?"

"Never been on one," Wesley carefully ate the nutrition bar.

"Don't worry, I'll show you how it's done," she leaned into to him rubbing his thigh, looked into his face opened her mouth.

"Sandra stop it! Don't tease the poor man, come on we got clean-up to-do."

"Catch you later," They leapt away.

Happiness filled a magic balloon in the blue hours, sun slowly setting behind Wake Mountain, silhouettes of birds. Dinner completed, the chef fired up the LNG faux wood fire and the old people drew chairs around. The girls piled all the mess into a plastic bin and left for his RV he followed but Sandra pushed him away, handing him his tablet he'd accidentally left on the rocks, "This is girl's work," she said. "They might want to sing something," she was gone, the door locked.

The tab. came to life with songs, Waltzing Matilda, I'm Henry the eighth, Long Black Veil. Not even oldies but nearly deadies, turning the place into a macabre karaoke bar. Not bad for no alcohol. No one drinks anymore. Wesley never drank, he vaped briefly 'till his Mom put a stop to it. But he always had a girl friend… he had one now …it's just that the shop didn't like her …didn't say so in so many words … but they didn't like her, she had no post-secondary training, worked in restaurants was thinking of going to nursing school, but didn't have the brains to get a loan, so she was stuck but he didn't have to be. *What was Sandra all about, who was she … how much money did she make.* His pay check was getting fatter and he expected the same out of a woman but… *I don't effin care…* she was in his mind. She was so damn healthy, she had it all …. but he didn't want to be played with.

He woke with the sun, a rooster crowed in his ear, audio hallucination from when he stayed on his great-grandfather's farm in Kansas, 20 years ago. Then he remembered where he was, the RV came into focus, the piles of stuff, major cleanup was in his future, probably that was all there was. Last night he tried to kiss Sandra but she pushed him away. Now he knew he was a good-looking guy, a favorite at the shop ... She played on him all night, bumping into him, hanging off him, her friend wasn't bad looking either, gave him a brief shoulder massage, but switch horses in the middle of a stream? ... nah ... he wasn't that desperate, he had a girl friend... Oh yeah he was in charge here, responsible for those bumbling old people, better get going.

He showered shaved groomed, got dressed grabbed the tab, ... 'Expect the girls to get breakfast in a quarter hour.' The screen cleared then he witnessed Sandra in the shower, couldn't look away, she was soaping all over, looked right at the camera, winked. then the screen went blank.

'Why play with me...' he texted.

'No play ... just a peek'

'A peek?'

'More to follow'

'More of what?' Wesley tingled all over but the screen wouldn't replay ... the girls at his door, he let them in.

A hike was planned for rock-pile spring. It was a strange anomaly, a pile of boulders with water flowing out from a distant aquifer, at a higher elevation hidden behind the earth's curve, it seemed magic, water at the top instead of the bottom. It was a little more than a mile each way, a long hike for the old people but central to their wilderness experience, the shop insisted on it.

It wasn't like leading children; these people were appropriately dressed, carrying water, watching their feet. *They're almost cute ...* especially the women, with simple appreciation, not a whole lot happening in their lives, they gazed adoringly at him, he was the big guy, theirs to steadfastly depended on ... leading them over and back.

The path twisted and turned, beautiful green vistas into the secret woods ended as the forest thinned from lack of soil. Piles of huge rocks they moved around, just challenging enough.

They paused midway, the incline, steep, the girls suggested they lead and he was to take up the rear. There he found the Johnsons, a retired farmer and his wife, they worked loss prevention. The shop let them stay together, and they were extremely effective ... unobtrusive and also quite old, supposed to be temps but became indispensable, reporting areas of weakness ... no one suspected they were behind a lot of stings.

"So what were you into before coming here?" Wesley found people over 65 interesting.

"Well, first I was a boat builder, then got into farming when my parents died and I took over their place." They moved slowly stopping to talk.

"Wood or Glass?"

"You mean boats … glass, composites, also steel pontoons … inflatables, anything there was a market for we did it all."

"You miss it?"

The old man stopped, looked at the sky, "Ya know I did, yes I did, miss the water, launchings, art of pa'fection, we did it right… both'er dangerous, farmin' and boat buildin'. I was a potato farmer, no animals … lot of mechanics same as with the boats, it carried over, those diesel engines," he paused smiling over his old love. "Now it's all new systems advances, components, GPS card' dinates, stuff dreamed of … they got … Always kept a few old tracta's on the farm, we'd dress-em, get 'em ready for fairs, yeah! We had a goodtime those old girls, they'd sit in the shed, peaceful, waitin' for me to start-em-up, then they'd make noise! Now everything's a snarl of chips and wire, rats nests."

"Much harder to work on."

"Yeah, they have the tools and testing, then they just swap out components, charge me $800. bucks. Had a 'ol 1940s Farmall an' a Case"

"You still have it?"

"Nah, arthritis and taxes took the place, we don't have a son, so now it's a 'green space' run by volunteers and refugees, only they don't grow potato they grow little bits of everythin' ... call it 'Future Farm, celebrating community.'" He made a bitter face. "It used to be just me and her, now the place is over run ... a regular anthill."

"But it's OK, we're happy here." his wife's bright little voice piped in. "It was so nice of the shop to take us in. I think the manager at Green Space had something to-do with it. And we're very comfortable, they gave us housing with a garden."

"That's descent of them."

"Ha, didn't know what they were getting, she's smart," he nodded towards his wife, "With her patrollin', watch out! Sees through the BS., got her own onboard GPS." He stood before Wesley; sinewy, long strong arms, circumspect in thought, with his plump wife smiling sweetly, he was the picture of health and intelligence, raw intellect, accumulated from years of clean living ... that gives certain elderly people the edge. "Our kid died in a motorcycle accident we have no grandkids."

Adopt me Wesley almost said. He had only his mother and she lived out of state. That's why finding the right girl, starting a family was important... eventually. "I'm sorry to hear that."

"It was awhile ago..." suddenly he stopped looked around at the trees, "you know there's a lot going on at the shop ... a lot of real sleazy stuff. I report it and nothing happens, nothing is done, except it gets moved to another area, then disappears but you think they stop it? I tell ya, these men have bad habits."

"What?"

"Listen, I can't tell you ... about that stuff ... but they don't give a hoot about you, me or anybody ... it's all a game to them, as long as we're the mouse. If I was young like you I'd get myself lost in a hurry. Just get out. We're in too deep but you're still on the edge." Suddenly he stopped sat on a boulder, "You go on we'll just stay here and rest a bit."

"I can't do that."

"You know nature has answers, stick close to nature and you'll be all right." He coughed. "Did you bring my pills."

"He really needs them, he's got life long asthma." He took a pill from his wife, followed by a swig out of his hydration pack, wiping his mouth with his sleeve, pondering the ground.

"Left over from sanding glass," he corrected, "but ... anyway lets push on, don't worry about the shop, they'll treat you OK a big handsome kid like yourself, it's just when you get old like us you start to feel it."

"You're doing great, and you've done a great job for them ... I'm sure they appreciate you, it's your undercover position, they can't exactly hand you an award at the annual ceremony."

"True ... come along Doris lets get to the top of this thing maybe there's a view."

"Oh dear my feet!" She sat down again and removed her shoe, uncovering a blister.

"Looks bad," because it did, skin already popped, her big toe's second joint totally inflamed. She looked pleadingly at him.

"The girls are carrying first aid, why don't we wait here, they should be down soon enough."

"OK but if you want to go see the spring, we won't keep you." She smiled sweetly ... gazed fondly up at him.

He gave her shoulder a reassuring pat, "Nah that's OK, what's that on your wrist?" She was wearing a silver bracelet with dog heads as charms.

"Oh that's how many Dogs we've had!"

"And she loved every one of them!"

Wesley smiled, he'd never owned a dog, *'poop machines' own one and you become a slave, mornings smelling their stuff... and you're supposed to pick it up!*

"They wouldn't let us bring him, might a spoiled their retreat," he stated sourly looking up the trail... "here they come..." Between boulders they watched a line of heads snaking down. "They'll be here pretty quick now," he adjusted his cap, she patted her hair, brushed her shirt.

They were 'at ease' around me! Wesley was flattered, happy for the old 'applied psychology' course.

Cook was leading. He was probably the youngest of the group, early fiftys with that smooth skin over weight people have, along with a light step and jolly expression he confidently kept everyone going. The girls together took up the rear. The next moment they were on them.

"Wesley, there you are...we waited," The red faced cook had made himself a walking stick.

"What's it like?"

"Worth it, the water's delicious, we all drank, its so pristine here, really unspoiled."

"One sip and you're young again," a wrinkly old guy made a sweep with his arm, the others seemed happy, animated ... they pushed around Wesley. More appeared and Cook stepped aside to let them pass ...thought the better of it, "Hey!" shouting, lets wait here for the nurses."

"Nurses?"

"Sandra and Jess,"

"Nurses, well that's great, we have causality here, this poor lady's toe."

"The group gathered round her ... expressions of sympathy had Wesley pulling back, *lets not over do it... it's a toe blister.*

"What's the problem?" Sandra was beside him, holding his elbow.

"Augh, augh."

"That poor lady has a painful sore on her right foot, Mrs. Johnson on the rock," the cook had presence of mind.

The girls sprung into action, fanny packs opened, first aid kits out, the audience of elderly felt well cared for, it was a group experience. The girls packed up, all evidence of medical help repackaged, zippers pulled, fanny packs buckled on.

"We better get back, stone soup night requires mental preparation and a big pot!" The cook started down the others followed.

"Want to see the spring? I can take you there," Sandra took his hand pulling him uphill.

"I… We …I," Wesley wasn't fully connected with mind or earth.

"That's OK," Jess said, "I can help them down."

"We're in good shape now," Mr. Johnson held a staff the cook cut for his wife.

'My foot feels much better, thank-you both, you've been just wonderful."

"You young people … need to enjoy yourselves," Mr. Johnson put it wisely. The rest left already, cook leading, Jess with the Johnson's slowly taking up the rear. Suddenly it was quiet … they were alone.

He reached for her clumsily but she laughed and sprung away, "you funny guy"

"Come on what's wrong."

"Don't you want to see the spring," she pouted, pulled his arm and ran ahead. He caught up with her and she led him down a side trail, then stopped, turned, "No cameras here," she looked desirously into his face but when he bent to kiss her, she pulled away, ran further down, looked around. "This is the spot."

"What do you mean."

"The perfect spot for it." He couldn't move, staring down at her. She opened her pack produced two small bottles of wine, squinted at the label reading off tiny print …. "look! made in Maine," handed him one. "Don't worry it's only 2%, I drink it all the time, got potassium and minerals added." Glowing with health, fluffy blond hair do, nails recently done, she was an office girl on vacation, enjoying her time. "Let's go right here."

Was he dreaming, this was too good to be true, she actually wanted him, wanted him all along but was better at details, girls are, and girls liked him, he was used to their attention. Sandra was better, high-octane. She'd spread out a blanket pulled him towards the ground, sheltered in the rocks, warm sunny, soft earth, she lay down, posed suggestively. He lay beside and she sat up. "lets drink to the day, this beautiful day … oh Wesley … I'm so happy. Are you happy? Oh Wesley, tell me you're happy."

He couldn't speak his body was on fire, but managed a nod of agreement.

"Well then drink up, drink," she pushed up on the bottom of his bottle until it was gone.

"VENUS FLY trap," his lips said because his head was buzzing, like a fly caught inside. His eyes refused to open. When they did he saw the rocks, huge rocks, each with a round shadow, moonscape, he'd left earth, had no memory …of …

the girl, he patted the ground like a blind man, but find her, feel her then fell back to sleep.

He woke again, this time his close surroundings came into focus. The blanket was gone, he was lying in dirt naked except for socks. He laughed, that's funny as he hated wearing socks, let alone shoes, always removing them first thing … but looking down he had the sensation he'd had it, been with her but couldn't remember …all he could remember was… the wine …did they spike it? Did she? What happened, there was evidence something did happen, he was feeling it but, *Christ this is weird, Was I date raped?*

"What you going to-do about it." a voice spoke inside his head. *Yeah what am I going to-do about it. Go to the cops? Help, I was date raped and that's the girl who did it.* He imagined their smirks, *poor guy*, they'd say, *better put some ice on that.*

His clothes lay in a neat pile, everything there, he didn't carry money or even cards. Nothing missing, a little dirty, he shook them and a cloud of dust appeared. He dressed slowly, skin sun burnt, uncomfortable, in places that were normally covered. He replaced his watch, picked up the tablet, waiting at the bottom under his clothes. The tab came to life and a scene started, like a porn movie only he was the star. *We did that? She's…wow …* Fascinated he replayed again and again, each time it went dimmer until zip it was gone. Gone. He hugged the tablet and started down couldn't wait to see her, forgive her if she drugged him …next time would be different.

It was in a special blue light that warns all creatures of approaching darkness, time to take shelter that Wesley arrived back at camp and found them gathered around a big pot. It was an eerie sight, the old faces under lit, showing off hideous bags and sags. They were chanting, "Into the Pot … Into the Pot…. all that's negative … I got to … throw it into the Pot!" He shook his head trying to see past the macabre to duty. He had to count them, make an accounting of all individuals, it was his responsibility, but the tab refused to pull up names and faces, so he left for his RV and second tab.

"Wesley where are you going," Sandra's voice said. She took his arm.

He paused while the earth righted itself and he managed to point at his RV.

"Oh why, don't you want to-do the soup, nobody's perfect, don't you want to leave troubles behind and start fresh?"

"I…"

"Oh Wesley," she squeesed his arm. I'm so sorry I left you, you were sleeping sooo peaceful, we had such a goodtime, you were so good," she giggled, "…oh Wesley tell me you're not mad at me …oh please … it hurts so bad to think you're mad…" they made it to his RV.

"Mad at what?" he'd studied interrogation technique.

"Oh, you know that … You were sleeping and I…"

"Right you couldn't wake me up." They'd made it up the stair and stood on his mini-deck. He didn't feel like going inside the RV, searching names on his other tab with her there, besides he had to clean up, change clothes, grit in the fabric was chaffing his sunburn.

"Oh Wesley, mind if I call you Wess,… OK? Wess? You can call me Sandy. .. I, I'm not that sure of myself, Wess, I'm… I'm you know … I'm not what you think I am, I'm really … very …oh you know …and couldn't exactly carry you down the hill. Sooo"

"What did you put in the wine."

"What do you mean …" what did I put in the wine,' what kind of question is that? You think I put something in the wine? Her voice started to rise."

"I…"

"What kind of an accusation is that?" She repeated loudly, the chef looked up started over, "How dare you, don't you understand what saying something like that means. I didn't put something, I didn't! I didn't!" She was red in the face, shrieking, the old people's faces pointed at them, enjoying the drama. The cook dropped what he was doing, bulldozing his way over. Wesley, (Wess) moved to place his hand over her mouth, when she put her finger there "shusssh, quick pretend you're kissing me." And she drew him down close, he went in for a real one and was pushed, she ran down the steps, took the cooks arm and led him away. The cooks huge torso and blocky shoulders a powerful combo Wesley'd rather not test. Sandra and Cook *bigfoot and little foot*, stood talking around the caldron watching him.

He quickly showered, changed, ate a couple nutra-bars and found the second tab. All the names and faces but as soon as he exited his RV it went blank. He was forced to go by memory and he was lousy at it. *Oh CERT why has thou forsaken me.* The only people he knew by name were the Johnsons and they were missing and the lady with the blank stare, Tuna something. She'd hung on his arm, a cold tired woman, until he passed her off to a couple… that was the last he saw of her.

Sandy was busy with Bigfoot gathering and labeling vegetables so he found Jess. 'Oh Jess, Have you counted the people."

"Counted the people," she repeated looking exaggeratedly confused.

"You know counted heads."

"Yeah, they're all here."

"Twenty-five"

"That many?"

"That's the correct count, twenty-four, including, me you, Sandy and Cookie … the driver left."

"I got twenty-one."

"Twenty-one."

"Twenty-one, oh I know that's because the Johnson's are in their RV, they've kitchen facilities you know. The other woman retired also. She had cancer you know, chemo, but a toughie, wanted to come." She looked steadily at him; he at her, they were silent for awhile.

"Maybe I better go check on them," he wanted to see the Johnson's again, they were the grandparents he never saw.

"I already did, they're sleeping now, so don't bother them," she directed. They stared at each other.

"How long have you known Sandy?"

"I don't know, why you don't ask her," she was breathtakingly rude, then smiled and said, "did you bring an item for the stone soup? We've extra if you don't."

"A stone."

"Don't be silly ... a vegetable."

"Ok ... what do you got?"

"Lots," she, placed her hands on her wide hips, wiggled and giggled, "We better watch it ... don't want to make Sandy jealous." He followed down a little path around a tree and up the steps of their shared RV, he'd been there before on his tab. There was the shower stall where he saw Sandra soaping her body, he closed his eyes for a second while Jess found him a potato. "Your supposed to attach, think hard at it so all your negative feelings go into the potato." Her deep brown eyes looked at the potato.

He moved close, conscious of being alone with her, out for easy revenge; fat girls are good that way... "Then what."

"You share it with the others, talk about hard feelings and throw it into the pot. Then it's brought to a boil."

"And ... we aren't expected to eat it?" She let him touch her, he pulled her close ... they used the same soap, he'd kill two birds with one stone, get one and get back at the other ...

"No," she giggled, "hey watch the hands ... I'm not into threesomes, and Sandra really likes you... she appreciates you so much."

"Next time I'll 'appreciate' her back."

"You mean you didn't?"

"Didn't what?"

"Appreciate Sandra"

"Kind a hard after she..."

"Everyone else does," she suddenly stopped, "I mean you're owned. Sandra wants you..." She gazed up at him in a deep unsmiling way, "Come on lets get back."

He stood in front of the door, anger and revenge filled his brain. "You didn't tell me what happens to the soup." He felt like shaking truth out of her but she had power he didn't... she was in with the CERTS ... What was her role ... pimp, prostitute ... *Doubt they're free...*

"We wait till it's cooled down and dump it in the compost heap.

"Sounds like a lot of work." *and counts as nothing if I can't remember....*

"Later we use the compost to plant trees. It's supposed to symbolize regeneration. You know like death and rebirth." She gave an odd giggle, "Let's see how your potato does." Wesley opened the door and followed her over.

"Into the Pot ... Into the Pot.... all that's negative ...I got to ... throw it into the Pot!" They were chanting louder and louder. He grabbed a nutria-bar and some water and sat on a rock.

Cook stood, his body casting a wide pillar, "I never really liked my first wife, just stayed married for the kids but it still hurt when she left me." the Cooks honesty started it off. He threw in a rotten onion. *At least he didn't sacrifice something good.* Wess stared at them... *who were theses people really.* A second man stood, large gut overflowing his belt. *Guess we're going to find out.*

"Into the Pot ... Into the Pot.... all that's negative ...I got to ... throw...."

"I used to smoke a lot of weed, get hammered too ... got really paranoid, thought the feds were after me..."

"Into the Pot ... Into the Pot.... all that's negative"

A woman stood, her hanging jowls wagging in the firelight. "I always hated my Mother." She quietly sat.

"Into the Pot ... Into the Pot.... all that's negative... we got to"

A man got up, frowned and said, "At my parents house we were having our driveway resurfaced and I parked my new car on the street. I was only seventeen at the time, spent summers working on it then some A-hole hit it and ran. I got on my bike and followed him for five miles, waited till he and his family were asleep ...and....set his car on fire!" The guy smiled with glee, "you should a seen it! Ka-boom went the fuel tank."

"Wait a minute, wait a minute," Cook put his hands in the air, "No arrest-able offences please, it would be my duty to report."

There goes the entertainment. Wess sighed, *hope they don't expect me to spill my guts.*

"Keep it simple, some negative thought that keeps you from advancing in your life. Negative thoughts are toxic …they make us sick," voice like a tuba, blasted compliance.

"No cause for worry," the old miscreant reassured, "statute of limitations expired thirty-two years ago, simple property crime anyway, arson with mitigating circumstances, my age, the fact that he hit and ran, besides his was an old shit box, I was doin' him a favor."

"Ok but lets keep it simple, we're talking about feelings here," Another warning blast of presence and authority, Wesley eyed him with envy. *He's obviously one of them; a CERT.* He looked around the crowd trying to find Sandy, saw Jess, laughing with some ugly old drake. Then they left together, he felt more than a tinge of jealousy, *watch out for the wine mister.*

"Into the Pot … Into the Pot.…. all that's negative …I got to … throw.…"

Wesley put his head down, they were recounting negative feelings about everyone and anyone they were close to! *Familiarity breeds contempt!* That's one reason why he liked space and was in someway reluctant to marry… What attracted him to Sandra wasn't the 'come-on' but that she kept pushing him away. He could live with that, An independent type, strong and OK alone by herself cause he loved being alone. He wasn't 'a loner' always shared an apartment with roommates …it was the desire to rest in his own space without interference that gave him strength to face the day. He needed a woman in his life, but not all the time.

Even though the cook remonstrated, these old people still found the need for mini tell-alls. It was depressing, so much hate.

"It's just like," It was Sandra's voice, "it's just like kind of hard to explain why I just, you know…I just really… oh gosh … please don't hate me …I really just like I really don't like dogs!" she finally blurted out.

Wow another mark in the plus column. This might work yet.

"Into the Pot … Into the Pot…. all that's negative …I got to … throw…. Wesley! Your turn."

Being last has advantages, some of the stuff he heard was blackmail material …his physiology minor kicked in … *Jump the shark* … "I really hate being alone. I get squirrelly after a few hours and a couple days later, I'm ready for a straight jacket. Solitary would kill me. I'm really a people person, My frame of mind has high people needs. I've always been awe… afraid of being alone." He smiled. His statement was excepted as truth for the most part, although some of the old farts eyed him mistrustfully; (*like hell you are*).

BACK AT HOME and work, all the craziness gone, Wess tried to retrieve normalcy. Got back with his girlfriend, then he was bored. *Too much of a good thing.* One thing positive at work was all the old people from the trip got their new uniforms. They had integrated enhancements in the joints as needed, behind the knees, inside the elbows, it was very humorous to see old heads and prancing bodies. But they loved it, just as he loved his visor helping with memory issues, the shop came through replacing deficits with enhancements. He didn't see Sandra or Jess. *They're company sluts Effem* he rationalized … But wanted her, fantasized about her, was ready for her, if he knew where she was, how to find her, make plans…

They had him doing inventory, totally tedious but important, he liked finding out what people buy and see progress …plus he liked seeing the old people whizzing around. The shop made use of their intelligence … desire to help. With broken bodies crowned in happy pain free faces, they appeared angelic, half human, the shop gave them 'wings'. He was called into a CERTS meeting, "keep an eye on them …they're very precious to us, loyal, intelligent, been with the company since inception."

"It works for them."

"Works for us too and Wess, keep us informed from the human level, ground floor observations. Who knows there's always a spot for a man like you on the inside." The head

CERT, arm across Wess' shoulder directed him to the door. "We'll be in touch."

Then they got them masks. There was an accident; someone lost an eye, so now they were all wore custom fitted full face masks.

They'd been some concern over the Johnson's and that other lady, Tuna or Tina, the sick one. A couple cops actually showed up, then a detective asked questions but the investigation was dropped when it was found they'd been moved to a different warehouse, gotten a promotion, he was happy for them, and the sick lady moved out of state.

One day he was talking to one of the masks, as he called them, the guy who set the car on fire, trying to see if he had more stories, inventory was dull, boring; task without end. The masks helped of course, he was their unit leader.

"Set any fires recently?"

"Fires?"

"Yeah burnt up anyone's vehicle?"

"Vehicle?"

"Yeah…"

"We had a fire in the fireplace this morning and my son has a car."

'Jeeze, never a dull moment at your place."

"We try and keep things polished."

"Ha, that's not bad, I'll remember that one."

"I'll remember two."

Wesley moved away. he felt no warmth coming from this person, was he real? Old people turning into automatons, differentiation faded, they were indistinguishable and seemed to be multiplying, dozens zooming around, lifting things, turning corners, no longer speaking.

Next day he tried peaking under one of the masks, but it was sealed tight. A couple boring weeks passed then one fell from a ladder and the mask popped off. Wess ran to him, one of his old people, but men came out of nowhere and he was pushed away. They didn't wait for an ambulance but lifted him on a cart, placed a rag over what looked like a black hole of wires and cards and rushed him away down the long central corridor.

Janitors emerged, swept the area, the other old people were unconcerned, went about business like nothing out of the ordinary. With no outward sign of disturbance, Wess was at a loss, wanted to talk to someone.

That night Sandra called, said she missed him, they had sent her to school and she just got back, "I spent the whole time thinking of us Wess, I missed you so much."

"That's interesting, as you didn't contact me and … summers over." That really bothered him he'd thought of spending July and August with her.

"Oh Wess, they wouldn't let us, said it was against company policy, you forgive me?"

"When can I see you?"

"Is tonight too soon, Ohh I can't wait, Oh Wess I've so much to tell you, you've been on my mind soo much!"

She gave him her address, it was in an odd part of town, outside of company housing, she had her own studio apartment.

Wesley prepared himself, brushed his teeth about 1ten times, dropped a tiny bit of meth, grabbed Viagra, not that he needed it, brought his own food, drink. *not taking any chances this time.*

She came to the door wearing shorts and a tank top, the same beautiful girl, perfect package, intelligent, playful. "So what's life like at the shop, I feel so out of touch, they sent us to China, can you believe? We wore oxygen masks the whole time except when we ate … with chop sticks!" She bounced provocatively, sitting next to him on a big soft wraparound couch. "Their country is so complicated and they're so proud but you wonder, wonder if they will ever really like us. Anyway it's not beautiful there." She became solemn, "We have it so good here, their lives are really hard, we couldn't do what they do … all that work, in those factories, day after day, ten-twelve hour shifts… and so foggy and smoggy, can't breathe normally."

The sound of her voice, her serious expressions had him seeing this other side he never imagined, that he liked and started to actually trust her a little more. "So now you're a 'social justice warrior'."

"No, oh Wess but .. we just got to care, that's what the Shop is all about, caring for people. They're so different over there it's all about work, working together, …they all have housing, we only provide 50% in the GOV/COM partnership, but they've got 100% and the people seem worry-free and grateful, really grateful but …they shame people for not working hard."

He moved closer on the couch, played with her neck hair, kissed her there, her eyes glowed with depth, he was ready but wanted to hold off, it's always better that way, so he began with his story… "Something strange happened at work. You know I'm in charge of the same group we took up north? They fitted them with the exoskeleton suits … there was a facial injury so they added masks. Those exoskeleton suits have elbow struts and a guy was about fifteen feet up on a sliding stair … and fell, the suit caught on something. Fact was he didn't fall with a thud … but kind of clattered, like a plastic toy and his mask fell off. I went to help but was pushed away, instead of following spinal cord protocol, collaring, back board …they threw him on a cart like trash, ran him out of there…

"Oh they've sensors in those suits, they knew what to do and maybe speed was important, Oh Wess I hope the old man was OK."

"If it was a man."

"Oh course it was a man! Why else would they go to all that trouble. They just care so much …and you know those people don't want to retire and some so disabled, I mean it must be terrible being them … but now they can work with our help. Other places think of nothing but their bottom line, loss cost prevention, heath insurance payments, our shop's people oriented, not replacement mad like the others."

"Then what's their end game, they can't kept it going forever. Eventually they'll wear-out for good." Wesley stared her down, dominated, she was getting flustered and he enjoyed it. She'd drugged him.

"And you don't understand," her voice rising, "we, I mean Central, tried to get young people to wear them but they refused but when we mentioned to the 'soon to be retired' they jumped at the chance. You see, Wess exoskeletons have internalized diodes so we get perfect feedback about warehouse needs, so we .. it can be..." She suddenly realized she'd said too much ...looked down red-faced with shame, "I mean those poor ... people... really wanted to help, you don't understand members of this age group they are so giving, ready to give... help progress... science. How else are we supposed to understand ... and progress and live the lives we're supposed to live?"

"Kind of an interesting way to replace ...them.

"Wess, you got it all wrong, we're doing it for them, that's how they are... they're that concerned with our lives, mine, yours ...everyone's.

THIS TIME HE remembered everything, this time he was fully conscious, but he had to get up and go, so headed for the bathroom. *Man is not a sex machine.*

Work concerned him, being with a girl who worked in the same shop enhanced the experience even if their thoughts were polar opposites. His real girlfriend seemed even further out in distant left field, *Sandra's a nurse already, worked in hospitals and she likes me, wants me at least that's what she says …acts … in a loud way!* He'd have to give his old girlfriend the bad news, but maybe not, *better keep it quiet, not hurt her feelings… women are pretty much interchangeable … and there were other girls…but… at least she doesn't spike my drinks.* He chalked it up to first time nerves; *Sandy's a keeper and she's getting to know me better.*

"You're good, Damn good" he said out loud to his reflection, shook his head at the thought, then washed his face, cleaning the night off … there was the shower … he stepped in, *Man this is a fancy place, filtered water,* at home it was full of chlorine.

He finished up, toweling off and thought of Jess, wanted to set things straight, he liked fat girls, studied his face in the mirror …flexed his muscles, struck a pose. Then started to snoop, wanted to learn more about Sandy, her clothes were on a hook so he went through the pockets and found the bracelet, the silver charm bracelet, with dangling dog heads belonging to Doris Johnson. *What the hell?* He thought of confronting her, demanding explanations but she'd know he was going through her stuff. So he slipped it in his pocket, *save it as evidence,* there was a strange fury in his bones, it all came tumbling out, the unimaginable reality, desire to seek justice, revenge… *they were my old people.*

He had to get out of there, collected his coat as quietly as possible but she woke, followed him to the door. They kissed goodbye, "you're the only guy I really care about Wess, I feel it in here," she thumped her heart.

"Then what's this," he held up the bracelet.

"That was in the lost-and-found ... you shouldn't snoop in my stuff", she shook a polished nail with odd tenderness.

"You like dogs..."

"Made into a bracelet...with names on each head," She held the jewelry examining it, then took his hand and dropped it in, closing his fingers around, watched him slip it back in his pocket, hands on her hips, "you can always give it to your girlfriend."

"Yeah, I might just do that."

"Or keep it with your other trophies."

"You're my trophy," he patted her ass, "Bye now."

The drive home took twenty minutes, he thought of who to call, from his RFID blocking life-wire. His chest hurt, head filled with tears ready to burst, all his old people turned to robots, killing them slowly... one at a time. He wiped his face, *I'll call Carol,* (his old girlfriend), nah she works nights but she's a goodhearted woman will know what to-do, doesn't need to know the whole story. She'll be totally on my side, then like fresh air coming into his lungs ... the reason the CERTS didn't like her ... *she was out of their control.*

He drove in a state of unreality, pulled into his parking space, last name HERD came at him, surrounded by street lamps, he fast tracked to his apartment, roommate on vacation, the place was as he left it except for the tab. *That wasn't here.* He looked around the floor, under the couch cushions, eyed the ceiling. *Someone's been in here.* He picked up the tab. and it came alive. He saw himself in a dark wood, or someone wearing his clothes, from the trip minus socks. The man in his clothes picked up a shovel and began to dig, the scene went fast forward until the man was at the bottom of a dug grave. He threw the shovel out, pulled himself up then retrieved what looked like a wrapped corpse, then another and another.

Wesley couldn't move, then ran to his bedroom, grabbing suitcase. scrunching clothes, wallet, keys, tax returns, PC, cell phone in his pocket, put on a coat he never wore and ran out of there, glad he opted out of the enhanced security package, remotely locked doors didn't happen, he fled to the parking garage, slipping his cell under the soft top of someone's truck bed, like it would actually throw them off…he knew it was over, that he'd been set up. He made it to his car, terrifying realization it wouldn't start, engine betrayed him, everything swirling, heart thumping like footsteps outside and suddenly cops were everywhere guns drawn. He was pulled from his vehicle, thrown face first on the cold tar, handcuffed. "Wesley Herd!"

Knee in the center of his back, he managed a shallow exhale, "yeah?"

"You're wanted as a person of interest in the murders of Doris and Jim Johnson, the rape and murder of Tina Murphy;

assault, rape and kidnapping of Sandra Cummings." They checked his pockets, found the bracelet.

He was placed in solitary, put on suicide watch ... alone. *That's one thing they can't take from me* ... not yet anyway. His mind crisp and clear. He had a story to tell.

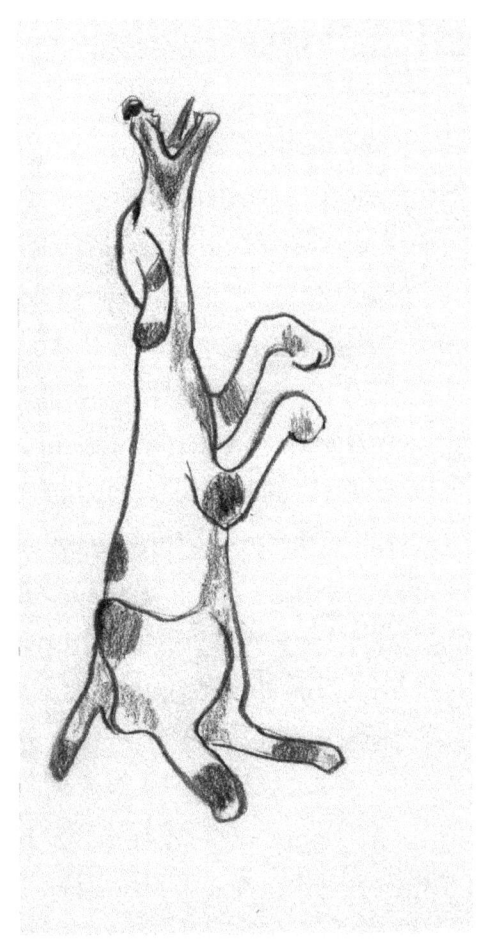

The Community

Debbie Caine

We were thrown in together as children, living in the Community, two little hyper-active red haired girls but she lived too far ... up on the Mountain Rd. Kids on the Shore Rd, where I lived were in opposing gangs.

I was five and asked over for a play date, she lived almost a mile away, way up on the hill. My Mom sent me by myself and laughed when I didn't make it. Debbie was mad at me ... I didn't have an explanation.

Later in Public school we didn't end up together, she tracked high; me low. third grade was our first time in the same class. It was an experiment to put smart and dumb together. Debbie was teacher's pet along with other smart kids. The teacher sorted us out and I ended up several steps behind.

Debbie was like me, really skinny, had to sit on her legs to reach the table in the cafeteria, but she was a fast runner and dare devil. The Mountain Rd. girls dared the Shore Rd.

girls to ride down the hill no hands. It was all frost heaves and potholes. I rode a friend's bike as I didn't have my own and made it half way. Boys were better at balancing, showing off, so we lost interest, went back to playing along the Shore.

The next day Debbie hit a rock, ... went over the handlebars and was fairly messed up, skin off a knee stitches on her forehead, out of school a couple days. A boy challenged her and she didn't back down. The Community was shocked, made a rule about it... a 'no hands' rule at the thought of losing her...

In junior high we weren't friends, I wasn't that polished, well dressed or academically inclined and she had all those things... a egg they called her, aced her scholastic standards, she grew tall, pretty ... athletic. My friends were more average also community girls in private school.

Public School stayed good until High School when many kids were sent away to boarding school and the community tinned out. The just completed High school was silent about the loss, built on an old quarry and gravel pit, a classmates Dad blasted the hillside... a whole show and tell of beautiful explosions.

Debbie didn't have to go through life alone; she had a brother and they were like fraternal twins. Ethan was a year older, everyone called him Caine, his name shouted across playing fields, he caught a ball and threw home. They lived with their Mom as their Dad was an important man in

Washington, two states away. As a result their family attended all public schools, to make their Dad look better.

"My Mom's almost completely deaf," Debbie said.

Her Mom, beautiful like a model, tall, blond, long legs but couldn't hear, for some inexplicable reason she lost hearing as a baby. Debbie took over parenting her two younger brothers, shepherding them to play dates, checking things out. Her Mom could talk but sometimes it came out wrong.

But that's all background. The Story really begins when our local juvenile delinquent, home on spring break from prep-school, threw an all night beer party at the boat landing. I was there with other sophomore girls and so was Ethan.

Shyly sitting on a pile of moorings hoping some boy would notice me, my face began to swell. That day I'd been over to a friend's house and used a sunlamp for the first time. I forgot all about it when Ethan sat next to me and was amazed when we walked around the field and he put his arm around me, "For Security," he said. Other couples were arm in arm and me with Ethan talking about sports and things.

Next morning I woke and my eyes were swelled shut, my face a mess. I heard a commotion outside and like a whirlwind Debbie was in my room. My appearance threw off her mission of figuring out what happened but she stayed long enough to realize nothing … and was suddenly gone, out the door, driving off.

Nothing happened but everything happened to me. I caught a glimpse of that feeling, then it was gone. I didn't hear from Ethan or go to beer parties again and figured it was a package deal, needing Debbie's stamp of approval.

My older sister Dani couldn't let it go. She was recently accepted as a day student to an all girls prep-school, and missed the H.S. dating scene, in gales of tears actually and disappointed at my big zero.

The flurry over Ethan ended when they picked me up walking home. Inside their car was an icebox, freezing me out ... but it was his car and they drove each day to school in it.

Later he began picking up girls with Debbie protecting the fount seat, four girls in the back, big old Chevy Impala. He sorted them out and picked one, not from the community but the cutest in school, after a Farrar Faucet cut.

He wasn't shy about displaying love, most boys were but not Ethan. And Debbie let it happen. I might of tried harder, dressed better etc. but I was a dunce and didn't grow up with the Mountain boys. I'd watched the Shore boys change from crazy bullies to sweet admirers. Ethan was a bolt from the blue.

Ethan and girlfriend were an item, it was obvious, he'd wait in the hall to walk her to class ... best looking pair in school. I hung out with friends, girls were less stressful and sillier.

One day everything changed, Mountain Rd and Shore Rd. came together in shock. Ethan drove home to the hill-top, sealed himself in their garage, sat in his Impala, turned on the engine and killed himself. Why? Blame came down and shut the community off, walled off guilt. Parents refused to talk about it. 100% mute. But my sister Dani and I blamed the three Moms. They used the same method, he must have been aware of their pain-free exit.

One found out her husband was gay, another's was leaving for someone else and a third couldn't get over the loss of her seven year old daughter who heart failed walking down stairs. More than eight years ago, an abnormal time, we lived through, stared at their homes but they were thirty-ish, old, blemished by time, housewives, in a development of fifty-five houses, town of six thousand, claimed three lives.

The Families threw out garbage, closed doors and moved. Kids picked through the trash, displayed trophies. I didn't ... why have a memento of something not wanted. We didn't want it to happen right? Trophies were for winners.

One of the Mom's liked me, I'd wished she was my mom. She planted flowers along our path to the bus-stop, she was gone but they came up every spring like she was smiling.

Caine was only seventeen and everyone was of like mind; don't ask but find out. Blond curly hair, bronze tan, molded on a heavenly planet... repossessed, not in the Community anymore.

On the late bus boys pretend strangled himself, slumped asphyxiated ... fake died ... tongue hanging out. Another kid pretended to have a seizure fell out of his seat flopped like a fish in the isle. "Help I'm dead."

"Cut it out," said the driver.

Then his best friend yelled so we had to hear, "Yeah he called me … tried to get me to come over … it was a mistake, he was expecting me … wanted to be found." He repeated it louder like he wanted me to say something, but I didn't. He was Ethan's best friend, shared confidences.

I told my sister and she said, "Oh, did not want to talk about it," At least not right away. She was in private school and jealous of my inside info … but then she found out had bragging right's to the truth, her best friend, still at the High school dug it up. Ethan's girlfriend wanted to date other boys. That was it. This was the early eighties … 'Walk Like a Man' was an oldie.

Everyone expected them to move, like the other three families but they stayed. Debbie got a ride to school with someone else, dyed her hair blond and curled it, like her brother's and lost twenty lbs. Her face was a mask, we never spoke but she knew I was watching her, everyone was. The girl who broke her brother's heart stayed awhile then switched schools.

Debbie's' hair grew straight red again but she didn't gain weight, walked stiffly in the halls, spoke to one close friend or not at all.

Gym class we were supposed to complete the aerial rings, go hand over hand swinging, eight rings and back. Letting go meant falling to the mats below. No one could do it … I got the farthest, half way back. Debbie's turn, she managed to swing and grab to the end … paused dangling, turned and started back. Girls exercised, the gym teacher stood, hands on hips, expecting her to fall but she made it, face set, swinging painfully. At that moment Debbie became my hero for all time.

We didn't think anymore of it, Ethan was a fluke, an anomaly, mistake, wasn't supposed to happen, if his best friend had shown up, he'd be alive if … if his Mom could hear… if his sister or Dad was home… but we were wrong.

Neighborhood Dad's weren't gun owners so it was carbon monoxide, gas stoves, hanging… girls and boys exited on pills, pills and alcohol, drowning, wrecks …. defenestration, disappearances. They were traced back to the community from boarding school, College, young married's, they did it in dorm rooms, during parties … exam week, on vacation, at home.

It was always, 'did you hear about so snd so,'… 'no really?' Then memories, when we last saw, spoke, when we were little, sitting in classrooms, playing on the beach.

Why did they kill themselves? And younger than Caine, in three separate incidents, twelve, fourteen, fifteen year old boys hung themselves… "It was a mistake," a Dad said, "he was playing a game … it was a kid game…"

The police didn't investigate that much. There wasn't a ton of cop cars in the drive way, or press holding microphones. Our community only had good people doing it, no intersection with murder.

We talked little, it wasn't grief, it was shock. Families went into solitary, tears behind doors. Kids were missing from bus stops, classrooms, teams, bleachers and later from college, jobs, marriages.

Why …with so many perfect parents, perfect upper middleclass development, Christmas sing-a-longs, Halloween parties, 4th of July parade … candle light flotillas. A big city suburb, noted for scholarship, where the smart kids lived, graduated from excellent schools, packed churches. We were a well dressed, caring, feeling community, known for Dads who made 'do it for the children,' speeches on memorial day, before the band played taps …

We blamed it on the fall, said it was gloomy. Winter was too long, Summers stressful, kids were under too much pressure, or not enough to-do, until everything became a contradiction and a nod was enough before turning away.

Years went by, trees grew huge, the Community became shadowy, hidden. Someone's wife shot herself and bang! Reality, thirty-two was enough, no more souvenirs.

We stood outside empty houses, as if waiting for them to return, some were multiples, happening days, weeks, years apart.

Vacancies slowly filled, we didn't tell them, or sometimes we did. So what if they bought into a graveyard, tombstones where happy families once lived, had friendships, birthday parties ... learned about life.

My mind blanked numb, couldn't focus, didn't care, why should I? They obviously didn't and compared to Caine, they were anticlimaxes, yet I kept a mental catalogue, everybody did.

I never appreciated my upbringing until later. My parents didn't like me, the only one with a long face. I was hit, jabbed with a boom handle, hiding under my bed. My sibs got new cloths, were brilliant; I was stupid, ugly, scapegoated ... assaulted. Nothing good was expected of me. I didn't try to be pretty or intelligent but was determined to survive and discovered the world wasn't like my family! Problems came with learning appropriate responses to others kindness. I begged God ...please help me love people and it worked. Love came into my heart and with it pain. I had to mourn all the losses and only then did I understand the suicides.

About the Author

Lucia Bartlett believes Northern Maine is a place of healing and peace, little settlements carved out of endless forest are her greatest love. She spends happy hours working in the woods with her family. She's also believes in the power of plants, that stars have answers and life is spirit. People struggle with humanity and purpose and Lucia's no exception. Her greatest wish is to give others a break, so they might live in her books for awhile.

Some may say Lucia's a satirist. She takes it well.

The Vampire Squid is her 3rd novel in a sequence following The King of Maine and The Donkey Club. The Donkey Club is for all ages. Add a year for The King of Maine and four years later the characters reappear in The Vampire Squid

The Vampire Squid is contemporary fiction, 'Papercuts' is the future; 2030 and 'The Community' is the past.

Lightning Source UK Ltd.
Milton Keynes UK
UKHW010724121021
392079UK00001B/239